Hyakumonogatari: Tales of Japanese Horror Book One

Richard Freeman

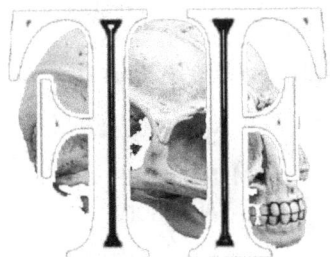

Fortean Fiction

HYAKUMONOGATARI: TALES OF JAPANESE HORROR
BOOK ONE

First published in Great Britain by CFZ Press 2012
Reissued 2015

ISBN: 978-1-909488-01-4

CFZ Press
Myrtle Cottage
Woolsery
Bideford
North Devon
EX39 5QR

www.cfzpublishing.co.uk

For Shigeru Mizuki, grand old man of the yokai

"Godzilla is the son of the atomic bomb. He is a nightmare created out of the darkness of the human soul. He is the sacred beast of the apocalypse."
—Tanaka Tomoyuki, producer *Gojira* 1954 Toho Studios.

"The Shadow-maker shapes forever."—Lafcadio Hearn

Contents

INTRODUCTION:

Hyakumonogatari in Japan

In Japan's Edo period, between 1603 to 1868, a party game became popular.

Hyakumonogatari Kaidankai, or a gathering of one hundred supernatural stories, involved the lighting of one hundred candles in paper lanterns on a table in a room. A mirror would be placed on the table or on the wall. The participants would then take turns telling stories of the supernatural, often involving yokai (broadly, ghosts and monsters), and often alleged to be true.

After each story, the teller would enter the room with the paper lamps and blow out one candle, and then look in the mirror. As more and more were blown out, the candle room grew darker. After the last candle was extinguished, a blue spirit called Aoandon was said to manifest, horned and fanged.

So popular were these parties that people would collect stories for them from all over Japan. They became a great resource of the preservation of Japanese folklore. The stories eventually became collected as books called *Hyakumonogatari*. During the Edo period, a high-ranking samurai named Negishi Shizue began collecting the local ghost stories told amongst the prisoners under his guard. Writing each tale down, he collected the stories into a large bag (bukuro); the collection was eventually comprised of more than 1000 ghostly tales. Negishi went on to publish this huge anthology in ten volumes entitled *Mimi Bukuro*, meaning 'Bag of Ears' ('Ears' implying tales heard). *The Mimi Bukuro* tales ranged widely in genre from the historic to the purely supernatural.

The interest in ghost stories in the late Edo period grew so much that the Japanese authorities banned them in 1808. They forbade the telling of stories that involved the following subjects:

- atrocities between men and women;
- crimes of bad women;
- fire daemons;
- heads flying about;
- animal and bird goblins;
- serpents winding round the bodies of people;
- dead bodies decomposing in water.

In his 1959 book *Oriental Humor*, Reginald Horace Blyth concludes the government ban was trying to suppress sexuality and bloodlust. It sounds almost exactly like the scaremongering of right-wing tabloids in the UK in the early 1980s, which led to the ban on 'video nasties'. Governments like to have scapegoats on which to blame social ills. No-one was ever harmed through the telling of a ghost story.

Despite the ban, the popularity of Hyakumonogatari, in book and game form, continued. Even now, when the game is seldom played, collections of ghost stories are still written. That is how this book came about. Previously I had written *The Great Yokai Encyclopaedia: An A to Z of Japanese Monsters,* in which I showcased the yokai, Japanese weird folkloric creatures and phantoms; the book remains my best-selling work to this day. Later I branched into fiction, writing the collection of horror short stories *Green Unpleasant Land: 18 stories of British Horror*. The book gained good reviews, so I decided to combine my love of horror and Japanese folklore into a book.

This is the first of four volumes, each containing twenty-five stories, to form the full one hundred required by a Hyakumonogatari Kaidankai. I hope the reader will find the strange entities within these tales a refreshing change from the ones in Western horror stories. As I bemoaned in the introduction to *Green Unpleasant Land*, our books and films seem to be dominated by repetitions of vampires, especially pretty teenaged ones. The pages of Hyakumonogatari contain no such things, and the entities of old Japan have more in common with the things that flop and crawl through the works of M R James and H P Lovecraft than they do with the wan and anaemic fare that passes for horror these days.

Richard Freeman,
Exeter, September 2012

1. Some Words with a Kappa

It was 4 a.m., and the last of the pachinko parlours and sushi bars had shut. Neon advertisements still flashed, but the traffic had almost all gone from the streets of Taito-Ku, Tokyo. A few late-night drinkers meandered home arm-in-arm. Some groups of drunken youths still sung the songs they had sung earlier in the karaoke bars.

Sado Abe was not tired. He could have easily hailed a cab or jumped onto the tube, but he preferred to walk. It was such a pleasant evening, and this was an area of Tokyo noted for its lack of crime and violence. Indeed, a couple of cheery drunks waved and wished him goodnight, as they trickled unsteadily down the pavement.

Abe worked for Taiyo Yuden, an electronics company. Five days a week he put in ten hours manufacturing high-frequency, multi-layer chip antenna. No-one could accuse him of laziness; in two decades at the company he had not lost a day's work. Abe worked hard and played hard; Friday and Saturday nights were his biggest blowouts. There was a full moon that Friday night, but it was obscured by the lights of the city and its tall buildings. He felt an urge to look up into the starry night and gaze at the moon. An idea formed in his head - he would not go straight home, but take himself down to Ueno-Koen Park and enjoy what was left of the night.

The park was the opposite way from his apartment, but the walk would only take him fifteen minutes. He entered via the main gate and wandered through the cherry groves. The trees were all in full blossom and lit by the fat, yellow spring moon. A slight breeze rustled the upper branches, sending the red and pink petals showering down like scented confetti. He wandered on past the galleries and museums, dark and silent in the night. Off to the far left he could make out the amusement park. At this hour, even the young lovers had abandoned the park and dragged their weary heads home.

He gazed up at the moon - it seemed closer and fuller than it ever had. He approached the long bridge that spanned the Shinobazu Pond. In truth, it was a small lake rather than a pond. The moon was reflected as a perfect circle in the waters, and lit the park almost as if it were day. Indeed, there seemed to be an almost violet, twilight feel about the place. He paused a few paces onto the bridge. He leant on the railings and watched the dappled and gold koi swirl restlessly in the pond below.

Suddenly, and as one, the fish vanished. They swam quickly under the bridge and away, as if disturbed by something. Looking up, he saw a shape in the water. At first Abe thought it was a rounded, smooth rock protruding from the surface, but, as he watched, he saw it move. Smoothly, it slipped through the water, and he realised that it must be the shell of a large turtle. He shook his head as he realised that this must be something that had escaped from Ueno Zoo. He had visited the zoo only two months before, when his nephews had visited him from Chiba. There was an impressive reptile collection, and this must be one of them; he recalled several kinds of large turtle. The animal seemed to be headed for the bank. It stopped in a small reed bed and pushed its way through. Realising that the turtle was coming ashore, and that there might be a reward for its capture, he ran down from the bridge and across the grass to the edge of the pond - it was then he realised that what he was looking at was no turtle.

The thing heaved itself up onto its hind legs. It was roughly the size of a five-year-old child. The body was encased in a shell, like that of a turtle or terrapin. The arms and legs were akin to an outsized frog, green in colour and slimy-looking, and its hands were almost human in form, save for the webbing between the digits. It clutched the half-eaten remains of a koi. The weirdest thing about the creature was the head - it was, by turns, reptilian and simian. The face and ears were formed like a large monkey, but, instead of a mouth, it possessed a horny beak. Its eyes were large and dark; they darted about restlessly. On top of its head, surrounded by a monkish fringe of hair, was a depression filled with a bluish liquid.

Abe skidded to a halt, his eyes growing round and his mouth flopping open wetly. He had drunk a fair amount, but not that much. A name for the odd little thing was dredged up from his childhood memories - '*Kappa.*'

The creature jerked its head up from the fish it was eating and looked towards him - then it spoke.

"You can see me, then? So few do these days."

Abe nodded mutely. He wanted to turn and run, but his legs seemed too weak.

"It's not that they can't, you know, it's just that you people have forgotten how to look. I blame television - no one can concentrate on anything longer than a few seconds these days."

"K-kappa?"

"Ah! Not many remember my name now, and those who do think I was just a myth."

The creature finished eating the fish and turned toward Abe.

"How the mighty have fallen. Once your ancestors gave me supplications of carved cucumbers so that I would not prey on their children and livestock; now I have to make do with eels and carp and the odd bits of food dropped into the pond. Sushi is not bad, but hamburgers are vile; gaijin food is tasteless and full of fat and chemicals."

Abe had calmed somewhat. The Kappa didn't seem aggressive, but rather chatty.

"You say that people don't see you? Most people don't even believe in you anymore."

"Sad, isn't it? Another little piece of magick gone from the world; it's not so much they don't see me, as they don't *notice* me. They can't see what they don't think exists - that's where science gets you."

"Then why can I see you?"

The Kappa seemed to ponder for a while before it answered.

"Who knows? Maybe the drink, mixed with the cherry blossom, mixed with the moonlight - something made your mind relax for a moment. Now you've learned the trick, you'll never forget - it's like riding a bike."

"You mean I'm drunk?"

"You might be, but I'm not a dilution, I can assure you."

"What are you doing here?"

"This is my home; has been for centuries. I remember Tokyo when it was called 'Edo.' And I remember when Edo was just a collection of mud huts. I saw the city rise, and I saw the park build up around me. You know that the park is dedicated to Ieyasu?"

This was a surreal moment. Abe was being lectured by a supposedly-non-existent water goblin. "Dedicated to whom?"

"Don't you know your own history, man? What are they teaching you in school these days? Ieyasu Tokugawa, founder of the Tokugawa Shogunate. Seven Tokugawa Shoguns ruled Nippon from 1567 to 1867; six of the seven are buried in the park."

The Kappa rocked back on its heels and seemed to be daydreaming.

"Yes, those were the days. Honour, bravery, a moral code - the samurai stood for it all. This was a land of legend until the gaijin ideas poisoned our world."

"What?"

"The foreigners. During the Edo period, there were hardly any in Nippon, save for a handful of Dutch and Portuguese traders - then you fools had to go and reinstate the monarchy. Right here in this park in 1867 was where the last Tokugawa loyalists made their stand against the restoration of imperial rule. They were defeated, and it's been downhill ever since."

"What's so wrong with foreigners? Japan is part of the international community - surely that's better than being isolated like we were during the Edo period?" As the words left his mouth, Abe felt the absurdity of the situation. Earlier in the night he had been drinking and playing pachinko with his friends; now he was talking politics with a legend.

"Look over there." The Kappa pointed to the silhouettes of the fairground rides in the distance. "The fair was part of the 1907 Meji Industrial Expansion. The government cast out the old ways of the samurai in its rush for westernization. The gaijin brought the black powder to Nippon years before. There is no honour in a gun; it is no weapon for a samurai. A sword or a bow and arrow require skill; there is no skill to a gun - anyone can pick it up and use it. Now we follow their ideas of industrialization, and our country is becoming lost in a forest of straight lines."

"But Japan leads the world in manufacture. We are one of the greatest market powers on the planet."

The Kappa seemed to sigh. "I recall when all of this was forest and, after that, fertile farmland - and now it is metal, concrete and glass. Where are my kind supposed to go now?"

"Your kind? I don't follow."

"The yokai, the spirits of old Nippon. There are only a handful of Kappa left in what was once Edo. Most live in storm drains. There are still Tanuki and Kitsunie, but they no longer shape-shift. The Tengu have retreated to the highest and most remote mountain forests. No one has seen a Sojo's ruddy-faced grin in a century. The last of the Yuki-onna are now reduced to haunting the fish lockers of Osaka. O-gon-cho, the great white dragon, has not been seen since 1834; he still sleeps under the lake of Ukashima at Yama-shiro, but his sleep is uneasy - each time he stirs, there are earthquakes and tsunami. Your scientists say it is the grinding of tectonic plates; I know better. There is little room for yokai in modern Nippon."

Abe suddenly felt sorry for the odd little creature. It looked forlorn and alone.

"Everything is finite, Kappa-san, everything has its time. Maybe the time of the yokai is gone. Perhaps there is no magick left in the world, and no room for monsters and spirits."

The Kappa nodded slowly. "Yes, perhaps you are right. Thank you, young man." It extended a rubbery-skinned arm, as if to shake its webbed, clammy hand in his.

Abe walked forward, bent over, and took the creature's hand. The Kappa shook his hand and looked up with its big, dark eyes. "Eel and koi get so bland after the years," it said. The creature's hand gripped with a strength that belied its small stature. Abe suddenly found himself floundering in the water. The creature drew close.

"I forgot to tell you," it whispered before dragging him under, "Some of us yokai are very adaptable."

* * * * *

One of the groundskeepers found Abe's body the next day. The police report reported death by drowning, exasperated by alcohol. His entrails had apparently been removed, and eaten via his back passage. They concluded it had happened after his death and was the work of eels - the only inhabitants of Shinobazu Pond capable of doing such a thing.

2. On the Couch

Before he opened his eyes, it felt as if the bedclothes had been drawn in too tightly around him. He knew that this was not the case; he had felt the sensation many times before, and knew what was about to follow. He opened his eyes and saw, as in all the times past, that his vision was now in shades of green. Before all this had begun, he had had no idea the colour green had so many varieties, so many subtle tints.

His arms and legs were bound tightly by the green bandages that swathed his body. His jaws were held shut and his mouth was covered, preventing him from screaming and, in turn, impelling him to breathe through his nose. He could smell the weird incense that was burning in the green-flamed braziers, and he could hear the low crackle of the flames. On the walls of the room he could just make out hieroglyphics and paintings of gods – Sebek, the crocodile God, was one; Anubis, the wolf-headed god of death, was another.

The three silent, grinning priests loomed into view and lifted his helpless body up. They dropped him, still alive and conscious, into the open sarcophagus. He was fully lucid, realizing that this horror was a dream. He was also fully aware that, if he didn't wake himself up, he would die. As the priest began to lower the heavy lid down, he arched his body in a mental strain to jerk himself awake. Darkness descended as the lid fell with a leaden clang.

Okuma Isamu sat bolt upright in bed. His body and the sheets that covered him were soaked in sweat. He realized, with an odd detachment, that he was screaming. Beside him, his wife Toshi rolled over.

"The dream again?"

He nodded, gasping for breath.

"It's every night now. You're becoming ill. It's time you saw someone." She crawled over and put her arms around him; he was shaking badly. "Do you still have that card you picked up?"

He leaned over to the bedside table and switched on a lamp. Opening a drawer, he fumbled for a while and withdrew a small business card. He had put this off for weeks, but Toshi was right - the recurring dream was affecting his health. He was a writer who had not written a word in five months; he had to do something about this. He looked at the card again.

Dr Enomoto Takemitsu
Hypnotherapist and Psychologist
Specialising in the treatment and prevention of nightmares.
1907 Kappabashi St
Asakusa

"I'll phone and make an appointment in the morning." He spent the rest of the night sitting up in bed with the table lamp on.

The doctor had been able to fit him in on a same-day appointment. That afternoon he travelled across the city to Asakusa Station and walked to Kappabashi Street. The street itself was almost a mile long, and was mainly a shopping area selling everything from paper lanterns to video games. The entrance to the doctor's premises was an unostentatious door with a small brass plaque. He very nearly missed it - it was squeezed in between a hardware store and a fast-food joint.

The door led to a corridor and a reception desk. The smiling receptionist waved him through, as the doctor had no other patients that afternoon.

He entered a larger room. It had several high-backed, leather-bound chairs and a matching couch. To the back of the room were large double doors secured with a heavy padlock. The room had an odd smell; Isamu could not recall where he had smelled it before, although he knew he recognized it.

"Mr. Okuma, welcome. Please have a seat." Dr Enomoto stood up from behind his desk to shake Isamu's hand. He was a tall, lean man with spectacles and thinning hair. Behind him on the wall were a number of framed certificates.

"Now, please tell me what seems to be the problem."

"I have been having a very bad recurring nightmare for over five months now - It's beginning to affect my health and work. I'm having it every night, and I'm losing most of my sleep. I'm finding that, if I fall asleep during the day, the dream comes back then as well - so there's no respite."

"Can you tell me about the dream? What does it involve?" The doctor sprawled back in his chair, idly chewing the end of a pen as he listened.

"Well, the weirdest thing is that it's all in tints of green. I normally dream in full colour, and I have heard that some people dream in black and white, but this is all in different shades of green - no other colours."

"Go on."

"Well, I dream that I'm being mummified alive and placed into an Egyptian sarcophagus. The worst part is that the dream is lucid; in the dream, I know that I am dreaming, and that if I don't force myself to awaken, I will die. Each time it gets harder to wake up."

The doctor leaned forward. "Very nasty, but not as unusual as you might think. This is a clear case of sleep paralysis - this is where the conscious part of the mind awakes from the REM mode of sleep, but the body is still sleeping for a while; ergo, the feeling of paralysis is often accompanied by the most awful hallucinations. But, it's relatively easy for me to cure."

"Really? The dream and my lack of sleep are beginning to wear me down, doctor."

"Yes, I can tell - bags under your eyes, sallow complexion. If you go on like this, you're headed for a breakdown."

"But you can cure me? How long will the treatment take?"

The doctor smiled. "Just one session of hypnotherapy. I've never yet come across a dream that I could not lay to rest with just one session. Just one day - just one glorious, magical day - and your life will be back on track."

He walked over to the couch and tapped its leather surface. "Shall we begin? There's nothing to be afraid of; it's a harmless process, and really quite relaxing."

As Isamu climbed onto the couch, he recalled where he had smelled the odd odour before - it was at the zoo. It was the smell of animals.

"Now, lie back, close your eyes, and relax. Imagine you are lying on a tropical beach in the sun. All you can hear is the sound of the blue surf gently lapping the silver sand. Just listen - listen to the sea. You are relaxing more and more. Your muscles go limp and you begin to drift off into a contented sleep. As I count backwards, your eyes become heavier still. Allow yourself to fall; nothing can hurt you. Five, feeling sleepy. Four, falling deeper. Three, deeper still. Two, you're in the land of nod. One, fast asleep."

A gentle snoring filled the room as Dr. Enomoto retrieved a set of keys from his desk drawer. He opened the padlock on the heavy double doors at the back of the room and swung them open. The musky, animal smell filled the room.

"Come on - come on, boy. Dinner time," he cooed, as if calling a dog. In the darkness, something moved. It shuffled towards the open doors and out into the room. It was an animal the size of a large pony. It had a dark-furred, plump body marked with pale yellow stripes. It moved on four short legs that ended in blunt claws; they scraped noisily against the tiled floor as it moved. A small tufted tail flicked to and fro. In the bright light of the office, the animal's small eyes blinked myopically - sight was not its main sense, smell was. Its short, tapir-like trunk rose up, sniffing the air. It sensed food, and its tusked mouth began to drool.

The creature trotted over to the couch and placed a questing trunk on the prone man's forehead. It began a glorious sucking. The wet slurping noise filled the surgery as Dr Enomoto reached forward and scratched the creature behind one of its elephantine ears.

"Good boy; eat heartily," he said, as the animal purred like an outsized house cat. After five minutes the beast drew back its trunk and, turning, waddled back through the double doors, its belly full. The doctor shut and locked them behind it.

Turning his attention back to the patient, he said, "And now you are waking up, feeling refreshed and well. On the count of three... one, two, three, awake!"

Isamu blinked and sat up. He ran a hand across his forehead. It felt damp, probably with sweat, but he felt better than he had in months.

"I... I feel great," he stammered.

"I don't think you will be bothered by bad dreams again. Now, you go home and get some sleep. I'll post you the bill."

* * * * *

Okuma Isamu was never again troubled by bad dreams. Dr Enomoto Takemitsu made a lot of money in his practice; so much, in fact, that he took a second expedition to the forests of southern Okinawa to find a mate for the beast he had captured there beforehand, the Baku - the creature that fed on nightmares.

3. Mouryo

There was a smell of tempura batter mixed with that of dumplings, fried eels' livers, public urination and warm sake, together with the voices of excited children rising up shrill over the deeper tones of storeowners eulogising their wares.

The tall man walked past the kabuki shows and tearooms, past archery boots, toysellers, barbershops, fortune tellers and massage healers. He paused briefly as two burly men involved in a brawl rolled in front of him, then continued on his way.

He ignored the stands selling agar jelly, white jade and rice balls - he knew where he was going.

This was the visual, nasal and aural cacophony that was the Great Fair at the Ryogouku Bridge. Spanning the Sumida River, the bridge linked the provinces of Musashi and Shimosa and, as such, was hub for traders, performers and assorted raconteurs.

The tall man walked through the maze of humanity as if he knew it like the back of his hand. He drew a few gazes; he was a head taller than most inhabitants of Edo, and his nose was notably larger than those of most of the people around him. The tall man had a slightly flushed complexion that, taken with the other elements of his appearance, lent him the demeanor of a gaijin.

Soon he drew close to his destination - a long wooden booth, its entrance covered by a thick purple curtain. Before it stood a chubby little man with greying hair, and, above him, a luridly-painted wooden sign proclaimed 'Yasuki's Yokai - The Obake Zoo.' On wooden boards outside the booth, various monsters were painted, somewhat ineptly, in bright colours. A small crowd had gathered around the man, who was shouting.

"See the strangest beasts on earth, captured from all corners of the kingdom! Are they the products of nature, or the spawn of Jigoku? See with your own eyes! Tell your friends!"

Money was changing hands and a queue forming. The tall man joined the queue. He threw his coins in the man's bowl and pushed aside the curtain. He found himself with the other people in a kind of antechamber. More pictures covered the walls.

The owner, Yasuki, passed the money bowl to a girl, who took it away; he then turned to the crowd.

"Ladies and gentlemen," he began, "I am about to show you some of the weirdest and most dangerous beasts ever to have been held in captivity. Please stand well back, as some of our exhibits are quite savage."

He moved over to a door.

"If you doubt the stoutness of your spirit, then come no further; these are not creatures to be viewed by the fainthearted!"

An excited whisper ran through the crowd.

"But the brave, follow me...."

He opened the door and walked through. The crowd followed.

In the next room was a large cage, around ten feet wide by ten feet long. At the back of the cage was a pile of straw. A few half-chewed cucumbers lay scattered around it. Sitting on the straw was an odd creature sipping half-heartedly from a bowl of water; it resembled a hairless monkey, save for the turtle-like shell upon its back. As the crowd entered, it looked up briefly, then returned to its drinking.

"Behold - the legendary water yokai, Kappa. This monster may look small, but it has the power to drag down and devour a full-grown horse or ox! The Kappa delights in tearing out human entrails through the anus and eating them. It is one of the most dangerous of all the yokai. It was captured after a long struggle in a pond near Tsushima in Nagasaki Prefecture. It had devoured many women and children. Men from the village entangled it in iron chains and dragged it out with a team of oxen. I myself bought the beast for my collection."

The small creature did not look very aggressive.

A child drew closer to the cage.

"Stay back, young man!", yelled Yasuki dramatically. "This yokai's power lies in its harmless appearance. It can tear you to shreds in the blink of an eye!"

The child drew back, alarmed.

"How do you keep it sedated?" one woman asked.

"A fine question; I'm glad you asked. The Kappa has two weaknesses a clever and brave man like me can exploit. Firstly, the Kappa's strength lies in a liquid held in its head; if this is spilled, the Kappa loses its power. Then, the Kappa is also addicted to the taste of cucumbers; if you carve your name in a cucumber and give it to a Kappa, it will never attack you."

There were rounds of 'ohs' and 'ahs' from the crowd. The tall man looked on impassively from the back.

"Now, my friends, on to our next exhibit in the Obake Zoo." Yasuki opened another door that led into another room. In it was a cage somewhat larger than the previous one. The back of the cage was obscured by shadows. Several scrolls were tied to the bars.

The people had all thronged in and were peering into the shadows. The tall man observed how Yasuki let them edge closer to the cage. Suddenly, a huge grey shape exploded out of the darkness with an animalistic roar.

The crowd fell back, yelling in alarm, as the bulky thing threw itself against the bars, causing the cage to rock. It looked like a huge, heavily-muscled, pot-bellied man, but its skin was ashen grey. It had a mane of wild red hair that fell from its head, and two curving horns sprouted up from the fiery mass.

It snarled, revealing sharp teeth and rolling its disturbingly-human-looking eyes. Crouching, it lifted a large, spiked iron club from the cage floor, and battered the bars whilst roaring.

Again, the crowd drew back.

"Fear not - the Buddhist sutras tied to those bars will keep him from breaking free," Yasuki reassured them.

"What is it?", a scared-looking man asked.

"This, my friend, is a genuine Oni, a daemon straight from the bowels of Jigoku. He was terrorizing a town on the island of Shikoku. It took the prayers of twenty monks to subdue him. Only the sutras are stopping him from bending those bars apart and pulling you limb from limb."

As the beast bellowed and stomped around its prison, the people looked suitably alarmed - all except the tall man.

"Come, there is much still to see."

Another door swung open. In the next room stood a cage whose bars were more closely-knit that than those of its predecessors. Inside was a tall wicker basket. Yasuki said nothing this time, but took a reed pipe from one of his sleeves and, lifting it to his lips, began to play. The high, eerie notes drifted across the room, like the refrain of some half-recalled childhood lullaby.

Something stirred inside the wicker. The lid of the basket slid off with a soft plop. From inside the basket something rose slowly into view. It seemed to be moving in time to the music. It was a wedge-shaped head, perhaps six inches long. It had large, ebony-dark eyes and scaly, leathery skin. As it rose higher, the watchers could see that it belonged to some form of snake.

It reared up maybe 18 inches or so, then halted. It swayed to and fro to the music, as if entranced. Its body was weirdly shaped; instead of being tubular in cross-section, it was strangely flattened, giving the appearance of a 'skirt' of scales running along its body. Sometimes the snake's mouth would open slightly, revealing a pair of long fangs.

Suddenly it swung its head forwards, mouth agape. A pale yellow liquid shot from its fangs, spraying the bars and landing on the floor only inches from the people, who cringed in terror - save for the tall man.

Yasuki stopped playing, and the serpent slid back into its basket.

"You have just looked upon the legendary Tsuchinoko, one of the most ancient of yokai."

"That thing spat at us!"

"It threw poison!"

"We could have been killed!"

The crowd was becoming agitated, but Yasuki played them like an expert.

"What is life without a little danger? Besides, I know how far the Tsuchinoko snake can cast its venom; I positioned the basket accordingly. It's not good business to kill your customers!"

A nervous laugh passed among the visitors.

"Accounts of the Tsuchinoko can be found in the *Kojiki,* Nippon's oldest surviving book. It is the most deadly of serpents, but it has a weakness for alcohol. We keep it calm with sakè."

"It looks like it needs a little more," said one woman.

The tall man scratched his chin.

"Steel yourselves, good folk, for other horrors await."

Yasuki turned on his heel and marched onwards into the next room.

The following cage was festooned with swathes of a whispy white substance. It hung in loops and curtains from the roof of the enclosure. In the far corner of the ceiling was a white bundle that hung in a pendulous fashion.

"This, stuff... is it...webs?", asked a boy.

"Very astute, my young friend; these are indeed webs. Please take a closer look."

The crowd edged forward. Now they could see what looked like bones in the webbing; they were from chickens and small animals. One was a cat's skull that stared out mutely from its sticky wrapping.

"What kind of spider spins a web that big?", someone whispered.

"A big spider," answered Yasuki, "none other than a real live specimen of a Tsuchigumo - an Earth Spider!"

Yasuki clapped his hands sharply together. From the hanging bundle of silk came a dry rustling noise, like dead leaves. All eyes were drawn up into the shadowy corner. A hairy body the size of a human infant rose up on eight fat legs. The hairy members arched and groped, the first pair emerging from the silken nest like shaggy sausages. The hair-covered giant was striped in brown and rusty orange. A head the size of an apple peered out, its six eyes shining like glass beads. It seemed to sway drunkenly on its legs for a time, and the head looked back and forth. Satisfied there was no prey to be had, it sunk back into the dark of the nest.

"It was huge!"

"What a horror!"

"It makes my flesh crawl!"

"This Earth Spider was one of a thousand young that tumbled from the belly of the great spider killed by the hero Yorimitsu. Its mother was the size of an ox and had eaten one thousand and nine hundred men. The stories will tell you that Yorimitsu and his followers hunted down and slew all of the queen spider's brood, but some escaped - and here is living proof! I captured this one myself. It had its lair in a ruined temple on Mount Ontake. Its poison is strong enough to kill a horse. We feed it on birds and small creatures."

Once again the host moved on, and the crowd followed as he opened yet another door. The tall man lingered a scant second longer, then followed.

In the next cage, a human-shaped figure sat in a chair. It was wrapped entirely from head to foot in white sheets; no part of it was visible.

"My friends, the last yokai we will see is the most tragic. This poor soul is half-human. His appearance may alarm you, but behind the grotesque visage is the mind and soul of a man. His heart is human, his eyes are human, his mother was human - but his father... his father was something else. Ladies and gentlemen, I give you – Umiwarawa!"

The figure stood up. The sheets fell to the ground around him, and there were gasps as they did so. The figure standing before them was a man, naked and hairless, but small, brown, squarish scales covered every part of his body, like the skin of a reptile.

"Good afternoon. My name is Umiwarawa," he said, bowing.

"He... he can talk," a man stammered.

"Indeed I can," answered Umiwarawa. "I am only a skin-deep monster. Beneath these scales I am not so very different from you."

"Then, why the bars? Why are you in a cage if you're not dangerous?"

"Ah, therein lies a tragedy; because of my alarming features, some people will actually attack and try to kill me in the mistaken belief I am a daemon come to devour them! You see, these bars are not for your safety - they are for mine."

"But, if you're a man, don't you object to living like this?"

"Yes, your dignity has been taken from you!"

"I thank you for your concern, but Mr Yasuki is my friend. He and his family are the only friends I have. My mother never recovered from the shame of birthing me; she died young. For many years I had to live wild as a thief and beggar on the streets of Beppu, until Yasuki found me and gave me a home. When you look like this, there are few occupations open to you, especially when people find out who your father was."

"And who was your father?", another man asked.

"My father was not human. He was the oldest and most powerful of the yokai. He was ancient when Mount Fuji first rose. He is the Water Father - my father was Mizuchi, the dragon of the Kahashima River!"

For once there were no gasps, just a stunned silence.

"The dragon god Mizuchi would occasionally release his seed into the river to fertilise the water and land, and any female dragons in the area - but if young women were bathing in the river when Mizuchi's sperm was released, then they would fall pregnant with a hybrid child, part man and part dragon. The child would have some dragon features, but this would depend on how much the dragon seed was watered down; the greater the percentage of dragon seed, the more like its father the child would be. Some were even fully-fledged dragons, who tore their mothers asunder in the birthing, then flew away. Others were part man and part reptile. I, sad beast that I am, have only a little of my noble father in me - these dull scales are the only mark he left upon me."

"And now, our tour is at an end," intoned Yasuki. "Be sure to return, and bring your friends with you." He bustled the crowd out through a back door, grinning and bowing, whilst Umiwarawa pulled the sheets about him once more.

Blinking in the sunlight, the crowd dispersed. The tall man went too, but he would be back.

The sun was setting and the crowds had left the fair, moving on to the brothels and taverns. Yasuki was closing up shop when the tall man returned.

"Too late, my friend. We're closed. Come back tomorrow."

"You are a fraud, Yasuki san," the tall man purred.

"I beg your pardon?"

"You heard me - a fraud, a faker, a charlatan; a mountebank, if you will. Your exhibits are a collection of artifice."

Yasuki almost choked.

"This is the finest collection of living yokai ever exhibited. Why, I captured most of them myself! The Kappa was from…"

The tall man cut him off.

"The 'Kappa' is nothing more than a shaved monkey with a dead turtle's shell strapped to its back. You keep it sedated with drugs."

"I, I… I…"

"The 'Oni' is an out-of-work sumo wrestler. He is painted grey and wears a headdress made from horsehair and oxen's horns. The brace of animal teeth in his mouth is a nice touch, though he needs to work on his bellowing - a real Oni makes far more noise."

Yasuki looked at the tall man with a mixture of embarrassment and disbelief.

"A *real* Oni?"

The tall man nodded and continued.

"The 'Tsichinoko' was a beautifully-crafted hand pupped from made from carved leather over a wooden frame. It was operated by your young son in the basket. The 'venom' was coloured water pumped out of waxed leather tubes from a pouch compressed by the boy. By the way, snakes are functionally deaf. They cannot hear music; it is the swaying of the pipe that attracts them."

"The 'Earth Spider,' 'Tsuchigumo,' was another puppet, this time operated via hair-thin strings attached to the head, body and legs, and pulled by one of your employees hiding in the roof. Carved wood covered in cat hair, unless I miss my mark. Its webs were made of muslin and silk."

"And, finally, we come to the son of Mizuchi, the dark water, the 'Water Father,' the dragon who spews death. He would not be pleased at your lies and mummery if he knew. Your man is no child of Mizuchi; he is but a poor soul cursed with a cutaneous condition that leaves his epidermis disfigured by callouses."

"You what?"

"His skin is diseased with growths that look like scales."

"Oh."

"A real dragon's scales are harder than diamond, and shine like sunlight hitting rain - but naming him Umiwarawa, after the merman, was a fine touch."

"Look, my friend, are you insane? Just what is it you are after?"

"To tell you all your exhibits are crude fakes."

Yasuki was getting angry; all he wanted to do was pack up and go home, but this madman was threatening his very livelihood.

"Nobuo," Yasuki yelled, "Nobuo!"

A burly-looking man with a shaved head emerged from a nearby tent.

"This man is accusing me of being a fraud. Please deal with him."

Nobuo grunted and lumbered forward. He swung a punch that the tall man stopped in mid-swing as if his massive assailant had been a child. The jolt ran through Nobuo's whole body. The relaxed look never left the tall man's face as he began to tighten his grip.

Nobuo screamed and fell to his knees. The tall man yanked him to his feet again, holding him aloft by one arm like a broken puppet; he then casually tossed him aside. Nobuo landed in a heap amidst some crates, fifteen feet from the tall man.

Yasuki had worked in fairs all his life and had known many strongmen, but he had never seen anything like this. The tall man did not seem particularly muscular, but his strength was immense.

"Look, this is my living! It's not harming anyone - think of it as theatre. If you expose me, I'll be ruined! I have a family. Look, I can pay you to keep quiet. All today's takings – here, have it."

He produced a bag of coins.

"You insult me, Yasuki san. I'm not interested in your money, and I don't want to close you down - even though you *are* a fraud."

"Then what do you want?"

"I have a proposition for you." The tall man leaned closer. Yasuki noticed how florid he looked, and how large his nose seemed. *Was he from overseas?*

"I have an exhibit for you. Not some puppet or drugged animal, not some deformed human being, but the real thing!"

"A real yokai? You can't be serious! There's no such...."

"There's no such thing? If you are so sure, come back to my tent and I will show you. I have a genuine Obake, one that I am willing to let you exhibit."

"And what do you want for it? What's in this for you?"

The tall man seemed to ponder, and looked almost wistful for a time.

"The belief in yokai is starting to fade. More people are abandoning the countryside and moving into the cities, like Edo. Yokai are vital to Nippon, they are part of her; if they fade away, part of Nippon fades, too. The gaijin come in their tall ships - they bring new things and new ideas. We need to keep hold of some of the old ways before they slip through our fingers."

Yasuki didn't fully understand, but he also didn't want to look a gift horse in the mouth. He would go and look at what this stranger had. It would probably turn out to be some foreign animal imported from China or the South Seas; nevertheless, it would attract interest, and he could spin some yarns about it.

"Very well. Lead on."

The tall man led Yasuki across the now-quiet fair. A few lanterns bobbed here and there, and the light from the cabins of the families who lived and worked there shone out through shutters. At the edge of the fair was a huge tent of purple canvas - Yasuki could not recall having seen it before. The tall man pulled open the flaps and beckoned him in.

The inside of the tent was partitioned off by a curtain. It was sparsely furnished with a few chairs, a table, and some scattered books. The tall man swept the curtain aside. In the hidden half of the tent stood a large cage, covered by canvas sheeting. There was an unwholesome smell emanating from the cage. The tall man took one end of the canvas and pulled it away from the cage. Yasuki noted that he stood well back from the bars.

The first thing that hit Yasuki was the stench; it was like old meat left too long in the sun. At the far end of the cage was a water bowl and a mass of gently-heaving straw. The tall man reached for a long walking cane, and struck the bars with a resounding clang. The mass of straw seemed to explode. A red thing that shrieked and shrieked, like a dying woman, leapt across the cage, a sinewy arm reaching through the bars to grasp at whatever was in reach. Yasuki jumped back in alarm, letting out a yell of his own.

The thing, seeing that there was no-one in reach, gripped the bars with its taloned fingers, and shook them so hard that the cage rocked. All the time it continued its high-pitched screeching. As Yasuki regained some composure, he looked at the animal properly for the first time. *Was it some kind of weird monkey?* No, it was totally unlike any creature he had seen or heard of.

It was the size of a three- or four-year-old child, but its limbs seemed possessed of an unnatural strength. It stood upright on two legs and was covered in a pelt of short, blood-red fur.

A mane of longer black hair tumbled down from its head and across its man-like shoulders. The face was flat, monkeyish, with a wide, thin-lipped mouth, now bared and showing masses of sharp teeth. Spittle and effluvia foamed out from its mouth like a rabid dog and fell to its chest. Above a flat little nose, two huge, nocturnal eyes shone a deep red. Weirdest of all were the creature's ears; they looked for all the world like an outsized-rabbit's ears. They rose up from the mass of black hair atop its head, and they would have seemed comical if not for the look of unhinged hatred on the creature's face.

The tall man reached for a bag on a nearby table. He fumbled inside, then tossed a brownish-red, shapeless object into the cage. Squealing with delight, the creature dropped down from the bars and grabbed the object, apparently some kind of meat. It now began a little dance as it crooned to itself, before ripping greedily into the flesh with a look of almost-orgasmic ecstasy on its detestable face.

"What in the name of Buddha is that?", murmured Yasuki.

"Nothing in Buddha's name - it is a Mouryo, a kind of daemonic yokai rabbit. It frequents graveyards, where it digs up human corpses and feeds on their rotting livers. In captivity, I feed it on animal livers procured from slaughterhouses. It seems not to mind, as long as I let them mature for a while."

"Where did you come by it?"

"I heard tell from some monks in Otofuke, way up in Hokkaidō, that some kind of creature was digging up graves and violating corpses in a cemetery on the outskirts of the town. At first they thought it might be wolves or bears, but, when they saw a Mouryo creeping amidst the tombs, they never went back. I used rancid livers to lure it into a trap. The townsfolk were quite grateful to me for having dealt with it."

"And you will let me have this for my show?"

"Of course. Won't it be grand to end your little tour with a *real* yokai after the parade of fakes you roll out?"

"It looks dangerous."

"It is. You must never dream of entering its cage. The Mouryo is not averse to fresh meat."

"How do you look after it, clean and feed it?"

The tall man pointed to a sheet of metal.

"When you need to clean the cage or change its water, you can use this to trap the Mouryo by sliding it through the bars and making a partition. It feeds exclusively on livers - you can buy these from any slaughterhouse for very little money. Throw them in through the bars; don't get within its reach, or it will tear your liver out whilst you are still alive. Remember, keeping this creature is like keeping a pet murderer!"

He lifted up the sheet of metal with a strange ease, and slipped it in between the bars and pushed. The Mouryo seemed too intent on its meal to notice. It cooed and gurgled like some horrid child. Once the sheet was through, trapping the creature in one half of the cage, the tall man twisted bolts on each side to secure it. The creature looked up briefly, then continued to suck and gnaw at the lump of flesh, smacking its narrow lips.

Between them, they threw the canvas back over the cage. At one end there was a handle, like that of a cart. For the first time, Yasuki noticed that the cage was on wheels. The tall man took up the walking cane and knocked away the wooden blocks from the wheels. Together they dragged the cage and its alarming occupant out of the tent and across the fair to Yasuki's exhibit.

* * * * *

Takings were up by 100%. The Mouryo was the attraction to end all attractions. Women screamed, men fainted, and children soiled themselves at the sight of it, but word of mouth got round and crowds thronged to see it. Yasuki always ended the tour with the Mouryo; it never dissapointed, flinging itself at the bars, desperately trying to reach the public in a hate-filled frenzy. It would foam and scream, and caper back and forth like a demented acrobat. Yasuki would toss it putrid liver, and he found that the beast could be trained - when he showed it the liver, it would dance a strange little dance. It rocked side to side, stamping its feet on the ground and turning in circles with its arms above it, as its mad red eyes stared out at nothing.

Yasuki's family would not go near the cage. The other performers and puppet operators could not bear to be near it - only Nobuo would help him with the creature. Both were careful not to come within reach as its scrawny but brutally-strong arms reached out from between the bars.

* * * * *

It was Nobuo who found him. The broken saké bottle told the whole story; Yasuki had been drinking more than usual lately. He had always been fond of liquor, but now, with the extra money, he could afford more than ever. Obviously, he had got drunk and wandered too close to the cage. He lay at an odd angle by the bars. The floor of the room was a carpet of red, and the hole in his back was large enough to admit two human fists. The lock on the cage was undone and the door open − a search of Yasuki's body revealed that the keys to the cage were gone. The Mouryo was nowhere to be seen, but a trail of inhuman footprints in the blood led away from the exhibit and into the night.

Sometime later, stories started to circulate of something digging up bodies in the local graveyards; most people put it down to feral dogs.

4. The Critic

It had been a good meal, but not an excellent one; good, but not good enough to stop him from tearing the establishment apart. The service was good, the restaurant was spotlessly clean, and the ambience was fine, but he had a reputation to uphold - he couldn't let his readers think he was getting soft.

Mori Hideki, you see, was a restaurant critic, and the most feared restaurant critic in Osaka. His column in the *Osaka Observer* could make or break an eatery, and he had broken far more than he had made. A meal needed to be transcendental before he gave it a favourable review; even then, he did it grudgingly. The fact was, Mori Hideki enjoyed giving bad reviews - he enjoyed the little power trips it gave him, and he enjoyed finding new and horrible ways to pick a restaurant and its food apart.

It was a good life being a restaurant critic, reviews aside; he usually ate very well (though he seldom let his readers know that). His meals and the accompanying drinks were free.

He had the admiration of his peers and readers, and the fear of the entire restaurant community of not only Osaka, but the whole of Nippon. He also got to travel the world and report back on the finest eateries on the globe. He had visited Jean-Claude Vrinat's peerless *Taillevent* in Paris, Heston Blumenthal's legendary *The Fat Duck* in the village of Bray in Berkshire, England, and Thomas Keller's *Per Se* on Columbus Circle, New York.

It was a life most could only dream of, and yet Hideki was only ever happy if he was criticizing someone else's culinary efforts. At this moment, he was mentally composing his review as he strolled through Dōtonbori, the finest restaurant area in the city.

As he wandered back towards the JR Osaka Loop Line to take a train back to the offices of the *Observer,* a smell hit his nostrils - Hideki was a foodie, and his nostrils were more bloodhound's than man's when it came to the smells of cooking. Smell is linked intimately to memory, and the scent now wafting under his nose sank deep into his psyche and transported him back 30 years to his mother's kitchen in Takatsuki - it was exactly like the smell of her home cooking. He smelled takoyaki, the octopus dumplings, exactly as she had cooked them, and kushikatsu, the cheese and vegetables deep-fried in dough. These were not the smells of street vendors or restaurants, but his mother's kitchen smells. Hideki had not eaten food like that in years; he had considered it fare only fit for bumpkins, whilst his palate had turned to grander delights. Now he felt his mouth begin to water, even on a full stomach. He turned and followed his nose.

The scent led him through a maze of little back streets he never even knew existed – as a critic writing for such a big paper as the *Observer,* the small establishments that filled the back alleys of Dōtonbori usually fell under his radar. Finally he came to it – a tiny, back-street restaurant whose sign proclaimed it to be *The Blue Dragon.*

The front looked grubby - the windows had not been cleaned in years, and prevented a clear look into the interior. The painted sign, a coiling sapphire dragon, had faded with age. The front door looked peeling and old – oh, but the smell! He pushed the door open and entered.

The wall of alluring smells hit him, and he began to salivate again. The place was busy, every table packed full of happy diners enjoying their food. A portly, smiling man with thinning hair approached. He was dressed in an apron and had his shirtsleeves rolled up.

"May I help you? Table for one, is it?"

"No, not today, but I'd like to book a place for next week."

"Certainly, sir," answered the man, producing a pen and paper from his pocket. "And your name?"

"Mori Hideki."

The man looked more than a little startled and took a step back, looking Hideki up and down for a moment.

"*The* Mori Hideki, of the *Osaka Observer?*"

Hideki grinned and nodded - he enjoyed his reputation, and liked to see restaurant owners sweat and squirm under his gaze - but this fellow seemed to gain his composure quickly, and offered a broad smile.

"I never would have expected that such a great man would set foot in my humble establishment." He bowed low, and seemed more pleased than apprehensive.

"Shall we say next Thursday? I can have the review in the *Observer* on Saturday."

"You do me a great honour, Hideki san."

"'Til next week, then. I will anticipate an excellent meal; don't disappoint me."

"We try never to disappoint at *The Blue Dragon*."

"I'm glad to hear it, my good man."

The owner bowed again, and Hideki turned and walked back onto the street. He mused, as he walked back towards the station, as to how different *The Blue Dragon* was to the grand, five-star restaurants he usually reviewed. It would be a pleasant change for his readers.

That afternoon he tore apart the restaurant in which he had eaten. Even though the meal had been fairly enjoyable, his review made it sound as if he had been eating excrement from inside an open grave; he was particularly pleased with the piece.

As the day drew on, Hideki found his anticipation of the meal at *The Blue Dragon* gaining. Could his enjoyment of eating actually be returning?

* * * * *

The portly owner greeted Hideki warmly upon his arrival.

"I have prepared a special room for you, so that the other diners will not disturb you."

"How thoughtful of you." Hideki grinned inwardly. He enjoyed being thought of as better than the masses.

His host led him past tables full of other diners to a door. It led to a smaller room with a table laid out ready for his guest. Hideki sat.

"I will bring the menu, Hideki san. Would you care for a drink?"

"Kirin Fukkoku beer."

"Certainly." He scurried off as Hideki made himself comfortable. The host, whose name Hideki had not even enquired of yet, was back holding a glass of beer and a menu within moments.

Hideki perused the list for a moment, and let nostalgia choose for him.

"Takoyaki to begin, followed by black cod with miso sauce, and pumpkin moci with ice cream to follow."

"An excellent choice."

Hideki mused on his choice as he sipped the beer. It was far more standard fare than his normal repasts, but he could write a piece on simple foods and nostalgic dishes from his humble past. Yes, that was a great spin - getting back to your roots.

The octopus dumplings were exquisite, the soft moistness of the dumplings contrasting with the chewiness of the tentacles. The cod flesh fell apart like an exotic flower opening, and melted in his mouth. The sweet stickiness of the mochi rice paste mingled with the pumpkin and the cool, persimmon-flavoured ice cream. Before long he was pushing the last dish away and smacking his lips.

"Was everything to your liking, Hideki san?" His host had reappeared.

"It was wonderful, the finest meal I have ever eaten!"

"That is wonderful; and would you like anything else?"

It was then Hideki realised that he was still quite hungry.

"Can I see the menu again?"

He ordered a second meal: kuhikatsu, followed by salmon in wild cherry, and adzuki beans with sugar, all swilled down with beer and rice wine. Again, the meal was delicious, but, again, he still felt hungry – ravenous, in fact. As always, the food was on the house, so Hideki ordered more.

Dish followed dish - tempura ice cream, yakisoba, chicken thighs in plum sauce, horse mackerel, wild boar stew, sukiyaki, deep fried pork cutlets, miso soup, hayashi rice, korokke... the list went on.

Suddenly, Hideki stopped. The chopsticks tumbled from his grasp. He realised that he had eaten enough for a half-dozen men, but he was hungry, more hungry than he had ever been in his life. It was a deep, gnawing hunger, as if he hadn't eaten in days.

"Is everything to your liking?" He looked up to see the restaurant owner grinning at him.

"I'm still hungry," Hideki whined.

"And so you will always be."

"What? I don't understand."

"Hideki, you live off other people's hard work, whilst never lifting a finger yourself. You scandalise good, honest folk, out of spite and the feeling of power it gives you. You eat the finest food in Nippon, and your thanks to those who sweat over it is to throw it back in their faces in the shallow, whinging, spineless little reviews you write. Do you realise how little you are? Do you realise how inconsequential what you do is? You take and take, and give nothing in return. Your overweening arrogance and cowardly peevishness has put hundreds of people out of work. Mr. and Mrs. Yasunaga killed themselves last year after what you wrote about them - did you know that? They had run their restaurant in this city for forty years! Well, now it's time for revenge. You will never enjoy another meal, Hideki, and you will forevermore be hungry."

The man held up a polished dish to show the critic his own reflection. Hideki recoiled in horror - his visage had changed beyond recognition. Gone was the chubby face and fine hair; what looked back at him was a mockery, grey skin barely stretched over a skull-like face. The eyes were little more than tiny balls of orange light in two deep, black sockets, and the nose was no more than a pair of slits. The mouth hung open, its long black tongue dangling over jagged, rotting teeth. Drool slavered from his tongue and mouth, coating his shirt. He raised a hand - it was a wizened thing ending in broken, filth-caked nails.

"Hideki san, you are damned - and I bid you welcome to a hell of your own making."

"What am I?" He managed to croak the words from the twisted mouth.

"Well, besides a cruel, petty, overpaid, vain, talentless hack, you are now a Jikininki."

"A wh-what?"

"A Jikininki - a hungry ghost. In life, Jikininki were greedy, selfish people. Now you are fated to be Jikininki forevermore, a cadaverous ghoul cursed with an insatiable hunger. Never again will that hunger be sated; never will you know peace. You will eat and eat, and yet be starving forever - starving to death, a death that will never come."

The man clapped his hands, and several neatly-dressed waiters began to clear away the empty dishes, whilst others brought more, overflowing with food.

Hideki pushed his face forward into a plate of sushi and began to eat, knowing he would never know the feeling of a full stomach again.

5. Enryö's Last Case

The old man looked at himself in the mirror, fussily adjusting his tie. If the young man had come all the way from Hokkaido University to interview him then the least he could do was look smart. He smiled to himself. 'Not bad looking for my age', he thought.

He walked over to the hotel window and looked out over the view of Dalian. The sun was glinting on the sea in Port Arthur in the distance. The port was taken from the Chinese then successfully defended from the Russians, Inoue Enryō felt proud that his country had come so far in such a short time. Not so very long ago it had been stagnating in isolation, crippled by supestition. Now it was one of the world's great powers. If felt that he, in his own way, had helped Nippon out of the darkness and into the light.

He glanced at his watch, the young man would be here soon. He felt more than a little flattered that the fellow had travelled so far to see him. There was a knock at the door. The lad was punctual, that was good. He walked over and opened the door.

Enryō san," the tall young man bowed low.

"You must be Tachibana Jin'ichi. How was the trip from Hokkaido?"

"Fine sir, fine. Thank you so much for allowing me to interview you."

"Not at all my boy, not at all. I am an educator and I always have time for those who wish to feed their minds. Now shall we sit?"

Enryō led Jin'ichi through to the sitting room. The young man set cut some pens and paper on the table.

"Sir, you have gained the nickname of yokai doctor or ghost doctor. For a man who has dedicated his life to dispelling superstition does this annoy you?"

"No, no", Enryō laughed, you see I look on ghosts and monsters as a sickness of the mind in the same way as a medical doctor looks upon physical disease as maladies of the body. Yokai grow from ignorance and superstition just as an ague grows from infectious diseases like malaria. So you see I am a doctor of yokai in that I cure these mental diseases by removing the cause, namely the old superstitions people use to cling to."

Jin'ichi nodded, furiously scribbling notes.

"Can you tell me how you first became interested in dispelling the ideas of ghosts and monsters?"

"I can well record the very occasion. It was in the early 1860s just before the Meiji Restoration. I was staying at a boarding school in the countryside some miles outside of Tokyo. A friend of mine needed to use the toilet in the middle of the night. He came back shaking with fear, saying that he had seen a monster in the kitchen, which you had to pass to get to the toilet. He was insistent that he had seen it. I managed to calm him down and finally persuaded him to take me to see this 'monster'. It had been nothing more than the silhouette of a stack of rice sacks. They had been piled up and, in the shadows, looked like a hulking beast looming out of the darkness.

Now this got me to wondering about ghosts and monsters. I thought if one monster could be explained, why not all of them?"

"So did you actively look into monsters before you began your formal training?"

"Oh yes, I recall another occasion from my youth. My parents had taken the family to Kyūshū for a holiday. I met some local men who were beside themselves with fear. They said that they had seen a kappa in a pond near the village. They were too afraid to go down there any more. My father and I took a look and found it was nothing more than a softshell turtle. It was a big one, granted, and covered in pond weed, but just a turtle nonetheless."

"So things like these began your interest in psychology?"

"Well the Meiji Restoration came about when I was ten years old. This whole rebuilding of Nippon, both as a nation and as individual people, dragged us out of the dark ages. As you know, Nippon had spent a long period closed to the rest of the world. This meant the country had fallen behind the rest of the world in scientific progress. Most people still believed in things long abandoned by folk in other countries.

The Restoration was a clean slate and I wanted to be part of it. I studied hard and became a psychologist. I wanted to know from where these peculiar fancies sprang, and why they were so persistent. I also wanted to slay these daemons of the mind to help my country.

Finally, in 1903 I set up Private University Testugakukan, what is now called Tokyo University."

"You must be very proud of your achievements."

"I am indeed, but by the same token I feel humble to have helped my country."

"Can you tell me about yokaigaku?"

Enryō rubbed his hands clearly warming to the subject "The study of monsters. I wrote six volumes on this. I have personally investigated over one thousand individual cases of monster, ghost and supernatural occurrences. On each and every occasion I found a rational explanation."

"Could you give me some examples please?"

"Good Lord, where to start? Well one of the most common reported paranormal occurrences was fox possession. When people began to act in an irrational manner they were thought to be possessed or bewitched by a fox. What they were actually suffering from was mental illness. People did not understand conditions such as schizophrenia, Tourette syndrome or narcolepsy. Imagine how these conditions must have looked to an uneducated peasant in a mountain village? I diagnosed a number of so-called fox possessions as forms of mental illness. Outbreaks of rabies were thought to be fox bewitchment as well.

People with physical deformities were looked on as being yokai or cursed by yokai. In the town of Tono up in Iwate, children born with deformities were thought to have been fathered by kappas!"

"I believe travel was restricted at one time as well," said Jin'ichi fumbling with his papers.

"Indeed. One had to have permission to travel outside of one's prefecture, and travel abroad was strictly forbidden to most people. This fostered an insular mindset and a fear of strangers. Outsiders coming into a village would often be suspected of being tengu; bird men!"

"It has taken me a lifetime, but I think I have just about stamped out these beliefs in all but the most backward backwaters. Now the promulgation of ethics through an institutionalised school system has put paid to the yokai once and for all. Children are now taught in schools that yokai and obake are nothing more than figments of the imagination. And do you know what else did for them?

"What?"

"The electric light," Enryō clapped his hands and laughed. "It's hard to believe in monsters with the lights on. They crawl away and die under the light!"

"So you think there are no mysteries to explore?"

"No, no my boy. There are real mysteries science needs to explore. We know nothing, for example, of the deep oceans or the dark side of the moon. These are real mysteries. Yokai are psuedo-mysteries. Once the cobwebs of ghosts and monsters are swept from our minds the true mysteries can be examined."

"Sir, did you ever, even once, think you might be wrong?"

"No, never even once. In all those cases I investigated, I never found anything 'supernatural'. What I did find was paranoia, delusion, delirium, illness and the odd sheet caught up in the wind at night."

"What would you do if I told you that you were totally wrong?"

"What do you mean, I don't follow you?"

"Oh Enryō san, you are so wrong. There are yokai. All your life you have been chasing shadows on walls when all you had to do was open up your eyes. In your mad clammering for modernity you denied what your ancestors knew to be true."

The youth had dropped his papers and now stood looking down at Enryō. Was he mad?

His eyes seemed to grow darker. Was it a trick of the light, but was his nose getting longer? He raised up his hands to show nails that visibly lengthened into bird-like talons. His fine dark hair rippled as it widened into a mane of black feathers. His jaw and nose stretched, looking for all the world like an opaque glass being stretched in a glass blower's furnace. Nose and jaws fused into a great black beak. His shirt and jacket shredded as massive, ebony wings unfurled and blocked out the daylight as they opened, filling most of the room. The eyes fixed on him, glittering like jet above the snapping, predatory beak.

"What do say you now Enryō san?" The creature croaked.

"T..t..tengu!" Enryō gasped as his mind struggled with taking in the thing standing before him. A thing he had spent his life disproving. He felt a sudden sharp, stabbing pain in the chest and a warm flush between his legs.

Inoue Enryō was found dead on the evening of the 6th June 1919. The verdict was heart attack though no-one could quite explain the look of surprise and horror he had frozen onto his face, or why he was clutching a raven's feather in his hand.

6. Letting the Dog in

The ferry from Takamatsu had been late. The sky was already bruising when the eight-mile crossing to Nao-shima had begun. The waters had become choppy, white horses breaking about the steamship's prow. Dr Matsushita gripped the rail and breathed in the sea air. It was said that his patient had not left the little island in the whole of her long life. So strange to think that she had been born, raised, schooled, courted, wed and had borne four children, all within the self-imposed prison of Nao-shima. Tanaka Yoshiko was 86, and although Matsushita considered himself a good doctor, he could not cure old age.

He had received the telegram that his elderly charge was weakening the evening before. He already had appointments to attend to at his practice in Takamatsu, but he left as quickly as he could, taking the new railway line down to the port and catching the last ferry to the island; this would, he realized, compel him to stay the night on Nao-shima. He sighed. It was not an unpleasant place, just a little - well, rustic. He had been surprised to find out that a telegraph could be sent from the little community - the Meiji Restoration had finally reached this little enclave. Above him, gulls cried mournfully as they returned to the shore to roost.

A horse and trap were waiting for him at the dock. The driver greeted him with a deep bow, and Dr Matsushita climbed aboard. The crossing had taken less than half an hour, but now the sun had sunken low in the autumnal sky. The horses' hooves cracked on the rough road that wound up to the Tanaka house - maybe the island was more resistant to progress than he thought. He passed one or two locals on the way, who nodded in greeting.

The trap drew up to the old, imposing house. It had been built in the mid-Edo, and now, in the twilight, Dr Matsushita could believe he had stepped back in time. There was no city bustle, no modern sounds of machines or industry. The air was scented with cryptomeria pine, and the only noise was the distant cawing of crows.

As he drew closer, he saw slips of paper pinned to the door. He squinted at the characters - Buddhist sutras. Telegraph or not, on Naoshima, the old ways died hard.

He rang the brass bell that hung beside the door, and presently a servant appeared.

"Dr Matsushita, my mistress is expecting you." He bowed lower than the trap driver had, and ushered the doctor inside. He knew the way well, along the corridors and up several storeys. Tanaka Yoshiko rarely left her chambers these days.

She lay on her futon, propped up by pillows. Her grey hair was tied neatly into a topknot. Her face was coated in thick, white makeup; it had cracked in several areas, giving the old lady the look of crumbling alabaster. Her dark eyes fixed on him, and her face cracked into a smile.

"I am sorry if I inconvenienced you, but I have no family left here, only my trusted servants."

"I came as soon as I could, Madame." He bowed.

"Doctor san, so good of you to come so promptly. I realise you must be very busy on the mainland."

"No inconvenience; it is a doctor's job to take care of his charges, my lady."

"But the hour is late, and you will miss the last ferry back to Takamatsu. I will have the servants make up a room for you."

"I have no wish to impose; I can find an inn at the village."

The old lady frowned and shook her head. "I will not hear of it, Doctor. I have brought you here, and it would be most remiss not to offer you my hospitality."

She clapped hands, made claw-like and bent with age and arthritis. He noticed her wince as she did so. "Make up a room and bring some tea and food for the good doctor - he has come a long way."

The manservant bowed and left.

"Come; sit." She motioned to a chair.

"What can I do for you, Madame?"

"I take it you have brought more medicine?"

He nodded. In his bag he carried her monthly supply of morphine.

"Good, good - but it is losing its potency. Do you have the other potion you mentioned?"

"I do, Madame Tanaka, but you must realise this is not a cure - there is no cure for old age."

The old woman gave a wheezing laugh and nodded.

"The first emperor of China, Qin Shi Huang, thought there was a cure for death. He was obsessed with cheating his own mortality. He sent out his court wizard and 3,000 virgins to find it. They got as far as Australia, but found no cure for death. The emperor even drank mercury because he thought it would preserve his body. Do you know how old he was when he died?"

"Fifty."

"I'm surprised he lasted that long." Madame Tanaka threw back her head and laughed. It was infectious, and soon the doctor was laughing too.

"All that effort, and the poor wizard Xu Fu ended his days here in Japan because he was too afraid to return home without the elixir of life. I've beaten Qin Shi Huang by 36 years, and I have never even left Nao-shima!"

"Have you never wanted to travel? It seems so strange that you have led such a long life on one tiny island."

"Everything I have wanted in my life I have found on Nao-shima. Wanderlust is for others. They are welcome to it - good luck to them. I have never once felt the urge to leave the island."

She must have seen the doctor's frown, because she continued to explain. "I know you must think this place is like a prison for me, but it is not. No, no, it is the very reverse. Nao-shima protects me; it is the bigger world outside I fear. I think it must be like that fear some have of wide open spaces - I believe you have a word for it."

"Agoraphobia."

"Call it what you will, the outside world can roll on without me It has taken my sons. The elder runs a fish factory on Osaka, and his younger brother imports art in Tokyo. When I die, there will be no Tanakas left on Nao-shima. I intend to stay a while longer."

"You must realise that the new potion I have brought you is somewhat stronger than the morphine you are used to."

The matriarch struggled to sit up. "My mind is in fine health, Doctor san, but my body is in ruin. It is an unpleasant situation. My joints and back cause me much pain, and I fear that I have grown, shall we say, 'accustomed' to morphine. Tell me more of your new concoction."

"It is called laudanum; it is a tincture of opium mixed in alcohol. It was developed in the sixteenth century in the West as a painkiller. In Europe brandy is used, but I have suspended the opium in sake."

He reached into his bag and produced a bottle of clear liquid. She smiled and nodded. "Ah, the fruit of the poppy; the old ways are often the best, Doctor san."

He nodded in agreement, but stopped himself as he recalled the sutras at the door. "I notice you have pinned up prayers at the doorway."

"When you are as old as me, you need all the help you can get." She laughed again. "Now I am getting a little tired, if you will forgive me."

"Of course, Madame, I will leave the medicine beside your pillow."

"Thank you. Your room should be ready now. I am sorry to detain you. You must be a busy man."

"I fear you are correct, Madame. I must away early tomorrow to make it back to my practice for opening time. I will probably be gone before you rise."

"No matter, Doctor, my man will arrange transport to the ferry at first light."

A servant entered the room and bowed. "Doctor san, your supper is ready."

He was led away to a pleasant meal of spiced duck and fruit with green tea, and then shown to his room. It was not long before Dr Matsushita was asleep.

The first rays of dawn awoke the doctor and he rose. Swiftly washing and dressing, he decided not to disturb the servants, but to let himself out of the house. He descended the stairs quietly and unbolted the door. As he opened the door, he saw something move in the half-light. There was a small animal beside the pathway. At first he thought it was a tanuki, but as it quietly approached he saw it was a small dog.

The animal resembled a Pekingese dog, with a long, dark coat that obscured its legs. It moved with a silent, gliding grace. It glanced at him briefly with large brown eyes in a flat, pug-like face framed with thickly-furred, drooping ears.

It must belong to Madame Tanaka, though he had never seen it before and she had not mentioned having a dog. The servants must have been up earlier than he thought and let it out to do its business. He lent backwards to open the door again, and the little dog slipped through into the hall.

He glanced at his watch; it had just turned 8 a.m. He walked down the path and waited for the horse and trap to arrive and take him to the ferry. He didn't have to wait long; the clopping sound of hooves heralded the arrival of his transport. The driver smiled as he helped the doctor onto the trap. It was the same man who had brought him there the evening before.

"How is Madame Tanaka?", he asked.

"As well as can be expected for a lady of her advanced years. She is suffering from arthritic pain, but the medicine I brought her will ease it. Tell me, how long has she had her dog? I have visited her a number of times in the past, but I have not seen it before today."

The man turned in his seat as he set the horse to trotting back. He had a puzzled look on his face. "Madame Tanaka has no dogs; she has no pets of any kind."

"That's strange. I saw a little dog this morning, and I assumed it was hers."

A dark look crossed the driver's face as he leaned back again.

"What sort of dog?"

"A small long-haired one; a Pekingese, I think."

"Where was it?"

"It was out on the path that runs up to the Tanaka house. I thought the servants had let it out, so I opened the door for it and it went back inside."

The doctor saw the driver's face visibly pale.

"What's the matter? It's only a little dog."

"It's not your fault, you're an outsider; you were not to know - how could you?"

"I'm not following you - have I done wrong?"

"The sutras at the door - they were to keep it out, but you opened the door and let it in. Maybe it's best this way - Madame Tanaka is old and beginning to suffer."

"What are you talking about, man? The sutras were to keep the dog *out*? Why on earth would she want to do that? Has she got an allergy to animals? She should have told me."

"No, Doctor, you don't understand - that was no ordinary dog you let into her house, it was a Keukegen!"

"A what?"

"A Keukegen - a yokai dog. It is a spirit of disease. One such creature haunts the Tanaka family - it comes to claim them. The Keukegen brings death to each member of the household. The sutras pinned to the door were to hold it back, to prevent it from crossing the threshold."

Dr Matsushita breathed an audible sigh of relief. He then began to laugh. "You worried me for a moment; I thought it was something serious!"

"It *is* serious - you have let death into the Tanaka household. Madame Tanaka will be dead by this evening."

"You can't possibly believe that - not even here, not even on Naoshima."

"I have lived here all my life, as did my father and his before him. Each time the dog appears, a Tanaka dies."

The doctor shook his head in disbelief. The Restoration had indeed not shone its light on this little corner of Nippon.

The rest of the trip was uneventful. He caught the ferry back to Takamatsu, and a short ride back to his surgery. Upon his arrival, his secretary greeted him and handed over a telegram.

"It came this morning. You must have still been travelling when it arrived."

He glanced down at the paper and unfolded it, reading the type.

'Dr. Matsushita, pleased be advised that Tanaka Yoshiko passed away this morning at approximately 8.06 am.'

7. Unknown Pleasures

In one corner, a pair of teenaged lesbians in *Sailor Moon* outfits were kissing passionately between excited, girlish giggles. Their hands explored each other's bodies as they broke off to stare loving into each other's doe eyes.

Close by, a man in a dog leash knelt at the pale, beautiful, bare feet of his austere mistress; he lifted them to his face and began to kiss and smell them. As he inhaled, first deeply, then frantically, his eyes rolled with dream-like ecstasy. His bob-haired mistress smiled faintly and took another drag on her Turkish cigarette, then spread her toes to scent mark her property.

A tattooed, muscular transman with a shaven head, wearing nothing but a leather peaked cap, had bodily lifted a genetic man up and pinned him to the wall with his body. He was planting a savage, invasive kiss on his willing victim's mouth, probing deep with his tongue whilst grinding his pussy against the man's crotch.

Another 'dom' had her nude slave across her lap like a child and was gently pulling a string of ass beads from his backside, popping the plastic spheres out one at a time. His bottom wiggled and twitched with each audible 'pop'.

Someone, gender unknown due to their getup, waddled past like a surreal S&M penguin. They were encased head to foot in PVC and were wearing a gasmask of some description.

Odd as these antics might have seemed to the casual onlooker who was not familiar with anything other than 'vanilla' sex, they were being largely ignored in favour of that night's floorshow at *Club Saliva*. A tall, round-buttocked, large-breasted shemale, her long ebony hair twisted into twin plaits, was deeply penetrating the anus of a man who crouched on all fours. Her ten-inch phallus rammed in and out of his greased fundament like a meat piston. Her egg-sized testicles slapped noisily against his much smaller ones. His own modestly-sized penis was stiff with delight; he moaned in pleasure, but his lustful vocalisations were muted by the fact that an equally-well-endowed ladyboy was eagerly thrusting her she-meat into his mouth. This second shemale was also naked, but her face had been made up to look like a geisha. Both of the transgendered amazons orgasmed with amazing synchronization, filling both of their slave's hungry holes at once.

Nakano Yutaka looked on disinterestedly and sipped his Singa beer. From the age of fourteen, Yukata had been a dedicated sexual deviant; from that first teenaged experience with a painted whore old enough to be his mother, sex had fascinated and obsessed him. He came from a well-off family and worked for a large law firm that paid well. He had spent a good portion of his wages in indulging in every sexual perversion he could. He was like a seasoned wine buff - Yukata could have written a sexual encyclopaedia if he had so wished. The trouble was that Yutaka had become bored with sex, disenchanted with fucking and all its associated games. He had done everything, and, like a stamp collector when his collection is finished, he felt hollow.

"Looks like all three enjoyed that." A tall man with a glass of sake had sat down beside him.

"I suppose they did," he answered, and drank more beer.

"You don't seem very interested in tonight's entertainment."

"Been there, done that - done it so many times I have lost count."

"You sound a little disillusioned, my friend."

"When you have done everything from bondage to bukkake, things start getting a little old. You know the old saying – 'nothing is new.'"

The man leant closer. "Surely there is *something* you haven't tried. People are coming up with new games and tricks all the time. Very inventive in that field, humans."

Yutaka looked at the man. *Was he mad or drunk?* He was a tall man with a florid completion and a long nose; he looked foreign and the UV lights in the club cast him in a weird relief.

"Surely the internet has something new to offer - it is the greatest parade of deviancy and aberrant sexual behaviour the world has ever seen."

"I'm a doer, my friend, not a watcher; voyeurism became a crushing bore for me before I had even left school. Any damn fool can squat in front of a computer screen, frigging themselves raw - what's the point? Reality or nothing. There is no 'virtual sex' for me."

"So, you have done it all?" The man sipped his sake like a bird taking water at a bird-bath and cast a disbelieving look at Yukata.

"Bestiality?", he enquired.

"I'm a committed animal lover."

"Hard sports?"

"Done that shit."

"Necrophilia?"

"I always had a stiff."

"Till some rotten bastard split on you."

Yukata almost choked on his beer at the man's joke. He was taking a shine to the stranger.

"So can *you* think of anything fresh in the sins of the flesh?"

The man grinned a tigerish grin.

"Oh, God, yes. You see, we are alike you and I - connoissuers of weird sex; worshippers at the altar of fuck. But I have been doing this longer than you. I'm older than I look, and I have discovered some strange things in my time - stuff a human mind, even one like yours, would never conceive of."

Yukata smiled at the man's compliment. "My mind can conceive of a lot, but everything it conceived of I have done repeatedly, endlessly, grindingly, till the lustre has gone."

"Ha, ha - the *lust*re; priceless. Let me get you a drink."

The man stood up. He was far taller than the average Japanese person. He moved gracefully through the crowd, avoiding the mistress riding her slave and controlling his direction and speed by reaching behind her mount and slashing at his exposed balls with her impressive nails.

By the time he returned with more beer and sake, the floor show had changed. A nude, female kickboxer, who could have been no more than 18, was wiping the floor with a middle-aged man in savage, erotic fight. She alternated between pounding his face and gut with her naked feet and fists; his attempts to fight back were swatted aside as if he were a child. Despite the bruised, swollen bloody mess his face and body were swiftly being turned into, his poker-stiff cock belied his enjoyment.

"What's your name?", Yukata asked.

"You can call me Tori."

"Well, Tori, I'm Yukata. Thanks for the drink. Now, have you any suggestions on how I can relight my fire as it were?" He lifted his beer glass to avoid a spray of blood from the floorshow.

"I have some special girls, Yukata - very special. They are unlike any other women you have ever met, and they can do certain *things*, exquisite things, to your body and your mind."

"Such as?"

"Not to be discussed here. Not in front of the competition."

"What do you mean? Do you own a fetish club?"

"Indeed, I do."

"What is it called?"

"*The Nest.*"

"I never heard of it"

"You won't have - it's *very* exclusive. We employ only a certain type of girl, and cater to a very select clientele; but, as I can see you are a man who really appreciates bizarre sex, I'm willing to let you in."

Yukata felt a vague stirring of interest for the first time in months.

"How much will it cost me?"

"Nothing, zero - this one is *gratis*, on the house, my friend. Here is my card."

The business card Tori handed him had a surprisingly-upmarket address.

"Be there at 10 p.m. tomorrow. Show them the card and say I invited you personally."

Tori finished his sake, bowed, and then walked away.

In the floor show, the girl was triumphantly standing over the man old enough to be her father. He was curled in a foetal, sobbing, battered huddle at her feet, whilst she, totally unmarked by the fight, raised her blooded fists on high. His pulsing erection was still clearly visible as it spat seed that mixed with his own blood.

* * * * *

The house was unremarkable; it looked like any other in the fairly affluent suburb of Tokyo. There was no flashing neon sign like there was at *Club Saliva*, but then, that was to be expected - this was a private club, after all.

When he knocked at the door, it was answered by a lovely girl whose kimono was embroidered with spiders. He proferred the card.

"Tori san told me to be here at ten."

She smiled and bowed. "Come on in; you must be Yukata. I will fetch Tori san." She bowed again and scurried off, her kimono giving her the illusion of sliding across the marble floor rather than walking.

He cast his eyes about the hall. On the walls were a number of paintings of naked women, all of them strange. One showed a naked girl against a snowscape - her skin was so pale that she seemed to blend into the background with only her eyes, hair, pubic hair and red lips showing clearly. Another showed a woman making love to a man on a large four-poster bed - she was straddling him and, unseen to him, a bushy fox's tail was sprouting from just above her shapely buttocks.

"You came!" Tori, who was dressed in black robes, came seeping down the corridor to the hall and shook Yukata's hand firmly. In the electric light of the hallway he seemed all the more strange; very tall, hook nosed and with ruddy cheeks.

"I have such a girl lined up for you. Her name is Hari. She comes all the way from Ehime on the island of Shikoku, and you would not believe the things she is capable of. You will never have had a lover like this in your whole life."

Yukata's interest was growing. He felt the spark of something stir deep down in his loins. It was something he had not felt in a long time - anticipation.

"The proof is in the eating of the pudding, as they say in England. Lead on."

Tori led Yukata down a flight of winding mahogany stairs and along a red-carpeted corridor to a high, arched wooden door. It looked ancient.

Yukata squinted at the characters carved into it. They seemed to be some kind of archaic kanji.

His host unlocked the door and swung it open. "If you would be so good as to wait, Hari will be with you momentarily."

The room had red carpets and red-painted walls and ceiling. There was a couch with red cushions. Red candles burned in the candelabra above his head, sending flickering shadows into the corners of the room. More candles shone from behind red glass lanterns, adding to the rugose atmosphere.

Tori shut the door behind Yukata, and he heard a bolt being drawn.

In front of him, another door opened; he had not noticed it before, so seamlessly had it blended in with the wall. A woman walked through the door. She was a little shorter than him, and quite naked. Her pale skin stood out against the ruby decor of the room. She had long, luxuriant hair that hung down to her waist in glossy black swathes. The locks seemed to have something at their tips like tiny beads. Her eyebrows were high and arched - they looked almost as if they had been painted on, like some kabuki performer's. Her eyes were large, dark and almond-shaped, her nose petite. Her lips were red as blood. The high-cheekboned face sat on an elegant neck leading to the white shoulders and pert, almost cone-shaped breasts. Her stomach was flat and her pubic hair had been dyed red and trimmed into a heart shape. Long legs led to elegant feet with cherry-painted toenails.

He felt taughtness in his loins as she slipped silently across the room and ran long red fingernails softly across his face.

"Undress." Her voice was something between a hiss and a whisper.

Excitement was now rising in him in a way it had not in years. He fumbled clumsily like a teenager, like he had that time with his art teacher in 'detention' all those years ago. He finally struggled, sweating, out of his apparel, and dumped it in an untidy heap on the floor. His body was a network of scars and piercings from a lifetime of sexual experimentation.

He opened his mouth, but she placed a finger on his lips.

"Shussssh!"

She began to kiss him softly, then more savagely, deeply grinding her hips into his. He reached down and encircled her perfect buttocks with his hands, then lifted her up. Her legs encircled his hips and she mounted him. She gripped his shoulders, her nails breaking the skin. He didn't mind; in fact, he relished it. She pulled her head back to look at him as he began thrusting into her whilst bouncing her up and down with his hands and hips.

Suddenly, he saw her hair rise up behind her as if pulled on invisible strings. It whipped up and danced about, writhing side to side, each strand with its own ophidian motility. As some of the long hairs drew close to his face, he saw that the 'beads' on the end were actually tiny swellings, each of which had now sprouted a fish-hook-like barb. Suddenly he felt a sharp pain in his cheek. One of the hooks had attached itself to his flesh and was tugging; then another strand and another lashed out like striking snakes, ripping into his face. He tried to pull away, but her legs tightened around him and her nails dug deep into his shoulders.

Her hair was now a black razor storm, hundreds and hundreds of them tearing at his face and neck in a frenzy. Her hair was so long that it could wrap around him and attach its predatory hooks into his back. He opened his mouth to scream, but hers was instantly clamped onto it; her serpentine tongue encircled his and held it fast.

He tried to push her away, but more of her hair coiled round his wrists and held them in a python-like grip. Now the hooks were being ripped free, bringing lumps of his flesh with them, only to plunge back in order pull more tissue from him. He mutely realised why the room was decorated in red.

A new pain exploded in his crotch. Her tiny pubic hairs were burrowing into his tender genitals like living, razor-wire worms. He felt the blood flowing down the inside of his legs.

The main door opened and Tori walked in, smiling.

"Oh, I see you are enjoying yourself now. I told you that she could do things you could never conceive of. Her full name is Hari-onago, but I'm sure that will mean little to you; no-one seems to study folklore these days. Suffice to say her hair is alive... and hungry."

* * * * *

Nakano Yutaka had always desired new and exciting sexual experiences - and perhaps that is why, when the police found his mangled corpse in a parking lot on the other side of town, he had the faintest hint of a smile upon his face.

8. Small Gladiators

The warriors circled each other, each wary of making the first move. Both looked resplendent in their armour as they skirted the sides of the arena, formidable weapons brandished on high. Each was weighing up the other for speed, size and strength; once the fight had started, there would be no mercy, no quarter given - this was a fight to the death.

The taller of the two struck first, unfurling with lightning speed and bringing his weapons down upon his more-squat foe. The enemy's armour proved too thick and the weapons failed to penetrate. He grasped at his foe, only to find that his foe grasped back, and with greater strength. The two grappled for a moment before the more squat and stronger combatant pulled the taller to the ground and brought his own weapon down again and again.

The taller fighter struggled to stand, but the squat foe held fast with a grip that was now crushing through his armour, even as the wounds he had sustained from the enemy's weapon began to take their toll. The taller gladiator collapsed, and the shorter one reared up in triumph.

The camera stopped. The scorpion began to devour the praying mantis, rending it asunder with its pincers and hauling the fragments into its mouthparts, while the mantis still convulsed with the venom flowing through its body.

"An excellent fight, one of the best yet." The youth behind the camera grinned as he peered into the glass tank in which the invertebrates had conducted their forced death struggle.

"That will be a great one for the site, Daichi," said his friend Ren, as he lifted the vivarium up and placed it back on the shelf. "The winner lives to fight another day, and star in another episode of *Bug Fights*."

The two boys stood in a large summerhouse. The shelves around them were filled with vivaria, all containing invertebrates. Living in rural southern Kagoshima was a bonus - the subtropical climate meant that bugs grew big. Daichi himself had captured the mantis in the woods near his home just a few days ago; the scorpion was a Middle Eastern species he had bought online.

Daichi's parents didn't know about their son's macabre hobby; they just thought he collected bugs, a phase most boys go through - but Daichi and his friends were filming invertebrates fighting to the death for their website, *Bug Fights*. The member's-only site was turning a pretty penny for the boys.

The summerhouse door swung open, and a third boy entered. "Otoya, did you get it?" asked Daichi. Otoya slipped off his rucksack and reached inside. He produced an angrily-buzzing jar.

"I sure did. Thank God this bastard didn't sting me! I hear it's like having a red-hot rivet shoved in your flesh."

He held the vibrating jar aloft, and the angry buzz could clearly be heard throughout the summerhouse. The sound seemed full of ire.

Inside the jar a Japanese giant hornet, the largest hornet on earth and the length of a finger, was trying to sting the surface of the jar. The yellow venom was clearly visible on the glass.

"God help whatever is fighting that," grinned Ren.

"Don't you worry. I have the very thing to give this evil little fucker a run for its money; just wait a moment."

Ren adjusted the camera as Daichi pulled down another vivarium and placed it on the table. Inside was a spider with a leg span that would have covered a dinner plate. It looked like an outsized hairy glove.

"A goliath bird-eating spider," Daichi smiled proudly. "It's from Brazil. I got it from a breeder in Osaka."

"We will need to be careful getting the hornet in with the spider. It's as fast as greased lightning," said Otoya.

"Ren, be ready with the camera." Daichi grabbed a cloth from a drawer and threw it over the vivarium. He took the jar and carefully unscrewed the lid. He gingerly lifted up the flap of the spider's container and slipped the jar under the cloth. Flicking the lid from the jar, he upended it into the vivarium and snapped the flap shut, as the hornet careered inside. He whipped off the cloth and shouted, "Roll!"

Ren started the camera as the hornet bumbled in a confused manner about the vivarium. It bumped a couple of times into the spider, who reared up, waving its legs defensively. As the hornet realised that it was still trapped, it became more aggressive, its buzzing louder.

The spider sprang forward, trying to grab the hornet in its flailing legs and drag it back towards the waiting fangs. The hornet was too fast; it dodged the spider's attack, then shot forward like a fencing expert who had seen an opening in his opponent's defence. Its cruel sting plunged into the underside of the huge arachnid again and again.

The spider, now looking clumsy, attempted to spring upon its foe, but the hornet avoided it with an almost lazy ease; the hornet then fell like a hawk on its prey, its impressive stinger now stabbing into the massive spider's back.

Finally, the bird-eater curled up its legs like a clenching fist, and lay still.

"Amazing," gasped Daichi. "I want to do a piece to camera now, Ren."

Daichi grinned into the camera. "Well, that's another exciting battle from *Bug Fights*. I hope you enjoyed it. You know, there are some dimwits out there who think what we are doing is wrong and that it's cruel to make these bugs fight each other. WAKE UP, YOU MORONS! Haven't you heard of survival of the fittest? Bugs fight each other and eat each other in their billions every single day! Here at *Bug Fights* the winner eats the loser - it's nature's way."

"Besides all that, there is a long tradition of insect fighting in China and Japan. Like cock fights, we kept crickets to fight. We kept them in intricate cages carved of ivory. We fight stag beetles, too - it's tradition. Back in China there was once a system of magic called 'Ku,' where insects were placed in a pot and made to fight; the winner was used for sorcery."

"So, with nature and history behind us, we need not question the morality of what we do. It's nature's way, and we turn it into great entertainment! So, don't forget to tune in for the next bug fight - it will be amazing!"

"That's telling them," Ren laughed. "Bunch of arseholes."

"Some people are just not grateful for all the time and effort we put in. Anyhow, that's a wrap for today. I'll upload these fights tonight. Let's get this place tided up."

The boys put away the vivaria and packed up the lights, microphones and cameras.

Ren and Otoya went home, and Daichi returned to the house for dinner. After eating, he sat on the porch in the warm summer twilight. He was about to go up to his room and upload that day's fights to his computer when something caught his eye.

There was a movement at the bottom of the stairs that led up onto the porch - an elongate form was animatedly scurrying about. Daichi half stood. Could it possibly be what he thought it was?

The thing seemed to be hunting. It moved in a rippling motion, occasionally stopping and raising up one antenna and waving it in a furtive manner.

God, it was indeed what he had thought it was! A mukade, a Japanese giant centipede, *Scolopendra japonica*. They were found only in the warmer southern regions of Japan. They had a reputation as savage predators with an agonisingly-painful bite; Daichi recalled reading stories of people cutting off their own arms to relieve the pain of a giant centipede bite. They were usually about six inches long, but this individual was a monster twice that size. Its grace was undeniable, moving its fifteen pairs of legs in a ripple that ran down its segmented, chitin-plated body like an ocean wave. Its antenna seemed to twitch endlessly in its quest for prey.

He had to have it for *Bug Fights*. The reputation of the giant centipede was legendary; they were even supposed to kill small rats! It was too far to the summerhouse; the creature would be gone by the time he got back - he had to think fast. Daichi, heart pounding, rushed into the kitchen. Opening a cupboard, he grabbed a tupperware box and fumbled in a drawer for some sugar tongs.

He raced back to the porch - the centipede was still there. He crept closer, slipping the top off the box. He knew centipedes were functionally blind, their tiny, compound eyes just picking up light and shade; the main sensory organs were the antennae. In one swift movement, Daichi snatched up the impressive arthropod with the tongs, grasping the tail end. Before it could twist around to bite, he dropped it into the box and snapped the lid back in place.

He raised it up to face level and peered through the transparent plastic. The centipede battered its plated head against the lid in anger at its imprisonment. He could clearly see the formidable maxillipeds, the first two legs modified into hollow, venom-injecting fangs. Its body was a deep reddish-brown, whilst the legs and the ever-curling and -uncurling antennae were a sandy yellow. The creature seemed like a concentrated mass of fury and bile. Daichi imagined it would take apart any other arthropod he set it against.

"You will be my new champion. Now, to get you a home fit for one."

Taking his prize back down to the summerhouse, Daichi selected an empty vivarium. He filled the bottom with bark chippings. He selected a piece of hollow log for the centipede to hide in, and some rocks and twigs for decor. Finally, he added a shallow dish of water.

Satisfied with his work, he carefully prised the top off the tupperware box and upended it over the vivarium. The centipede slid out and scuttled into the hollow log. Taking no chances, he slid the glass lid back onto the vivarium and cellotaped it down. He then found a rock and put it on the lid for good measure.

"Now you'll stay put. Tomorrow's your big day, Champ."

He uploaded the day's battles to the *Big Fights* website, noting happily that the counter had now registered over one million visitors.

He phoned Otoya and Ren, excitedly telling them of his find. The pair were almost as excited as he was, and both promised that they would be over the next afternoon to help film the fights.

Daichi did not sleep well that night; he was too excited. The thought of pitting the centipede against a tarantula or a scorpion thrilled him. He rose early and decided to inspect his collection before the others arrived.

He stopped at the doors of the summerhouse - both had been smashed clean off their hinges, and were scattered like so much matchwood across the garden. A few tattered pieces of wood hung to the frames; it looked as if they had been forced outward.

Rushing inside, he found his collection in disarray. All of the vivaria were shattered. As he sifted through the wreckage, he could not find even one of his gladiators - every single bug was gone. Had someone stolen them? No, if that were the case, the thieves would have taken the tanks intact along with their occupants; it must be vandals from the animal-rights nuts. He had been getting more abusive e-mails from them lately; some had even threatened violence. The bastards had wrecked his whole setup - it would take months to build up the collection again.

Daichi heard a movement behind him, a sort of dry rustle accompanied by a soft clicking. A shadow fell over him. He turned slowly around.

Half-in and half-out of the summerhouse was the centipede, *his* centipede, only vast. It reared up like a cobra ready to strike, towering ten feet off the ground. The remaining twenty feet of its length ran out of the door and onto the lawn. *How had it gotten so huge? How could it* **be** *so huge?* An arthropod so massive should not be able to move or even breathe.

He froze as the swaying head moved closer, the ripple of clicking limbs sliding it across the summerhouse floor. His racing mind half-recalled something from Japanese legend - a monster called 'O-mukade,' a giant, man-eating centipede.

The antennae, now each as long as his legs, uncoiled and began their endless twitching. One of them brushed his face, and he barely stifled a scream.

His fear-instilled paralysis was broken, and he dived to one side as the dustbin- lid-sized head struck - the scything maxillipeds closed on air instead of flesh. He made a run for the doorm but the monster was faster. With blinding speed it had whipped round, and its awful head was now blocking the doorway. Before Daichi could scream, a section of the plated, multi-legged body had grasped him from behind. The spiny legs wrapped about him like a trap and held fast.

The head came close and paused for a while, a foot from his face, then the curved maxilliped stabbed into his chest, pumping in the warm, paralysing venom. He felt the warmth spread throughout his body. The creature released him and he fell stiffly to the floor. The impact hurt him, but he could not cry out. He was perfectly conscious, but could not move so much as a muscle. The pain from the wound in his chest was acute.

The O-mukade withdrew to the doorway and looked like it was waiting. There was a scurrying noise, much softer than that made by the monster, a subdued scuttling that was getting closer. Suddenly he saw what was causing it - bugs, thousands upon thousands of insects and other invertebrates, were swarming past the O-mukade and into the summerhouse, like a living carpet.

Spiders, scorpions, millipedes, mantises, beetles, crickets, ants, cicadas, fat white grubs, seething maggots - all came tumbling and flopping toward him in a living tide. In a trice they were upon him, crawling on his flesh, tickling his face with tiny legs and hairs, walking over his unblinking eyes. A fat grub was forcing its way between his lips; it felt like a cold, rubbery sausage as it slipped into his mouth. At the same time, a cricket the size of a small mouse began to eat his left eyeball.

* * * * *

Ren and Otoya called at the house that afternoon. Daichi's mother told them that he was busy in the summerhouse, and that she hadn't seen her son all day. They found the summerhouse in a state of disarray, and Daichi himself sitting in a chair in the midst of the chaos.

"Daichi, what the hell has gone on here?", shouted Otoya.

"I think he's asleep," said Ren.

Ren walked forward and shook Daichi. He flopped like an old sack in the boy's grasp. Then, out from his mouth, his empty eye sockets and his ears the creatures began to pour. Maggots fell like confetti, grasshoppers bounded and spiders scampered - Daichi seemed to deflate as the tides of bugs crawled from his carcass. Finally, the body seemed to fall in on itself like a deflating balloon, until only skin was left.

Behind them, the boys heard a strange sound, a sort of dry rustle accompanied by a soft clicking....

9. Yanari

Tanaka Sakura had never liked the house - not since she first laid eyes on it. It seemed cold, hostile and, somehow... *outside*. Her husband Ichiro was a spice merchant; they were not poor, but neither were they rich. After the birth of their son Masa, they needed more room. The house should have been a godsend, but it was just wrong - it felt hostile.

Ichiro's uncle had passed away suddenly and left the house to his nephew. Uncle Aoi had been found at the bottom of a flight of stairs; he had fallen and broken his neck. It wasn't the fact that her uncle-in-law had died in the house that bothered her - it was something else, almost as if there was something in the house itself... something unseen.

The country house was much bigger than the little place they had back in Kyoto, but it would be hard to adjust to small-town life. Shigaraki was a town close to clay beds; it was well-known for pottery, and little else. The house sat several miles out of Shigaraki and had a somewhat lonely air to it.

They never had many servants; they were just not rich enough. Old Naho, the cook and cleaner, had elected to stay with her children in Kyoto; she was nearing the age of retirement anyhow, having served Ichiro's late mother. Wataru, the stableboy, had gone with Ichiro; her husband had loaded up his horses and left for Osaka, to sell and buy spices.

Ichiro was sorry to leave his wife, but the money he would make in the markets of Osaka would last for months. He had told Sakura she would be fine - Shigaraki was a quiet little town with hardly any crime. She must lock the doors and shutters at night, but that was just common sense. He had left enough money for both her and the child, and some extra to take on a new servant.

He heart fell as she watched him ride away on that morning. During the day she busied herself attending to Masa, who had recently learned to walk, and to tidying the house - the furniture had been left *in situ* and had accumulated dust and cobwebs. In the evening she lit lamps, and after dinner tried to read, but found she could not concentrate on her book, so she took herself and the child to bed early.

Sleep evaded her. She tossed and turned, jumping at every little noise. She chided herself for such stupidity; it was an old house, and bound to creak in the wind.

In the morning she took Masa into the town to buy groceries. The locals in town seemed friendly enough - some women stopped to make a fuss of Masa. She bought rice, meat, bread and vegetables. One woman asked if she was new in town. Sakura told her she was married to Ichiro, and had moved into his uncle's house. The woman's face seemed to darken, but she said nothing.

She stopped at a teashop and struck up a conversation with a girl there. Again, on hearing where she lived, the girl seemed nervous, and did not want to talk anymore. Sakura finished her tea and rose to leave; as she did so, she heard the girl speaking with another girl from the tea shop. She only half-heard the whispered conversation, but caught something about a Shinto priest cleansing the house.

When she arrived back home, one of shutters in the front room was open - she was sure she had locked them before leaving. With her heart pounding, Sakura checked every room in the house - she found nothing. No items seemed to be missing or disturbed. She told herself that she had not bolted the shutter correctly, and a breeze must have forced it open.

She played awhile with Masa and read to him before preparing lunch. After she had eaten, she went into the garden to check on the birds - she had brought four ornamental doves with her from Kyoto. Ichiro had specially built an aviary for them in the garden.

As she approached the aviary with seed and fresh water, she noticed that the wooden dowelling that formed the bars of the cage were broken. They were snapped, and some had been pulled from their brackets - something had forced its way into the aviary. The birds were gone, but there were blood and feathers on the floor.

What could have done this? The garden led onto woodland and countryside. It was unlikely to have been a bear or a wolf; they seldom left the mountains and deep forests. They also avoided humans. Besides, a big animal would have made more of a mess. Was it a tanuki or a kitsune? Raccoon dogs and foxes did approach human habitation, but would either have been strong enough to snap the dowelling like this? She went back inside and locked the doors and shutters.

That night, as she sat reading, she heard something scratching at the kitchen door. At first she thought it was her imagination, but, as she strained to catch the sound, it came again - this time more distinctly. It sounded as if something was scrabbling to get in at the door. It sounded hideously inhuman, but low down against the wooden panel; that meant whatever was making the noise must be fairly small. Steeling herself, she took up a lantern and a broom. She crossed the kitchen, her heart in her mouth, and unbolted the door. She got ready to swing with the broom as the door swung open and revealed ... nothing. She raised up the lantern and in its amber light she thought she saw something move in the bushes. She did not get a good look at it, but she was sure something had been there, watching.

Could it have been one of the monkeys from the mountains? They usually moved around in large troops and were not active at night.

She re-bolted the door, then checked on the other doors and shutters. She looked in on Masa; he was sleeping soundly. Now he was walking, she would have to keep an even closer eye on him. She grew cold at the thought of him wandering off alone whilst that thing, whatever it was, was roaming around the garden.

Later that night it came back. She sat bolt upright in bed. The thing was on the roof. She was sure she could hear small, clawed feet skittering across the tiles. Whatever it was seemed to be looking for a point of entry. It moved back and forth across the slanted roof. Sometimes it seemed to leap; other times it ran in short, sharp bursts. It seemed too heavy for a cat or an owl. She got up and gently took Masa out of bed without waking him. She sat awake in her bed, holding her son, as the scratching noises from the roof seemed to grow more insistent. They carried on until dawn; at first light, they seemed to fade away.

She needed another person in the house with her - it would be the only way she would feel safe. She took Masa into town again and enquired after employing a girl as a live-in maid. There seemed to be plenty of young girls around, but none were interested, even when she mentioned how good the wages would be. The girls all turned away, shaking their heads and muttering under their breath. Several times she caught the same word – "Yanari." Where had she heard that word before?

Back at home, the word went round and round as she cleaned. She knew she had seen the word in one of her husband's books. Ichiro was a bibliophile, and he had collected books on his travels around Nippon. Sakura knew she would have no peace until she found out what "Yanari" meant. She left the cleaning and went to her husband's study.

Three hours later, she found what she was looking for, in a book by the woodblock print artist Toriyama Sekien. *Gazu Hyakki Yakō* was a parade of a hundred types of daemon found in Nippon. All kinds of grotesque and bizarre creatures were illustrated in its pages, and it was only one of four volumes on the subject. The Yanari were illustrated as tiny daemons; they looked like the giant Oni, but were little more than knee-high. They looked like distorted humans with wide, demented grins on toothy mouths. The Yanari had ape-like faces with hairy eyebrows and short horns. Their hands bore three fingers ending in sharp claws. Several of the little monsters were shown tugging at the wooden supports of a house's porch, whilst others attacked the structure with tiny hammers.

The text revealed that Yanari were usually invisible, but manifested themselves through knocking, scratching and other inexplicable noises in old houses.

Sakura dropped the book in horror. *Could there really be one of those creatures, a Yanari, lurking in the grounds of the house? No wonder no-one wanted to work here.* The house was infested with evil, and the local people knew it - they had more sense than to come there.

Maybe it was a Yanari that killed uncle Aoi. The image of a stunted Oni tripping the old man up at the top of the stairs, and capering about in delight as he fell head-over-heels to his death, flashed into her mind.

Thankfully, it had not actually got into the house since she had been there; well, not as yet. She recalled the half-heard story of a Shinto priest cleansing the house - maybe it was his spells that kept it from crossing the threshold. Tomorrow she would go to the town's temple and seek out the priest. She would learn what went on in this house, and if she and her child were safe; if not, she would have the priest come back and drive the Yanari away for good.

She moved Masa's little bed into her room that night. She also took a knife from the kitchen and laid it next to her futon.

The last couple of days had taken their toll on Sakura. She had not slept in over 48 hours, and the strain of keeping an eye on her son was adding to her weariness. At least he did not cry at night like some children. She lay in bed waiting for the sounds to come again, but they did not. Finally, her eyelids grew heavy, and she fell to sleep.

She awoke from a dreamless sleep with a jolt. Instinctively she knew something was wrong. Hardly daring to breathe, she strained her ears for the slightest sound in the blackness. It came from down the corridor, a soft patter of sneaking footfalls. *The Yanari must have found a way into the house! The priest's magick must be fading.*

It scurried, then stopped; scurried, then stopped. It sounded as if the creature were looking for something. It seemed to be moving from room to room. She could see it in her mind's eye, a tiny bundle of hate and rage looking somewhere between an insane monkey and a stunted, diseased man. She heard it draw slowly closer along the corridor. She thought she could even hear the tiny monster's breathing.

Sakura fumbled in the dark for the fruit knife she kept by the bed. She stifled a sigh of relief when her hand closed around its handle. *Would a knife stop a Yanari?* She vaguely recalled reading something about iron being effective against spirits. She bit down on her tongue to stop herself from screaming as the thing stopped outside her bedroom and opened the sliding bamboo and paper shōji. It was entering the room where she and her son slept. As her eyes began to adjust to the dark, she could vaguely see the shape of the creature, bipedal and midget-like. The thing paused, then turned her way. It rushed at her, but she was ready. Sakura thrust the knife out with every ounce of strength she possessed, aiming for the creature's chest.

Just as the blade struck home, the little figure spoke one word; it said "mummy."

10. The Brides of Mizuchi

The cold air of a January night in Okayama Prefecture made Yosida Daisuke's breath rise up like serpents of smoke. He looked up at the wall - it was ten feet tall and topped with razor wire. Why would a private health spa want razor wire? Reaching into his backpack, he removed the ladder and the wire cutter. He unfolded his ladder and propped it against the wall. Scrambling up, he peered furtively between the nasty coils. He could see the extensive ornamental gardens and, in the background, the dark hulk of the main house where the spa was situated. A few of the lights were on, but there was little activity.

"Ah, well," he murmured to himself, "here goes nothing."

The cutters made short work of the wire, which fell away in tangled strands like daemonic wool. He replaced the cutters and hauled himself up to balance unsteadily on the wall. Crouching, he pulled up the ladder and turned slowly round, placing it on the opposite side. He descended as quickly as he could. He folded the ladder up and slipped it into his pack whilst praying he hadn't been spotted. He'd never make a burglar - he was too slow and clumsy.

Daisuke ran for the cover of the bushes, then caught his breath. He thought himself mad; he was a 45-year-old accountant from Takahashi, not James Bond. He almost turned back, until he thought again of the reason he was here - somewhere in that dark, looming building was his daughter.

Misaki should never have left Takahashi; it was a beautiful, historic town, but, like all teenagers these days, she wanted more - she wanted to see a bit of the country. Misaki was a bright girl and had won a scholarship at the University in Okayama City. At first Daisuke and his wife had not worried; after all, it was hardly as if the city was on the opposite side of Nippon. And Misaki was sensible as well as bright, not the sort of girl to get herself into trouble - but they had been wrong.

Misaki had come home with her head full of queer ideas. At first her parents worried she had joined some sort of weird cult. She insisted that it wasn't any kind of religious sect, but a *private* and very select spa and fitness club. Though she had shown no previous interest in such things, Misaki seemed to be obsessed with the Tatsu Springs Health Spa. Only a few people were considered for membership, most of them young women. This fact alone had rung bells in Daisuke's mind. *What was really going on in there?*

It was all down to that awful man - handsome, suave, silver-tongued, rich and, Daisuke was sure, utterly malignant, Kawakuro Ryuunosuke seemed to exert a sinister influence over women. He was always surrounded by an entourage of girls, and Misaki had become one of them. Ryuunosuke was the owner and proprietor of Tatsu Springs. He had apparently brought the land, including the natural springs, a number of years ago, and built an extensive house around the springs themselves. Daisuke had seen the literature he gave out - glossy pamphlets full of pseudo-scientific nonsense about the rejuvenating and invigorating powers of the waters of Tatsu Springs. A lot of young girls had joined Ryuunosuke's health club and ended up living there, never returning home.

In the early days there was a lot of suspicion surrounding Ryuunosuke and his organisation. After the Sarin gas attacks of the Aum Shinrikyo cult in 1995, the government kept a closer eye on such organisations. Ryuunosuke had been more than accommodating, and a police search had revealed no illegal activity. The members, both female and male (of whom there were a small number), claimed to be resident at the spa of their own free will - there was no sign of brainwashing or drugs. Tests on the spa's water found no element that was foreign or unexpected in spring water, and, as Ryuunosuke's club charged no membership fee, he could not be prosecuted for profiting from false claims about the spa's supposed miraculous properties.

But there *was* something very wrong about Tatsu Springs. On her first visit home, the spa was all Misaki talked about. She mentioned nothing about her course, social life, or any friends outside of the other Tatsu Springs members. She seemed to be spending more time there, fully fifty miles from Okayama City, than she was at university - and she would not shut up about how wonderful Kawakuro Ryuunosuke was.

She wrote letters home as well. Her parents were shocked and appalled when she told them that she was dropping out of university to be with Ryuunosuke at the spa full time. There was no phone connection to the place, and letters posted to her were ignored. The final straw came when she wrote to her parents telling them that she was getting married; she was not marrying Ryuunosuke, and did not deign to tell them whom she was intending to wed. She told them that she was sorry that they would not be able to attend the wedding, but it was strictly for members only. Her mother had been tearful at the news, but her father was angry - and suspicious.

Spa or no spa, this had smacked of cult. The daughter he knew and whom he had seen come into the world would never have written words like that of her own volition; she had been hypnotised or brainwashed somehow.

At first Daisuke had hired a private detective from the city; he claimed to have rescued kids from cults before. He told Daisuke he intended to infiltrate Tatsu Springs and find out what was really going on. If he could get Misaki back, he would.

Daisuke never heard from him again; his mobile phone and landline both seemed dead. When he returned to the man's office in Okayama City, it was empty - the landlord said he had vanished without paying his rent, and the office was to be leased out to someone else. That left just one person to help Misaki -him.

He ran from the trees and ducked down behind an ornamental bush. As he knelt, he noticed something - the ground beneath his knees seemed warm. Indeed, the whole of the expansive lawns around the house were free of frost; streams of steam were steadily rising from them. *Was the place geothermally active?* He recalled nothing about that in the spa's pamphlets.

Glancing around, he ran toward the house. Something came hurtling out of the darkness, something fast and muscular - it was a tosa, a huge fighting dog, a breed renowned for savagery. It did not bark; this was an attack dog, not a guard dog. It moved with a speed that belied its almost bear-like bulk. Daisuke fumbled in his pocket frantically and produced the can of mace just as the dog flew at him, all sinew and teeth. The blast caught it in the face, but its momentum slammed Daisuke to the ground, knocking the air from him.

The huge tosa was shaking its head from side to side, pawing at its face and rubbing its snout against the damp grass. He knew the effects would not last long; he gathered himself up and made a last rush for the house.

The lights in the lower windows were all off. Pressing himself against the walls, he slipped round the building trying each window he came to. All seemed locked from the inside. Turning a corner to the rear of the building, he saw a flight of metal stairs running up to the second floor. He wondered if it was a fire escape. Scrambling up, he winced at the noise his boots made on the metal steps as he climbed. At the top was a heavy door. He tried the handle and found it locked.

Daisuke had cursed the weight of his backpack on the long walk from where he had hidden his car, but he was glad he had brought all his tools. He inserted a crowbar between the door and the frame, and heaved back on it; the wood gave only slightly, so he redoubled his efforts. On the fourth try, the wood splintered and the door swung open.

He entered into a plushly-carpeted corridor. It was still unlit, but the moonlight gave enough illumination for him to see that the walls were hung with traditional art. As he slipped along the corridor, he noticed pieces by Kuniyoshi, Sekien, Okyo, Hokusai, and several others; whoever he was, Ryuunosuke had to be incredibly rich if these paintings were originals. All of them depicted creatures from Nippon's ancient legends - fevered ahborrences, imprisoned on canvas by ink and paint.

He slipped along the corridor and through an unlocked door at its end - another passage, as richly decorated as the first. This corridor led off in two ways. Light was pouring from beneath the bottom of a door some way to his left; he gently opened it. Daisuke found himself looking down over a huge room. He was in some sort of viewing area that overlooked the springs themselves. This was the heart of the building, what the house had been constructed around. Peering through the glass panels, he saw circular pool of clear water. In the centre was a jagged peak of rock that rose up some twenty feet. From its tip spewed bubbling crystal water that cascaded down into the pool below.

Some kind of ritual was going on below him, and he crept closer to get a better view. A group of men in black, hooded robes were standing behind a naked girl of pale, doll-like beauty, who could have been no older than eighteen. She had some kind of symbol painted on her belly - it was not native kanji or hiragana. To one side of the group on a raised plinth stood Ryuunosuke. Daisuke had recognised him from photographs in the group's pamphlets. He seemed to be reading from some vast, worm-eaten volume supported by a lectern. Daisuke strained his ears to hear what was being said through the glass. Ryuunosuke was speaking in no tongue Daisuke recognised. The words seemed more like animalistic noises formed by inhuman vocal chords; the man seemed to spit and croak them out.

The girl appeared to be drugged in some way. Her eyes were glazed, and she had an ecstatic look upon her face. Ryuunosuke closed the book and motioned to the girl. She walked forward, beaming, and entered the water. She waded in up to her waist.

The waters foaming down from the rock fissure suddenly changed colour and constancy. The water became thick and white, oozed down the rocks, then billowed out into a great cloud as it mixed with the clear waters of the pool. The girl walked forward until the ever-expanding cloud of white water surrounded her. She threw back her head and let out a long moan.

A hand fell on Daisuke's shoulder with a powerful grip. Before he could yell, he was slammed bodily into the wall. His attacker was a tall, burly man in a high-necked black shirt. Daisuke pulled the mace out of his pocket, but it was kicked from his hand before he could deploy it. The man pulled him to his feet. He lashed out, grabbing his assailant's shirt collar and ripping it away. The shirt tore open and fell away, revealing the man's arms and chest, covered in glistening black scales. Dasiuke screamed in horror at the sight as the man's hand fell on his neck with a chopping motion, like a blunt axe.

He awoke with a throbbing head and sore neck. He was being supported by two large men, both in the same high-collared black shirts. Before him, with an arrogant smirk on his face, stood Kawakuro Ryuunosuke.

"Yosida san, I have been expecting you for some time."

"How did you know I was coming?"

"When Misaki wrote to you telling you of her marriage, I knew you would come. Did you really think it was so easy to break into here? We allowed you in so that you could see your daughter."

Dasiuke struggled wildly, but the men's grip seemed inhumanly strong.

"Where is she? Who the hell did she marry?"

"Misaki's husband is someone of great influence and power. Your daughter could not have asked for a finer husband. Even now she is heavy with his child."

He thrashed wildly against his captors.

"She's pregnant? Already? What the hell is going on?"

"Nature's miracle is what is going on." Ryuunosuke grinned broadly. "I will take you to your daughter, Yosida san. I'm sure she will be overjoyed to see you, her father, when she gives birth."

He turned and walked away, motioning for the men to bring Daisuke. They dragged the shaking man out of the room and along another corridor. They entered another room, this one darkened. Ryuunosuke twisted the dial on the wall and raised the light levels. A low moan rose as the room became illuminated in a sickly yellow light.

Misaki lay upon a bed in the room. Her body was distorted almost beyond recognition. Her stomach was so vastly swollen it reminded Daisuke of a bloated queen termite. The balloon-like sac of her belly dwarfed her prone body. The skin was stretched paper-thin and was translucent. It was filled with a yellowish liquid in which some serpentine thing twitched and writhed.

"Misaki, what have they done to you?"

She turned her head towards him and smiled like an imbecile. Her eyes shone with the lustre of madness, and drool coated her pillow.

"Daddy, you came! You came to see me!" She sounded like a little girl on her birthday. "You came to see your grandson. He wants to come out and see you."

Misaki threw back her head and screamed - her father couldn't tell if it was in agony, ecstasy or both. The thin membrane that was her outlandishly-stretched stomach exploded in a yellow liquid blossom. She fell back, motionless, on the bed as her child uncoiled itself from within the ruins of her body.

It was a serpentine creature some ten feet long. Its elongate body was coated with black scales tinted with a sapphire tinge that shone even through the coating of viscera. The creature stood on four legs, each ending in claws like crystal daggers. On its back, above the first pair of legs, two wings like ornate fans, unfurled and stretched. It had a head somewhere between a horse's and a crocodile's in shape. Red barbels, like those of a catfish, grew at the sides of its nostrils; the buds of horns were sprouting on its cranium. A forked tongue flickered between rows of razor teeth to lap up the amniotic fluid that coated it.

It then turned its attention to the corpse of its mother and began to feed, biting into the tattered flesh with a lustful crunching.

Daisuke felt a hot, wet flush between his legs as screaming rang in his ears; the screaming, he realised, was his own.

The creature looked up from its awful meal and regarded Daisuke with green eyes that glittered with an unnatural intelligence.

Then it spoke one word. "Grandfather," it said.

Mercifully, he fainted at this point.

Daisuke awoke and for a moment considered whether these perverse events were some kind of twisted dream, then he opened his eyes. He was dressed in a white smock and lay upon a bed covered by immaculate white sheets. He wondered dimly if he was dead and this was some kind of afterlife. Then the door opened, and Kawakuro Ryuunosuke walked in, all smiles and charm; if this was the afterlife, then he was Jigoku.

"Yosida san, you are with us again. This is good - we have much to talk about."

Daisuke tried to lunge for the tall man, but found his wrists and ankles had been strapped to the bed.

Ryuunosuke ran long fingers through his shiny black hair.

"You murdering bastard! You killed my daughter!" He strained against the straps until his wrists bled, hot tears obscuring his vision.

"She was not murdered. She died like, so many of her sisters, bringing wonder into the world; she sacrificed her own life so that something great could walk the earth again."

"She was ripped apart by a monster, from the inside," screamed Daisuke.

"Not by a monster - by a newborn god. I can see that I will need to explain to you the nature of your late daughter's husband." He stood and began to pace up and down the room as he lectured.

"Her husband was the god Mizuchi. He and his kind came to earth from the stars long before the first hominid screeched and jabbered on earth. They dwelt in a universe that existed before this one. When that universe wound down and came to its end, Mizuchi and his kin threw themselves through the black, howling void of time and space to manifest in this universe. The people of the Jamon period knew and venerated him. His worship has come down through the aeons to the present day."

"You're utterly insane. You worship some kind of lizard?" He pulled madly against the bonds again.

"Since when do lizards bear wings and speak? My sanity is quite fine. When I call, my god answers; does yours? Tell me, then, who is mad - you or I?"

"What are those things?"

"In their own universe they were known as the Lloigor. Here on earth they have many names: in China they are ying lung, in Mongolia they are called luu, and here in Nippon we called them tatsu or ryu - but the name most humans call them now is 'dragon.'"

"The tatsu sleep all across the earth. They can hibernate for hundreds of years, but their sleep cycle is coming to an end. The Great Mizuchi will soon walk the earth again with his children and the faithful. Mizuchi's brood swells even now."

Daisuke thrashed and screamed. Ryuunosuke waited calmly until his spasms had subsided.

"Mizuchi resided in the depths of the River Kahashima. He began to repopulate the Earth with his kind. He would release his milt into the river water where women bathed and impregnate them. They would give birth to the children of Mizuchi; how much the children resembled their father depended on how much the Kahashima diluted his seed, or how far the women were from the source. Some were born as full-blooded dragons, like your grandson; others were human/reptile hybrids. If the seed was very dilute, it manifested only in the children's skin."

He unbuttoned his high-necked shirt to reveal a skin covered from the neck down in glossy black scales. He lent forward over Daisuke and licked his face with a long, forked tongue.

"You and I are *family.*" he whispered. "But enough of this, we have things to attend to."

He clapped his hands sharply, and two large men entered. One held Daixuke still whilst the other unstrapped him. Between them, the scaled brutes held him fast and tied his hands.

"Come, the god awaits." Ryuunosuke swept through the door and Daisuke was dragged after him. They seemed to be heading down into the cellars of the building.

"The caves under this building are truly vast. The rock has been gnawed away by the spring waters for millennia. Water is the oldest and most powerful of elements; given time, it can dominate and destroy all of the other elements. Water is Mizuchi's element."

They walked down flight after flight of crudely-carved, badly-worn stairs lit by flickering torches that illuminated petroglyphs depicting horrific things that Daisuke tried not to look at. The steps ended in a cathedral-like cavern. Braziers cast freakish shadows over the queer rock formations. It seemed as if the rock itself had melted like tallow and reformed into these grotesque shapes.

The men pushed Daisuke towards a great canyon in the cavern's floor. Looking down into the velvety blackness, Daisuke became giddy - it was as if the monster fissure had no bottom. It seemed to fall away into eternity.

Ryuunosuke walked over to a great coiling horn shaped like a gaping-mouthed dragon. It was cast in bronze and painted green with verdigris. He breathed in deeply and then blew the dragon horn. It released a long, hollow, mournful wail that echoed throughout the chamber. The men holding Daisuke stepped back from the edge of the chasm quickly.

"IA! IA! LLOIGOR!", Ryuunosuke bellowed out in invocation.

Deep below there was a great exhalation in the darkness, as if a mass of gas under pressure had been released. Up from the abyss shot a jet of greenish vapour. Dasiuke tried to turn his head away, but he was caught in the cloud; it smelt of rotting violets and left a stinging sensation in his mouth and nostrils.

"The breath of the god - you are indeed favoured." Ryuunosuke and his lackeys had moved to the back of the cavern. The normally-confident Ryuunosuke sounded almost afraid.

Daisuke found his muscles tensing and locking, freezing him to the spot as if he were made of stone. His face was angled down, looking into the pit; try as he might, he could not turn his head away. It was as if the vapour had not only frozen his muscles, it had heightened his senses to an almost unbearable degree.

In the bowels of the earth something was moving, something unfathomably huge. He heard sounds from the pit - sounds like titan coils shifting, like great claws gouging stone, like ribbed wings unfurling, like steely teeth scraping against one another.

Looking down into the sea of darkness, he could make out two green dots against the black. With an appalling languidness, the twin lights gradually drew closer.

"The god Mizuchi blesses the spring waters with his fecundity; he demands that we offer tribute in return."

As the green lights rose through the darkness, Daisuke realised that they were eyes. His frantic mind tried to reason just how large the creature behind those eyes must be. Something else was moving through the shadows, reaching up from the chasm.

A long, red form reared up over the lip of the crevasse and kept rising. It was slick, shiny and as thick as a tree. It reached up almost to the roof of the cave and swayed back and forth like a cobra before the motion of a snakecharmer's pipe. At its termination, it split in two - Daisuke realised that it was a tongue! It flashed down in one swift motion and licked up the little man like a toad snatching a maggot from a fly-blown corpse - then it was gone, back into the fathomless lair.

"Eat hearty, Father," said Ryuunosuke. Then he turned back towards the stairs. He had more pamphlets to print and distribute around Okayama University.

11. Sea Beef

"Ten, nine, eight, seven, six, five, four, three, two, one - Happy New Year!" Nakamura Goro raised the glass of sake to his lips and swallowed the hot liquid in one gulp. His colleagues, who had themselves consumed much of the rice wine and Kirin beer, cheered rowdily.

"Just because we're away from home doesn't mean we can't celebrate properly." The others cheered again, raising glasses and cans. The table around which they all sat was testament to a fine meal, of which any of the men's wives would have been proud: boiled seaweed, fishcakes, mashed sweet potatoes with chestnuts, simmered burdock root, o-zōni soup with mochi rice cakes, and sashimi arranged to resemble the form of roses.

The room lurched slightly, rattling the table and bringing the men back to reality. For a short time at least, some of the crew had forgotten that they were aboard a ship in Antarctic waters thousands of miles from Nippon. There was, of course, a skeleton crew up on the deck and on the bridge; they would be celebrating later.

"Look, the Kadomatsu has fallen over." The first mate, Inoue Jiro, stood up unsteadily and righted the little decoration of bamboo and Japanese apricot sprigs. "We can't have the kami upset - not with the luck they have brought us so far."

"I'll drink to that.", piped up Katō Kaede, the chief harpoon operator. "A hold full of sea beef and a hole in those self-righteous bastards' sides!"

There was even more cheering from the crew of the *Shonan Maru.*

The whaling ship, one of a fleet from Osaka, had been in the Antarctic Ocean for nearly two months now, and had caught and 'processed' over one hundred minke whales. The Japanese Institute for Cetacean Research exploited a loophole in the International Whaling Commission's moratorium. They stated that the whales they hunted were for scientific research rather than for commercial consumption; tons of 'sea beef,' however, found its way into the markets of Osaka.

The 2009/2010 journey had been doubly successful, as the *Shonan Maru* and her crew had experienced a resounding victory over the anti-whaling group Sea Shepherd. The crew had blasted the environmentalists with high-pressure hoses and used loudspeakers attached to helicopters to bombard them with high-pitched sound.

Three days ago, the *Shonan Maru* had 'accidentally' rammed the Sea Shepherd vessel, the *Steve Irwin*, tearing a hole in the ship's hull below the waterline and impelling the crew to radio for help, putting them out of commission for the whole season; the *Shonan Maru* was now free to proceed with its task un-molested.

Yes, this had been a very good expedition indeed, Captain Nakamura thought to himself. Soon they would be returning home, but there were still a couple of profitable weeks left in the whale rich Antarctic waters. It was worth being away from your home and family, even at this time of year, if you only needed to work ten weeks or so in every twelve months.

"Remember, guys, we have to be up in the morning, and you don't want to be on deck with a hangover."

Viewed from above,the *Shonan Maru* looked like a single grain of rice on a vast blue carpet, its leaden bulk dwarfed by the enormity of the ocean. Pull the point of view further out, and the huge ship was lost like a mote of dust in the endless blue. It ploughed a straight course unfettered by the ice that for half the year held this part of the ocean in a steely, impassable grip. The Antarctic summer not only freed the waters of ice, it gave 24 hour sunlight. 24 hours in which to spot, hunt and kill whales.

The morning of January 1st was bright and clear. The sea was mirror calm and had changed from blue to a bottle green. Yamada Katsu stood on the upper deck, binoculars raised to his eyes. He was scanning the waters for whales, searching for the tell-tale ejection of air when they surfaced to breathe. The famous 'spout' was, of course not water, but the warm breath of the breaching mammals. The sight and even the sound could be detected from miles away. But today, as yet, there was no sign of whales or indeed any life, just endless, calm, green water.

A dot appeared on the horizon, not in the water but in the sky. Katsu tried to focus on it. *Could it be another helicopter sent by those insane green activists? Don't the bastards ever give up?* He was about to report the sighting to Captain Nakamura when he realised that the object he was observing was not a helicopter. As it drew steadily closer it resolved itself into the shape of a bird, but what a bird! Its wingspan was huge - no wonder he had mistaken it for an aircraft at first sight.

Tracing its course, Katsu identified it as a wandering albatross, its twelve-foot wingspan being the greatest of all living birds'. He had seen them whirling over the southern seas on past journeys, but had never gotten a close look at one. It seemed that the bird was flying directly towards the *Shonan Maru*; perhaps it was attracted by fish stirred up in the ship's wake. The bird glided, flapping its massive wings lazily from time to time. It was a dirty, slate grey - it had none of the brilliant white and light grey plumage he had seen in wildlife documentaries. Even the beak, usually a vivid yellow, was the same ugly grey. The edges of its wings looked ragged, reminding Katsu of a tatty kite.

The filthy avian circled the ship on its moth-eaten wings peering down at the deck. Suddenly, and without warning the ragged pinions folded and it fell into a dive.

Katsu dropped his binoculars and fell to the deck a heart beat too late. The filth-caked beak ripped his cheek to the bone as the force of the impact sent him skidding across the deck, trailing blood. Before he could recuperate, the bird had turned and dived again landing with a great 'plop' in a clumsy tangle of rotting feathers and flailing wings several yards away. It waddled over and began savagely pecking at the stricken man. He threw up his hands to protect his face and the knife-like bill began slashing his palms and fingers.

Katsu's screams had alerted several other crew members who scrambled onto the upper deck to help him. The albatross span round, releasing a sound like a death rattle. It spat a black ichor at the men, who leapt back as it spewed out across the deck.

It hopped towards them, its razor beak flashing out like a foil. The nearest man fell with a scream as the beak ripped into his leg. The second, Kaede the harpoonist, tore off his thick coat and flung it over the huge bird's head. As it staggered about he straddled it and gripped the beak in his brawny, weather-beaten hands and twisted viciously. The bird fought with immense strength. Kaede recalled reading somewhere that birds were, technically, feathered dinosaurs, and hence many times stronger than a mammal of the same size. He could well believe it, as the bird bucked and struggled beneath him. Despite outweighing the albatross many times, it was putting up an impressive fight. Several other men came to his aid and grasped at the wings; after being knocked back several times they managed to pin the wings down. With the extra weight, Kaede heaved and twisted again - he was rewarded with a resounding 'snap,' and the great bird sagged beneath him.

"What the hell is going on here?" Captain Nakamura was up on the deck and was greeted with the sight of two men lying prone, the floor awash with blood and ichor.

"This bird," answered Kaede, "it attacked Katsu. He needs medical help."

The big man stood up, pulling away his coat to reveal the scraggy, mired seabird, its neck hanging at a crazy angle. Almost as soon as the weight of the men had been removed from it, the bird reared up again, releasing another throaty rattle and a jet of black liquid. It scuttled forwards on feet whose webbing was full of holes. The distorted beak continued to snap at the legs of the men.

"What's wrong with it? Look at its eyes!", shouted the captain, staggering away from the horror. For the first time, the men noticed that the bird's eyes were tiny, black, and dessicated - like raisins. They seemed to have no moisture in them.

One of the other men who had fled returned with an axe. He swung it down with as much force as his shaking arms could muster. The bird's head was totally severed, and flew across the deck with the beak still snapping like a demented mousetrap. The oily body blundered about, wings thrashing, until heavy axe-blows broke them; finally the body collapsed, twitching, into a heap.

In the sick bay, Katsu had been given ten stitches to his left cheek after the wound had been comprehensively washed to prevent infection. Naoki, the man whose leg had been pecked, had got off more lightly, but still had his wound disinfected.

"Just what the hell happened back there, Katsu?" the Captain asked.

"Like I said, Captain, I was on the lookout for whales when I saw an albatross. It came closer, and I noticed that it looked - well, dirty; diseased, even. Before I knew what was happening it was on me, attacking me. It's all a blur after that, to be honest."

"I saw some pretty strange stuff out there, Katsu. I've been at sea for thirty years, but I've never come across anything like this."

Katsu gingerly touched his stitches and winced. "I've heard of seabirds attacking people if they think their eggs or chicks are under threat, but I never heard of an albatross just ripping into someone, unprovoked."

"There's more to it than that, my friend. Whilst you were flat on your back, I saw Kaede break the thing's neck with his bare hands, but it just kept on coming at us as if nothing had happened; then, one of the other men hacked its head clean off, but it was still moving about."

"Can't chickens live for a few seconds after their heads are chopped off?"

"It was thrashing around until he beat its wings and body to a pulp with the axe; even then the carcass was still twitching! What's more, there was no blood. The bird was hacked apart, and there was no blood!"

"Do you think it could be some sort of disease? Something like rabies, that makes them go mad or affects the nervous system?"

"I've no idea, but we put the carcass in a plastic bag so that Professor Itō can dissect it. If anyone can tell us what's going on, he can. The damn thing was still twitching in the bag! Until we know what was wrong with the bird, I want you to stay in the sick bay. We can't afford an outbreak of some kind on the ship."

Katsu nodded in agreement and climbed back into his sick bed.

Every whaling ship in the fleet had a zoologist or marine biologist onboard. It was supposedly so that they could dissect and study the bodies of minke whales; in reality, it was little more than a feeble veneer to give the illusion of scientific research and respectability to what was, in actuality a commercial venture.

Professor Itō Wanatabe of Osaka University was supposedly studying whale lice - parasitic crustaceans found only on cetaceans. Some of his colleagues claimed to be studying the stomach contents of whales, or even population numbers. Actually, he had done little research whilst on the *Shonan Maru* aside from preserving a few whale lice in jars of formaldehyde. He had relished the chance of dissecting something new when the Captain brought him the specimen. He was even more intrigued when he heard the strange story that accompanied it.

Captain Nakamura knocked on the door of the Professor's onboard laboratory, then entered. He found the old man bent over his dissection bench. He looked up. His face seemed worried and, if Captain Nakamura had not known better, frightened.

"So, Professor, can you tell me anything about this yet?"

"I can tell you that we need to head back to Osaka and get everyone onboard this ship into quarantine."

"You mean the bird has some kind of disease?"

"I can only assume so, but this is unlike anything I have ever encountered before. The bird you brought me is indeed a specimen of *Diomedea exulans*, the wandering albatross. When it arrived in my lab, its head had been removed and wings broken. There were several deep gashes in its breast, but it was still moving."

The old man stood and opened his arms in a gesture of confusion. The Captain could see that his white apron and rubber gloves were stained with the ichor.

"The carcass that was brought to me was twitching; I had to pin it down on the table."

He moved to one side, and the Captain saw the remains of the dissected bird pinned down to Itō's workbench like some avian Christ.

"I found that all the organs were desiccated: heart, lungs, liver and so on." He held up what looked like a shrivelled apple in a jar.

"This is the heart - there was no blood in the bird's blood vessels. In fact, the only liquid I could find apart from the waterproof oil coating the feathers was in the stomach. It was the same black liquid that the bird apparently vomited out when attacking the men on deck. I am currently analysing it, but it appears to be composed of moisture from the organs, as if, in the desiccation process, the liquids were drained into the stomach for some reason.

"And yet the bird still moves, even with the bits hacked off it, like the head. Against all known biological principles, it was *moving!*"

"Couldn't it just be the nerve endings firing, like in a headless chicken?", asked the Captain, echoing Katsu's earlier question. "I've been told that mounted insects can twitch four hours after being pinned down to a piece of card, even after having been inside a killing jar."

"No, you don't understand. Nerves are just pathways for electro-chemical impulses. These operate muscles, but they could not work in a desiccated medium - it would be like expecting a bit of old leather to move around."

"Well, how do you explain it, Professor?"

"I can't; I can only surmise that this is some sort of disease, perhaps a pathogen of some kind utterly unknown to science, which gives the appearance of life after the host organism has died - but such an organisation of the host body is totally unprecedented."

"You think we are in danger?"

"Possibly, but we are dealing with unknowns here." The scientist began to pace up and down.

"We have to get back to Osaka and into quarantine until we know more about this condition, and if it's transmittable to humans."

The Captain looked doubtful.

"Professor, we have two good, clear weeks left in which to catch more whales. We get paid by how much whale meat we bring home. For a lot of my men, this is their only job."

"Captain, would you like to be held responsible for the possible outbreak of an unknown disease in a major city? If this something new and virulent, it could grow into a pandemic."

"Then aren't we better out here, where we can't infect anybody? It's only for a couple more weeks,and the men who were attacked by the bird have been ordered to stay in the sick bay. This way, if anything develops, we can radio ahead for advice. It's better to isolate the ship out here than back at port."

Professor Itō shook his head.

"Very well, but on your own head be it. I'll run some more tests on the bird. Make sure the doctor keeps an eye on the men in sick bay."

Back up on deck, a relative calm had returned. Men were posted about the ship, scanning the horizon for whales. One of them, Tanihashi Shinobu, saw something huge and grey heave from the water some three miles out, to starboard. Focusing his binoculars, he saw the tell-tale spout. This was no minke; judging by its massive size, it could only be one species of whale - the blue. He reached for his walkie-talkie and contacted the Captain.

Moments later, Nakamura was on the deck beside him, looking through the glasses at the creature.

"It's a blue whale alright - god, the size of it! I've never seen one so big."

"Are we going to go after it, Captain?"

"Of course! There is as much meat on that one animal as in two dozen minkes."

"But the blue whale is one of the protected species. We're only supposed to hunt the minkes."

"This is your first journey, isn't it, Tanihashi?"

"Yes, Captain".

"Then you wouldn't know, but once rendered down, whale meat all looks the same. We just cut the blue into smaller bits. Who's to know?"

He lifted his own walkie-talkie and barked orders into it.

"All hands to deck! We have a whale. Hunting stations, everyone! Katō is still in the sick bay, so Sasaki Masaru, you take his place. Steer starboard and don't lose sight of him."

The massive ship turned with surprising swiftness, and cut through the water like a knife, after its huge prey.

Nakamura kept the beast in view through his binoculars as they chased it. He had seen blue whales before but, even by their standards, this one was a monster. It was hard to judge size in the open sea, as there were seldom objects to compare things to as there were on land; a life at sea, however, had given Nakamura a better gauge of size than most men. Calculating the distance, he reckoned the beast must be well over 150 feet long - that was almost a third longer than the largest specimen ever captured at 108 feet. Nakamura had thought all such giants long gone, erased by the harpoon decades ago.

As the *Shonan Maru* drew closer still, he could see that there was some sort of cloud following the whale. He adjusted the focus of the binoculars and saw that it was a huge flock of sea birds. They were following the whale, probably to capture the fish that the great beast stirred up as it swam.

Up at the harpoon, Sasaki Masaru readied himself for when they drew into range. He had harpooned many whales before, but nothing this size. *God, Katō will be jealous.* He gripped the trigger of the harpoon with sweaty hands, wondering if even an explosive-tipped device such as this could put paid to such a titanic whale.

The ship was now closing fast, its powerful engine bringing it ever closer to the ponderous sea giant. Nakamura noticed that there was some kind of slick in the water around the whale; black and oily, it ran from the creature's flanks and formed a floating ring about it. He wondered if the animal had encountered an oil spill; he hoped not, as the meat would be ruined.

The whale heaved up out of the water like a volcanic island surfacing during an undersea eruption. The head and body then went under as the huge tail rose with a spray of dark water. The flukes must have been 30 feet across. The flesh on them looked ragged; perhaps the beast had been attacked by killer whales. He recalled seeing footage of a pod of killer whales attacking a blue whale, like wolves attacking a moose - the orcas had torn the blue whale to shreds. It had occurred in the Sea of Cortez.

The beast had a network of scars running across its flanks - badges of past conflicts, no doubt. A whale couldn't grow that big without being incredibly old. The average blue whale had a life span akin to that of a human, about 80 years. The bowhead whale could reach 200 years. Lord alone knew how old this cetacean Methuselah was! Nakamura realised he could be looking at the largest and oldest animal ever to have lived on earth. A scientist would have looked on in awe and wonder, but to Captain Nakamura, the giant whale meant only one thing - money.

"Get the harpoon ready," he barked into his radio.

Sasaki swung the harpoon cannon round and secured the beast's frankly-un-missable flank in his sights. He pulled the trigger that released the harpoon itself. The lethal device arced out, trailing its line, and pierced the grey, oily hide of the mammal. The explosive in the tip was detonated by the impact and erupted inside its victim, sending out barbed hooks to anchor itself into the flesh.

The distorted flukes hit the water with a deafening crash as the whale pulled away. The harpoon line went taught, and then the multi-barbed harpoon was ripped away from the whale's side bringing with it a dining-room-table-sized chunk of shrivelled, lifeless meat that flopped into the sea like a dried-out bull's carcass. There was no blood.

"The meat!", shouted Nakamura. "Look, it's the same as that bird, desiccated. It's got the same damn disease. Get the Professor up here."

The whale turned again and drew closer. Through the binoculars, Nakamura could see its tiny, dead eyes rolling in their sockets. The whale spouted, but it was not carbon dioxide - it was expelling out some foul yellowish gas born of internal decay. The men turned back from the railings of the ship, gagging as the vile, acrid stench burnt into their nostrils. Some doubled up and vomited onto the deck.

It was not only gas that was released, but a fine spray of black ichor that fell down on the *Shonan Maru* like a liquid, ebony rain. It clotted into the men's hair and ran down their faces and necks. It had the texture of machine oil and the smell of an open grave.

Nakamura felt a hand on his shoulder and turned to see Numasaki Akio, the oldest crew member, at his side.

"Bake-kujira" the old man shouted.

"What?"

"Bake-kujira - a yokai, a spirit."

"What are you raving about, Numasaki?"

"My father saw it off Shimane Prefecture back in the 1930s. It's a zombie, an un-dead whale, a spirit of the ocean. It is sent to punish whalers who hunt too many whales. It has a following of un-dead birds. The thing that attacked us before was just a scout. Bake-kujira sinks whaling ships. We stayed in the polar sea too long; we should have gone back before the turning of the New Year, but we were greedy. We stayed on too long, took too much - we are all dead men now."

The Captain was about to berate the older man for speaking such childish drivel when the air was split by an unearthly noise. It was a high wail that descended into a deep-bass booming that they felt in their bones and guts. The awful cry rang out again, making them fall to their knees with their hands over their ears.

"Bake-kujira - it is calling. That is the voice of the zombie whale." Numasaki was shaking and his eyes were wide with horror.

The noise did indeed sound like a distorted mockery of whale-song.

"He is calling down his entourage."

Nakamura had forgotten the cloud of birds circling high above the whale; he looked up in time to see the ragged creatures begin to dive. There were all types of sea birds: herring gulls, fulmars, frigate birds, albatrosses, and gannets, not just birds found in Antarctic waters. It was as if the creature had swum all the world's oceans like some cadaverous Moby Dick, collecting sea birds from across the globe as it went.

Sasaki, at the harpoon, was first to be hit. A rancid gannet smashed into him like an organic kamikaze, knocking him to the deck. In an instant it was joined by a pair of dead terns; the three decaying birds stabbed into his face and eyes with matter-coated beaks.

Elsewhere the birds were raining down in fury of stabbing bills and raking talons. What had once been a pelagic cormorant fastened itself to old Numasaki's neck, rending the flesh with its cruel, fish-spearing beak; the old man tried desperately to dislodge the bird, and appeared to be doing some kind of weird dance as he struggled with the horror. The cormorant was joined by a massive skua that split the man's balding skull with one brutal peck. As he fell, more birds were upon him, like vultures about a kill on the African savannah.

Some of the men had tried to run for the ship's helicopter, but were being forced back by rotting pelicans. A colony of decomposing boobies had taken up roost on the chopper's blades.

Some other men had leapt into a lifeboat and pulled the tarpaulin across themselves as they lowered it into the sea. The birds did not follow; for a time the men thought themselves safe, but something launched itself from the water like a missile - it was an emperor penguin, and more of them followed. The zombie penguins waddled about the lifeboat, slashing the tarpaulin and the flesh of the men beneath it.

The emperor penguins were soon joined by other species - gentoo, rock-hopper, king and chinstrap. Soon the weight of the dead birds forced the lifeboat under, and the floundering men were easy prey for the nightmare penguins.

Nakamura needed to get to cover, and made a run for the bridge. A family of dead puffins latched onto his arms as he scrambled up the stairs. He smashed them against the metal steps and railing, stamping them underfoot as they fell. Even as his boots descended on them, they turned to stab and peck with dead beaks. Kicking the flapping corpses down the steps, he made it to the door and pulled it open; even as he slammed it behind him a petrel smashed into it with a sickening crunch.

Several injured crew members were already in the bridge; some of them were kneeling in prayer. Sea birds were hurling themselves against the re-enforced glass of the windows; the glass was becoming opaque with the black ichor that ran down it. As a black-browed albatross smashed into one of the windows, the glass began to crack.

Captain Nakamura shook off his shock and, with adrenalin-fuelled speed, rushed across to the wheel and span it around. "We have to pull back now! If we retreat, they might leave us alone!" Even as the words left his lips, he did not believe them.

The *Shonan Maru's* engines groaned in protest as the ship did a tight turn to try and escape from the yokai whale and its army of zombie birds.

Out in the ocean, the Bake-kujira saw its prey attempting to flee - it would not be cheated so easily. The rage and fury and hatred of every whale killed by mankind resided in its colossal bulk. The tattered tail, as broad as a city bus was long, powered it forward, surging through the water like an icebreaker made of dead flesh.

The Bake-kujira rammed the side of the *Shonan Maru,* and metal folded and ripped like so much paper. On the bridge, Nakamura and the others were thrown to the ground, whilst the ship pitched crazily to starboard. Below, in the sick bay, men were tossed from their beds and cabinets up-ended, sending pills, bottles and medical equipment cascading across the floor.

In his laboratory, Itō was hurled across the room. A soup of formaldehyde, broken glass and whale lice spread across the floor as his specimens were tossed from their shelves.

Nakamura staggered to his feet and tried to gain control of the wheel, which was spinning madly. He realised that the monster had rammed them badly, damaging the ship and shifting the ballast.

He peered down from the odd angle of the vessel and saw the giant whale. The brute was even bigger than he had at first thought; it was as long as his ship, and probably as heavy. The *Shonan Maru* was 175 feet long and displaced 491 tons, but the monster had tossed it around like a toy.

The zombie whale seemed to be swimming away. The birds were following it. Nakamura thanked the gods; he did not think that the ship could take another blow like that.

"Someone see if the radio is working! Call for help!"

One of the dazed crew members staggered over to the radio and began to examine it.

Nakamura glanced back out of window, and saw, to his horror, that the Bake-kujira had not retreated, it had merely swum away in order to turn and gain speed for another attack. The beast thundered through the ocean, a marine locomotive powered by vengeance and rancour.

Spray arced up around the beast as it gained speed. Nakamura tried to hold onto the wheel, but was hurled across the bridge like a doll as the monster struck. The screaming of tortured metal filled the air. The side of the *Shonan Maru* gave way in a huge gash as the hull was rent asunder.

Water exploded into the ship below deck. It spewed down corridors, smashed open doors and washed away men, furniture and equipment alike. The cold Antarctic Ocean was entering the *Shonan Maru,* filling it, a bitter water weighing the ship down.

Captain Nakamura held his left arm. It hung at an odd angle, obviously broken. The adrenalin overwhelmed any pain he might have felt. He staggered over to the window. The ship was badly listing now, and he could plainly hear the roaring of water as it poured through the great hole that had opened in the side of the ship like a mortal wound. Instead of lifeblood flowing out, the ocean, the lifeblood of the Earth, was flowing in.

The Bake-kujira had swum away and turned again for another attack. This time the leviathan did not ram the ship; it leapt from the water, a living mountain of decaying meat and ancient bones stronger than steel. Hundreds of tons of whale meat came down on the *Shonan Maru* as the creature hit her amidships.

The back of the *Shonan Maru* was broken; the weight of the Bake-kujira and the water already inside of her was too much for the ship. Whale and whaling ship vanished below the surface, sinking in less than sixty seconds.

There was a great swirl as the displaced water crashed upon the surface, followed by the air being forced out of the stricken ship in great bubbles. There was then a profound silence. Finally, something surfaced - the dark mass of the Bake-kujira risen in silent victory. Its collection of birds reformed round it like flies about a carcass. It called its eerie cry, then forged off into the endless waters in search of more prey, a justice machine that ran on vengeance.

12. Primary

The sun was beginning to draw close to the horizon. Slats of amber light shone through the blinds and fell across the crisp white sheets. The room was still. Barely an hour ago, it was full of life; people from all over Hakodate, and indeed from all over Hokkaidō, had filled the room with colour and noise.

Wakasa Ichiro had been gratified that so many people had come so far to see him - his two daughters and his son (the latter who had come all the way from Osaka), his six grandchildren, four great-grandchildren, and finally little Riko, his great, great granddaughter who was only 18-months-old. Then there was the mayor of Hakodate, and dozens of well-wishers from the city. Reporters from several papers (including the *Hakodate Observer*, at which he had worked for over thirty years) had turned up, as well as a film crew for the local television station. His age caused interest, even in a country whose population was the longest-lived in the world.

The cake had been huge, by necessity, to hold 100 candles - he had counted them all before failing to blow them out. He was getting a little out of breath for things like that, but not too old for a nip of his favourite sake.

The papers had asked questions about his youth - *what had it been like growing up in the 1920s when Hakodate had been given city status?* He spoke of the great fire of 1934 that killed over 2,000 people, including some of his friends and relatives; he was one of the young men who had helped the overburdened rescue service, helping to save many lives. He still bore the scars from the burns he received to his hands, though the wrinkles now masked them - time erased all things. Some asked about his time serving with the army in Borneo and Sumatra during WWII; he had spent a good part of the war recovering from a snakebite that nearly killed him. After the war, he became a reporter and progressed onto travel writing. He had seen much of the globe, from England to Bolivia, from Tasmania to Botswana - his life had been an interesting one. Ichiro had always meant to write an autobiography, but had never gotten around to it. He still had boxes of notes all banged out on that creaky old typewriter of his - he never did get on with computers. He supposed it would be down to one of his children to write his life story now.

Ichiro told his guests that he had felt blessed. He had escaped death a number of times in the war, and had seen many of his friends die young, then outlived those who were left. He had a good wife, Noa, who had passed away five years ago, and who he still missed. but he had a good family. He had lived for many years now with his eldest daughter Takako and her husband, both of whom cared for him very well. He spent most of his time in bed now, but he was still able-bodied enough to putter around the garden for an hour or so in the warmer months and admire the view out over the bay.

The party had taken it out him, even if it was enjoyable; he needed a little rest now. Just as his head began to nod, the door of his room swung open. He looked up and saw the silhouette of a child standing in the doorway. It must have been one of his great grandchildren - perhaps the child had left something behind and returned to retrieve it.

"Toru, is that you? Did you forget something?"

The child shook its head. As he drew closer, Ichiro could see he was a boy of perhaps six years. Ichiro realised that the child was not Toru, or indeed any of his family's offspring.

The boy was curiously dressed, looking very old-fashioned. His hair was drawn back into a topknot. He had geta sandals on his feet that clacked on the floorboards as he walked, and a plain kimono with an obi. In his hand he held a wooden staff taller than he was.

Ichrio thought that he may have been a child brought in by many of the local well-wishers that had visited him.

"Have you lost your mother and father?"

"Yes," the boy answered, "a long time ago."

The boy drew closer and sat down on Ichiro's futon. He looked somehow familiar. *Was he a relation?*

"I waited for the others to leave before I came, so we could talk in peace." The boy's voice sounded young, but he spoke like an adult.

"Do I know you, young man?"

"I hope so, Ichiro san; we spent many happy hours together."

Ichiro sat up in bed and looked more closely at the boy. Something stirred in his memory like a carp in the leaf-strewn depths of a pond, but seemed to slip away again.

"Whereabouts was that, my boy?"

"At the old house up on Gagyūzan."

Ichiro started at that name. He had not heard it in a long time; Gagyūzan, Mount Cow's Back, the old name for Mount Hakodate - Ichiro and his parents had lived in a house in the foothills when he was a boy.

"How did you know I lived there?"

"I live there, too."

"You live in my old house? How wonderful." Ichiro beamed; he had not thought of his childhood home in many years.

"You lived there with Wakasa Takayuki, your father, and Wakasa Chika, your mother, and let's not forget dear old Raikou, your Japanese spitz."

Now Ichiro was genuinely puzzled.

"How can you know all this?"

"The three of us used to play together in the cherry orchard behind your house."

"How old are you?"

"I am six years old."

"Then how could you have possibly played with me? I was born in 1910."

The little boy leaned on his staff and smiled.

"I have been six years old for one thousand and seven hundred years."

"Who are you?"

"Come now, Ichiro san; don't say you cannot remember me, your old friend Hajime."

The old man shook his head.

"Hajime? But I thought you were just a...."

"A dream? In a way, I suppose I am."

"You were an imaginary friend I had when I was living up on the mountain. We were higher up than most other houses, and I didn't see other children as often as I would have liked."

"So you dreamed me up as a playmate - that's what they all tell themselves as they grow older. Tell me, Ichiro san, how old were you when you last saw me?"

"About eight, I suppose."

"Yes, that's the age when I fade from the view of most children. You see I was not an imaginary friend, I was a real one - I was your home's Zashiki-Warashi."

"The parlour child? That's just a myth."

"No myth; is this real enough for you?"

Hajime reached forward and touched the old man's cheek.

"You are so wrinkled now, so old."

"And you're so young."

"No, time does not touch me, but I am far older than you, Ichiro san. Your house was one of the oldest in the city - it dated from the 15th century - but other houses stood there long before, and long before them was a Buddhist temple, and before that a Shinto temple. New religions build over the old; go far enough back and you will find the first religion."

"Back then there was a religion in Nippon that has long since been forgotten; only vestiges of it are known to people today. The Chinese visited Nippon in the third century by the Roman calendar, and they took a few notes on it. There was a high priestess who lived alone in a temple mound where she communed with the gods. One man was allowed to visit her - he transmitted the messages of the gods she gave him to the people.

"She was a very beautiful girl, and her existence was a lonely one. After a while, as she grew into womanhood, the inevitable happened - she had a child with the priest. Both were supposed to be celibate; they hid me for as long as they could, but after a few years I was discovered. The people grew angry and lost faith in my mother. They demanded a sacrifice - me. I was killed and buried under the temple so very long ago."

"Were you scared?"

"I was too young to know what was happening. The other priests gave me some kind of drug; I felt no pain when they slit my throat, it was just as if I were falling to sleep. From then on, my spirit was charged with bringing luck to the temple, and to whatever building stood on its site after its walls had turned to dust."

"One thousand seven hundred years is a long time. The world changes so much. When I was a boy, a living boy, this country was still filled with magick. Dragons swam in the seas and rivers. Nue and Tengu haunted the forests and mountains - man seldom sees them now.

"All that time I have played with the children in the temples and houses - novice monks, the boys and girls of the generations of families that have lived there. But the curse of the Zashiki-Warashi is that our playmates forsake us; our friends forget. You see, only a child can see a Zashiki-Warashi, until they reach the age of eight or so - then we are as invisible to them as we are to adults. It is a lonely existence knowing your friends will only last a few short years. I have seen hundreds of children come and go whilst I stay, unchanging and alone.

"There are no children in the house now. The man who owns it is unmarried; he seldom visits, except at weekends with his mistress. I think it is time the old house had children in it once more. The cherry trees are in blossom. Come, Ichiro san, little Raikou is waiting to play with us again."

As the last rays of the sun gave the horizon a purple glow, two children walked away from the house in the city and made their way up to the mountain.

13. Flutter

The night was clear. The bluish starlight lit the road ahead, almost as if it had been daylight. The lack of cloud gave the air a sharp bite though - it was well into October; the nights were drawing in and becoming colder, even in the south. The rōnin pulled his cloak tighter around him.

In the distance, wolves howled. He fingered the handle of his shōtō, the short sword that accompanied his longer katana. He had seen wolves on the road from Kokubu, grey shapes that slid in and out of the trees like ghosts, but they had not attacked; not so the black bear that had come crashing out of the bushes to tear the throat out of his horse. He had been pitched down a slope and cracked his head. By the time he regained consciousness, the bear had gone, leaving his steed half-eaten by the roadside.

His head still throbbed, and he limped. His pack was heavy on his back. The rōnin cursed his luck; not just the bear attack, but the untimely death of his master in Kokubu. He was now compelled to look for a new master, and had left to ride for the city of Kagoshima, where he hoped to find employment. Once a samurai - now nothing more than a rōnin. He spat into the shadows.

For the last three nights he had slept under the stars, building a fire and gaining what warmth he could from that; thankfully, it had not rained. There were few on the road, but the handful he had met had told him of an inn halfway between Kokubu and Kagoshima. The rōnin gritted his teeth and pressed on.

Eventually he saw a light ahead, and hoped his luck had changed. As he drew closer, he saw there was indeed an inn, set back a little way from the road. It was quite small - just two storeys and a stable - but he was glad to see it.

The rōnin pushed open the heavy door and entered. By the light of many paper lanterns and fish-oil lamps, he could see the little inn was surprisingly full. Tables and chairs were arranged around a central fire pit. Most of the tables were occupied by patrons eating and drinking. Few looked up as he walked in; he liked it that way - there was no honour in being a rōnin. He sat on a wooden stool by the bar. The man serving was little more than a youth.

"Do you have a room for the night?" he asked.

"We are very busy tonight, sama. I will need to check and see if any are left."

The rōnin was pleased at the honorific with which the boy had addressed him, and guessed that he had noticed the swords he kept beneath his cloak.

"Are you the landlord?"

The youth blushed.

"No, sama, my master and mistress have been away buying supplies in Kagoshima. They should be returning later tonight."

"I would like some food as well, and warm sake." He took several copper mon from a string at his belt and dropped them into the youth's hand."

The boy bowed.

"Very good, sama." He hurried away.

The rōnin relaxed, slipping the pack from his back and enjoying the warmth of the hearty fire that bathed the inn in a warm glow.

Service was good, and soon he was sipping from a bowl of warm sake. Not long after, a girl brought a meal of rice, vegetables and beef, followed by tofu flavoured with honey.

The youth reappeared and bowed once again.

"You were in luck, sama. We have a room and it has been prepared. If you would care to follow me?"

The rōnin followed the boy up the stairs and along a corridor to his room. The inn was old-fashioned, lacking the more common sliding shōji made of paper and bamboo - the doors here were solid wood. The boy unlocked the door and showed the rōnin inside. It was simple but clean. Floored with tatami mats, it had a plain table, an oil lamp, and a futon. There were bolted shutters on the far wall.

"Is it to your liking, sama?"

The rōnin nodded, entering the room and placing his pack in a corner.

"Do you wish to retire, sama?"

"Not yet; I think I will drink a while longer."

The boy handed him a key. Locking the door behind him, he walked back down the stairs to the bar.

He was drinking his second bowl of sake when the door of the inn swing open and a fat man entered. He had the look of a merchant, and a number of pouches hung from his belt. He wore a fine silk kimono and carried no luggage. Behind him was a tall, lean man with a large backpack; there was a sword at his side and the rōnin assumed he was a bodyguard in the pay of the merchant.

"Boy!" the fat merchant bellowed. The youth came scurrying over.

"I need my horses fed, watered and stabled. I also need two meals, drinks and a room for the night."

The boy reddened at the cheeks and bowed.

"My apologies, sama, but we have no rooms left."

"No rooms? What do you mean, boy? This is the only inn for miles around! My man and I have been a long, hard time on the road - I need rest."

"But sir, all our rooms are booked for tonight."

The merchant's hand fell to his belt and produced a pouch, which he shook. There was a chinking of many coins within.

"I can make it worth your while, boy."

The youth looked at the pouch and thought.

"We do have one room, but it is very old and has not been used for quite some time."

"That doesn't bother me."

"It will be quite dusty now; we will need some time to clean it."

"Then I will take my meal whilst you prepare it."

"There is only room for one in the room."

"My man has a ground roll; he can sleep on the floor outside my door."

A serving girl was passing, and overheard the exchange.

"Yuu, you can't give him *that* room!"

"There are no other rooms, Kotone. What do you expect me to do? Send him back out onto the road on a night like this, with the wolves and bears?"

The girl pouted.

"I'd rather take my chances with wolves and bears than spend a night in there."

"Never you mind, Kotone. Fetch the stable boy to attend to out guest's horses."

The girl walked away and the youth turned back to the merchant.

"I apologise for that outburst, sama. She is a little highly-strung, and dislikes the idea of a guest staying in such an untidy room. If you will follow me, I will get you some food and drink."

He led the way to a recently-vacated table, and the merchant and his minder sat down. The rōnin, who had overheard the conversation, discreetly watched and listened, his interest piqued. Sake and food were brought to them and they ate in silence.

About half an hour later, the door swung open once more and a middle-aged couple walked in carrying bags and bundles. The youth, Yuu, and several girls went over to help them. There was a short, whispered exchange, then the man shouted, "You did what?!"

Pushing Yuu aside he rushed over to the merchant's table and bowed low.

"Many pardons, sama, but I believe my incompetent apprentice has booked you into a substandard room."

The merchant smiled patiently.

"It really doesn't matter. I've travelled all over Nippon and I'm sure I have stayed in much worse rooms than the one you speak of."

The man, whom the rōnin assumed must be the landlord, looked worried and shook his head.

"With respect, sama, I cannot insult you by allowing you to sleep in such an unworthy room."

The merchant chuckled. "Where else is there for me to go at this hour? Would you turn me back onto the road in the dead of night? Besides, I have already paid for the room."

"I will gladly give you your money back, and the drinks and the meal can be on the house."

"No, I am tired and I need to sleep. Besides, what is so bad about this room anyhow? Your boy said it would be cleaned up."

"It's not a case of cleaning the room up," he said, lowering his voice.

"What, then?"

The landlord looked at his feet, clearly embarrassed. His wife came over to join him.

"Sama," she began, "the room you have been given at the end of the corridor is… haunted!"

The merchant burst out in a laugh so loud it turned all the heads in the inn.

"Haunted? Haunted! I thought there was something seriously wrong with the room!"

"Please, sama, not so loud," said the landlady.

"It is bad for business," the landlord added.

"You would deny me a room on account of superstition?"

The landlord held his head in his hands.

"Sama, you do not understand. The ghost that haunts that room is dangerous. We took over running this inn from an old man nearly twenty years ago. He warned us of that room, but we ignored him. Every single person who has ever slept in the room has been found dead in the morning - not just old people, but the young and healthy. The medical men said they were suffocated. There were investigations, of course. Some thought we had killed the travellers to rob them, but they never had any valuables missing. Soon the inn got a bad reputation, and people stopped coming here. We even had a priest in to perform an exorcism, but it did no good. In the end, we just locked the room and never used it again. I can't believe Yuu was so stupid as to let you have it."

"The boy is just greedy," snapped his wife.

"You are worrying over nothing. I will have my man posted just outside my room; if anything happens in the night, I will just call him."

"Is there nothing we can do to change your mind?"

"Nothing. Now, if you please, I am weary and wish to retire."

Yuu lead the merchant and his guard up the stairs.

Soon after, the rōnin made his way to bed. He glanced along the corridor to the door at the end, and saw the bodyguard asleep on his bedroll, blankets tight around him. He unlocked his door, undressed and slipped into the futon. Soon he was asleep.

He awoke from a dreamless sleep and saw that morning light was filtering in through the slats of his shutters. A loud noise was coming from along the corridor, a banging and shouting. He quickly dressed and went to investigate.

The bodyguard was banging on his master's door and shouting.

"Come, quickly, somebody! My master is not answering!"

The landlord emerged from his quarters, rubbing his eyes and frowning.

"Get the key, you fool!" snapped the guard.

The landlord fumbled in his pockets and finally found the correct key. With shaking hands, he pushed it into the keyhole and turned. Entering the room, he gave a strangled gasp and stumbled back.

"Oh, no, not again! I warned you, I warned you!"

The guard pushed his way past the shaking landlord, and the rōnin followed. The merchant lay across the futon like a beached whale. His eyes bulged in their sockets and were rolled back. His fat tongue protruded from lips that were blackened. His cheeks had a bluish pallor. His arms were raised to his chest and his fingers were locked in *rigor mortis* as if he had been trying to tear something away from his face and neck. The rest of the room seemed undisturbed.

The merchant's man spun round and drew his sword.

"Murdering bastard! You had him killed for his money and invented this stupid story to cover it."

The landlord backed away.

"No, I tried my best to dissuade him from taking the room."

"Wait!" cried the rōnin, "Have any of his money or goods actually been taken?"

The man wandered over to where the merchant had piled up his bags and pouches.

"No, it doesn't look like it."

The rōnin turned to the landlord.

"Apart from the merchant, you had the only key?"

He nodded.

"And you," the rōnin addressed the bodyguard, "you were beside the door all night?"

"Yes, I was."

"Then how could the landlord have gotten past you, even if he had wanted to?"

The bodyguard scratched his thin chin.

"He could have come through by the shutters."

The rōnin walked over to the shutters and examined them. The bolt was still drawn and there was less than an inch of space beneath them.

"Still locked from the inside."

"Is there no other entrance?" asked the guard.

"No, there is no other way in. I have told you - it is always the same in this room."

"Did you hear anything during the night?", asked the rōnin.

"Nothing much," said the man. "I thought I heard something fluttering at one point, like sheets in the wind, but it was not loud. I thought nothing of it."

They covered the merchant with a blanket and, between them, carried him out of the inn. The guard borrowed a small cart to transport his body back to Kagoshima, and was on his way before breakfast.

The landlord and his wife were beside themselves with worry.

"We are ruined; we are ruined!", the landlady repeated.

"They will send people from Kagoshima to investigate. Word will get around again. We had just shaken off the bad name - now men will come and blame us for this man's death."

The rōnin put his hand on the landlord's shoulder.

"I saw that room. The shutters were locked from the inside and the guard was in front of the only door. No-one could have gotten in or out."

"Like I said, it is a strangling ghost. It kills anyone who sleeps in that room."

"I will put a stop to whatever is doing this."

The landlord shook his head.

"How can you fight a ghost?"

"We don't know that it is a ghost."

"What else could it be?"

"I intend to find out, if you will let me."

"Heavens, no," exclaimed the landlady, "we cannot afford two deaths in as many nights."

The rōnin smiled.

"The merchant was old, fat and unarmed; I am young, strong, and well-armed." He pulled aside his cloak, showing his impressive swords.

"Sama is a samurai?" exclaimed the landlady.

"I fear that now I am but a lowly rōnin - but I still try to uphold samurai principles. Let me stay in the room and I will lay this 'ghost' of yours low."

The couple looked at each other, eyes full of doubt.

"I have no master, no family - no one to miss me should I die. If I do die, bury me in the woods with my swords and you may take what money and other goods I have. If I live, then whatever is visiting that room will not trouble you again."

"If you think you can help us...." began the landlord.

"I can. Now, can you tell me any more about that room."

"I know nothing of the inn's history, other than that it is very old; but sometimes, at night, my wife and I - if we pass the room we can hear a soft noise."

"Like a fluttering," added the landlady.

"Very well. Tonight I will sleep in the haunted room. I intend to stay awake all night, so I will sleep in the afternoon. Wake me an hour before dusk."

The sun was already low on the horizon when the rōnin ate a simple meal of rice and chicken. The landlord gave him the key and wished him luck. He lit the fish-oil lantern in the room, and then examined his surroundings more closely - four thick wooden walls; one door, which he locked behind him; and the bolted shutters. He pulled the bolt aside, noting how stiff it was - it couldn't have been used in years. He heaved the heavy shutters open; they too were stiff on their hinges. He looked out and could see the waters of Kagoshima Bay glistening in the distance and the black hulk of Sakurajima, the volcanic island, on the horizon.

He closed the shutters and bolted them once more. Bending down, he looked at the tiny slit beneath them, too narrow to admit even a mouse. The rōnin toyed with the idea of some kind of poison dart being shot through the gap, but the idea was absurd; the shutters were on the second storey and the would-be assassin would be shooting blind through the tiny gap. Besides, he had seen no mark on the merchant's body that could be equated with a dart, nor had he found a dart at all.

Perhaps a venomous snake like a nihon-mamushi had crawled through the gap. Snakebite could stop a man's heart and turn his skin blue - but if that were the case then the animal would have had to have slithered out again, for it was not in the room. It was getting colder, and most snakes would be about to hibernate. Nothing seemed to make sense.

The rōnin read from the few books he had in his possession for several hours. Soon he lost track of time. There was noise from downstairs that eventually subsided. He heard the guests climbing the stairs to go to their rooms. He sat, still and silent, in the golden glow of the lamp. In the wee small hours, his head began to nod.

The yūjo moved closer to him, loosening her kimono. She had untied her hair and it fell down in an ebony cascade. He could feel her breath on his neck and her fingers brushing his cheek. They felt so soft ....

His eyes snapped open; the oil lamp had burned down low, reducing the light in the room. Hardly daring to breathe, he turned his eyes to the right, where, in his dream, the courtesan had been stroking his face. Something flat and white hung in the air, level with his head, and trailed off into the shadows. In one fluid movement, he rolled to his left and leapt to his feet.

The thing swept down like a striking cobra, hitting the floor where he had been a second before. In the dim light, he could see that it was an elongate, flat, white form, over 30 feet long and about 18 inches wide. The end of it was still sliding under the narrow gap beneath the shutters. It appeared to be a great length of cotton, unrolled and crawling about with an unnatural animation. It was now moving what the rōnin took to be it's head end to and fro across the floor, as if searching for prey. Frozen in horror, he watched as it slowly draw closer. He saw what might pass for eyes in the folds and creases close to its front.

The rōnin recalled a story from his childhood, a weird phantom that took the shape of a roll of cloth. The Ittan-momen was said to coil about is victims like some vast serpent and suffocate them; that was the story, but now, here, that same children's tale was hunting him in strange fluttering, looping movements.

The Ittan-momen rose up again, taller than a man. Its rear end had now slipped through the shutters. It resembled some gigantic flatworm, grave-white in the half-light. The cloth phantom swayed side to side and then struck. Its movement was a pallid blur. It coiled about the rōnin in an eyeblink, pinning his arms to his sides. What passed for a head enveloped his face, covering his mouth and nose. It adhered to his skin like a death mask, stifling his breath.

The rōnin fell backwards, and the cloth coils crept up his legs to pin them helplessly together with a strength that fabric should not possess. He strained against the mummifying convolutions that bound him, but as the breath left his body, he became weaker. His desperate thrashings were subsiding. The rōnin's head swam. He could not reach his katana, but his left hand was free, and he reached for his shōtō.

His numb fingers grasped the handle and pulled it from its sheath even as the cloth horror squeezed harder. Blindly, he slashed and stabbed at coils with what little movement was left in his wrist. He felt them give, and began to cut deeper. The rōnin felt warm liquid against his leg and thought he had cut himself. The Ittan-momen was slackening its grip and unfurling. The cloth mask was peeled from his face, and he sucked in air in great breaths.

Looking down, he saw that the blood was not his, but was flowing from the gashes he had cut into the cloth monster. Now it was slithering away, trying to find the shutters and a means of escape. It had expected another flabby, unarmed victim, not an armed rōnin. The creature rose up and, with fluttering undulations, took to the air. It floundered clumsily in the small room, and the rōnin feared it would knock over the lamp and set the inn ablaze.

It was making for the shutters once more, but the rōnin stabbed down with his shōtō, pinning the fluttering horror to the floor. It now looked like some ghastly kite as it tried to reach for the narrow gap through which it had gained access. Drawing his katana, the rōnin slashed and hacked at the cloth; ghost or not, it bled. The Ittan-momen turned back and tried to strike at him, but in the small room it became entangled in its own long body.

Again and again the katana flashed, until the thing flopped to the floor in a growing pool of blood. A few undulations ran along its length like the ripples of a stream. Finally, it lay still.

There was a banging at the door.

"Sama, sama, are you alright? We heard a commotion."

He unlocked the door and let the landlord and his wife into the room. They gaped at the dying Ittan-momen, still trickling blood. A small crowd of patrons had gathered behind them.

"Your strangling ghost will be of no more trouble." The rōnin indicated the tattered, bloodstained remains.

"What was it?", the landlady asked.

"An Ittan-momen - an animated, malevolent length of living cloth, a supernatural entity. It gained entrance into the room by a small gap under the shutter and killed anyone it found sleeping here."

"But why did it come here, and where was it from?" The landlord mumbled more to himself than anyone else.

"That I can't answer," said the rōnin. "Perhaps it was some curse or enchantment laid down decades ago and long since lost to time. Maybe, like some old servant, it kept returning here to do its duty long after whoever caused it to come in the first place had died - we will probably never know."

"How can we repay you?" The landlady was fumbling in a bag of money.

"Keep your money. My horse was killed by a bear on the road. I am travelling to Kagoshima; I would be grateful if you could take me the rest of the way in your cart."

The landlord and his wife nodded in agreement.

They burnt the remains of the Ittan-momen behind the inn. It gave off an acrid black smoke that seemed to last an unnaturally long time. The rōnin was given a hearty breakfast of fruit, eggs, pork and sticky rice, washed down with the finest sake, all on the house.

The landlord took the rōnin on his cart to the bustling centre of Kagoshima, where the latter hoped to find a new master.

As he left, the landlord thanked him once again for his courage.

"I never even asked your name," he said.

The rōnin smiled. "My name is Ryuu," he said.

14. Gama

It's a funny thing, playground lore; I often wonder if anyone has written a book on it. Not the old rhymes and games, but the stories and rumours. Some of them are countrywide, like the 'slit-mouthed woman,' or the ghost who haunts a certain cubicle of the girl's toilets (in our school it was third from the left). Others are unique to the area.

I grew up on the edge of the small town of Kawakita. It is near the coast of Ishikawa Prefecture, and lies on the north bank of the Tedori River. Mostly Kawakita is a quiet town, but once a year, on the first Saturday of August, we hold the Tedori Fire Festival. Our little town boasts the largest bonfire in Nippon, at 150 feet tall. Drummers beat their drums to drive insects away from the rice fields, whilst villagers hold up torches and 10,000 fireworks are let off.

Save for that single day, Kawakita is a sleepy town.

Maybe it was the very sleepiness of the place that started the stories. On the edge of a little town, there is not much for children to do except tell stories. I recall that, as a girl, one of the creepiest I ever heard was 'the house of the red snake.' It centered around a large, old, tumbledown house that lay between Kawakita and the coast, some miles out of town. We didn't know why the house had been abandoned or who once lived in it, but that didn't stop us telling stories.

Yuto was a boy in the year above me who relished telling ghost and horror stories. One day he explained to a crowd of children who had gathered around him why the old building was called 'the house of the red snake.'

"It was a fine, grand house in the 1920s. It was owned by a professor of zoology, who lived in it with his wife and children. The professor worked for the university down in Hakusan. He used to go abroad collecting specimens; sometimes he brought back live ones for zoos. In 1923, he took an expedition into the jungles of Sumatra. One of the animals he brought back was a baby python. He kept it as a pet at his house; he fed it on mice at first, and as it grew he gave it rats. The snake grew bigger and bigger and, as it grew, he had to find larger animals to feed to it - rabbits, then goats then pigs. The professor would spend hours talking to the snake as if it were a pet dog."

"Soon the python was thirty feet long. The professor kept it in a special room. One day one of his servants, a maid, entered the room by accident. The python grabbed her and wound its muscular coils all round her body, and squeezed the life right out of her, then it swallowed her whole. There was no trace of the girl, so the professor told the authorities that she had simply ran away."

"They say that after it had eaten the girl, the python shed its skin - and its new scales were blood-red. Well, all was fine again for a while. The professor put new, heavy padlocks on the doors, but a few months later one of the professor's own children stole the key and went to see the red snake, despite being warned never to enter the room. Just like the maid before him, the great serpent seized him in its awful jaws, with the rows and rows of needle-like teeth, and then coiled around him."

"Did it eat him too, Yuto?", asked one little girl from the first year.

Yuto was warming to his own story and smiled horribly; I recall he loved frightening children with his tales. "Why, of course it did, Rin! It crushed his body, and then swallowed him by stretching its horrible jaws over him and gulping him down its great maw. The professor's wife demanded that he get rid of the horror, but it seemed like the professor had gone mad - he claimed the red snake was speaking to him. He said it was a Kami, a spirit of nature. He believed that it would one day grow into a dragon.

"Well, his wife told him that she would have him put into the madhouse, so he dragged her down to the room and fed her to the snake. When his daughter asked what had happened to her mother, she too was taken to the red snake.

"The servants soon followed. One by one they vanished, but the professor was so respectable that no-one thought anything untoward was happening. The professor told people that he had sent his wife and children on a tour of England!

"As the snake grew and grew, it needed more food. He bought whole cows from farmers, and the serpent gobbled them down; finally, it grew so big that it smashed out of the room, splintering the thick oak door like matchwood. The professor could not control it, and the red snake ate him, too."

"Now the great serpent had the house all to itself. At night it would slither about and ambush travellers on the road outside. Soon no locals would go near the place after dark."

"Yuto, is the red snake still there in the house?", piped up a little boy.

"Why, yes, it is, Eita. The red snake still lives in the old house, and it feeds on vagrants, tramps and wanderers who are tempted to spend the night there. I've heard tell of one old vagabond who managed to escape from it - he said it was a huge, blood-red serpent, dripping venom and crawling from room to room in search of its prey."

"Rubbish!", I shouted out loudly.

"Oh, yes, and what would you know about it Teiko?" He snorted. Yuto hated having his stories spoiled, especially by a girl.

"Well, for a start, pythons are tropical. It gets cold up here in winter - how would it survive?"

"Maybe there are hot springs under the house that keep it warm. Besides, if it really is a Kami, then it wouldn't be worried about the cold, as it would be a spirit animal."

"And another thing," I said, undeterred, "pythons don't have venom, so how could the old vagabond have seen it dripping venom?"

"I didn't say it had venom - it was the old man's story. Anyhow, it might have been dripping with water, if it had come up from underground springs."

"You're just making it up," I snapped.

Then Yuto dropped his bombshell. "If you're so sure of yourself, why don't you spend a night up there, in the house of the red snake?"

The other children gasped, and as one turned to look at me.

"Well," he said, "are you scared?"

"O-of course not; there's nothing to be scared of unless you're frightened of woodworm and rising damp." I'm sure that I didn't sound very confident.

"Will you really go and sleep in the snake house?" asked Rin, the little girl who had spoken earlier.

I felt myself flushing as all the children's eyes were on me. Yuto was smirking appallingly and expecting me to back down - I just couldn't let him win.

"Yes, I'll spend a whole night in that stupid old house - and what's more, I'll take pictures to prove I did it. I'll go and sleep there this weekend!"

That wiped the smile from Yuto's face. I was glad of the sound of the school bell that ended playtime - it cut short any awkward questions from the other kids.

I spent the rest of the day worrying about what I had gotten myself into. I couldn't concentrate in my classes. *What would I tell my parents? Did I really have the nerve to stay in that old house overnight?* I didn't believe in a word of Yuto's red snake story, but the prospect of staying in the house on my own was not appealing.

I was lost in my thoughts whilst walking home until a voice jerked me back into reality.

"Hey, Teiko, I hear you're sleeping all night at the red snake house on Saturday. Can I come?"

It was Chiyo; she was my best friend in school. She lived close by me and was a bit of a tomboy. If anyone was climbing trees, stealing cherries or making rafts to float off down river and explore, you could be sure it was Chiyo.

"I don't know Chiyo, I said I would, but..."

"Come on, you can't back out now. The whole school is talking about it. Besides, you don't want Yuto getting one over on you, do you?" She had a point. I could already see his sneering face.

"But what will I tell mum and dad?"

"Just say you are staying over at my house. I'll tell my parents the same thing; then we can go together. We can take torches, drinks, food, and sleeping bags; we can make a fire in one of the old fireplaces. It will be great fun! Besides, I know more about ghosts and monsters than you, so it makes sense to have me coming along."

I knew it was pointless arguing with Chiyo, once she had her mind set on something. Secretly, I was more than a little glad that I didn't have to stay up there on my own.

Saturday rolled around with uncanny speed. I had asked my parents if I could stay over at Chiyo's and they were fine with that, I had stayed over at her house many times, and she at mine. Chiyo had likewise told her own family that she was staying at my house. We were glad that neither set of parents had thought to ring the other to check.

We met up at the edge of town. We both had rucksacks, sleeping bags, torches and food. I had a thermos of tea, as it was October and there was now a distinct chill in the air. Chiyo had brought a little, old-fashioned kettle to set over the fire once we had it going.

I had 'borrowed' my dad's instamatic camera and had bought some film for it that afternoon in town. There was no use in sleeping in the house if we could not bring back proof.

We wandered along the quiet road, leaving the town behind us. We didn't speak much as we walked. Chiyo looked as if she was looking forward to the whole affair.

An hour or so later, the bulk of the house rose up from beside the road. I don't know much about architecture, but the place did look very old. It had the traditional pointed, tile-covered roof and was several storeys high, with rickety verandas running around the outside of each storey. The posts and beams that held up the roof still seemed stable, but the window shutters hung loose and the sliding door had rotted through.

We approached through the old garden, now grown wild with cherry trees gnarled with age and flowerbeds given over to the chaos of nature. Here and there lichen-covered jizo statues squatted, half-hidden by the tall grass.

We climbed the steps up to the first veranda and walked through the doorway into the imposing hall. No-one had been here in some time, that was apparent - a thick layer of dust lay upon everything. We moved around the ground floor rooms first. The place must have been impressive once; the rooms were large, but now they were empty. What little furniture remained was rotting where it stood. Great blotches of damp discoloured the walls.

I began taking snaps with the instamatic, impatiently waving the photographs around as they developed. The images of decay slowly took form, like manifesting ghosts.

"Hey, look at this." Chiyo was calling me from an adjacent room. Putting the pictures into my rucksack, I ran to her. She was pointing to the floor. There in the dust was a long mark, as if something heavy had been dragged across the floor.

"Looks like someone has been here after all, and not long ago," I said.

"No," Chiyo answered, "look again; there are no footprints. It looks like something was slithering along the floor - something big."

"You mean...?"

"A snake - a big one. I've seen the tracks they make in the dirt and mud on wildlife films."

We followed the trail. I could tell Chiyo was nervous, as she had stopped speaking. I took several pictures of the weird track as it meandered from room to room. I had the feeling that whatever had made the track was looking for something.

"Look Chiyo, we have some pictures - let's go back now. We can camp out in the woods near town. If there really is a big snake here, I don't think it's safe to stay."

Chiyo had turned noticeably paler, but she shook her head.

"Come on, Teiko, where is your sense of adventure? Don't you want to solve the mystery?"

"I don't want to get eaten! Look at how wide the track is - it must be huge!"

The width of the drag mark in the dust would have indicated a snake as big around the middle as I was. I shuddered to think how long it must be.

"Well, at least let's see where the trail leads," she said.

We searched all of the lower floor, following the track through a number of rooms. It seemed to stop at some heavy iron doors in the floor. They looked as if they lead down into a cellar. Chiyo took hold of the handle, a great ring of iron, and heaved at it.

"No, don't!", I shouted.

It was far too heavy for her to lift anyhow.

I took a closer look at the doors. They seemed to have some kind of writing on them. It was old and rusty, and hard to make out, but I didn't recognise them. They were not kanji, that was for sure. There was something else on the doors - a patch of clear, sticky, viscous liquid. I prodded it with a pencil, and it clung in loops and strands as I pulled it away.

"What on earth is this stuff?" I asked, pulling a disgusted face.

"Maybe its ectoplasm," said Chiyo.

"What?"

"You know, the stuff ghosts are supposed to be made out of; mediums produce it whilst in a trance. Perhaps the snake is a ghost."

"I don't think ghosts leave trails in the dust; this is getting weirder by the moment. Maybe we should leave."

"Look," said Chiyo, "whatever made these marks didn't seem to go upstairs. Let's take a look around on the next two floors and choose a room. We can light a fire in one of the old fireplaces; if a python does come, which I seriously doubt, then it won't approach a fire. I swiped these from home." She produced a cigarette lighter and a handful of firelighters.

We looked round the second and third floors, and found no marks in the dust. We selected a room on the third floor to stay in. I still didn't feel comfortable with it, but I didn't want to seem like a coward. The shadows were lengthening now, so we gathered some bits of wood from the garden (the stuff in the house all seemed too damp) and piled it up in an old fireplace in the room. Soon we had a nice blaze going, and a pile of wood to feed it that would last the night.

As the light began to fade, Chiyo hung the kettle over the fire, and we ate our sandwiches and biscuits. Gradually we began to relax. In the warmth of the fire, the idea of a giant snake lurking in the house seemed absurd. Something had make the track in the dust, but it could easily have been a person dragging a sack or something behind them, rubbing out their own footprints as they went.

I took a few more pictures, and Chiyo and I talked and sipped tea well into the night. Finally I began to nod. Chiyo was still awake but she looked drowsy. I glanced at my watch - it was well past midnight. I snuggled down in my sleeping bag and was soon asleep.

I awoke with the feeling of something warm and damp on my face. Without opening my eyes, and still half asleep, I raised my hand to my face. My fingers met with a warm, gooey substance on my cheek. I recognised the texture.

I opened my eyes. The room was lit with the ruddy glow of the dying embers. In the reddish light I looked at my fingers; they were smeared with a gelatinous, clear liquid. I realised it was the same stuff I had seen festooning the heavy doors of the cellar. The realisation jerked me into wakefulness.

I rolled over on my side to look for Chiyo. She was no more than four feet from me, staring at me with weirdly-bulging eyes. She seemed to be trying to say something; her mouth was moving, but no words were coming out, as if the air was being squeezed from her - then I saw why. Coiled several times around Chiyo's body was a huge red snake. Its ruby skin seemed to glisten wetly in the light of the embers. I couldn't see its head, but the snake was huge; its coils lay across the room and out of the door, into the darkness beyond.

In seconds I was out of my sleeping bag and had snatched up a penknife from my rucksack. I leapt onto the snake and began to plunge the penknife into its side. The flesh seemed warm, slippery and rubbery, not at all like the snakes I'd held at the zoo. The tough flesh turned back the knife. Chiyo was thrashing wildly and turning purple as the coils squeezed tighter. I grabbed a piece of wood from the fire and thrust it into the embers, praying that it would light. Soon the wood ignited and I rushed back to my struggling friend. I held the burning stick to the muscular coils. The response was swift; the red snake retreated from the room, but it held fast to Chiyo, dragging her with it.

I snatched up my torch and ran out into the hall. The snake was already dragging Chiyo down the stairs, her body thumping hard against the steps, a slick clear trail being left in the snake's wake. The creature seemed fantastically long - I could not see its end. It seemed to wind off down the stairs and around the corner. I scrambled after it, around the corner and down another flight of stairs to the ground level. I followed the retreating snake and Chiyo through several rooms until the serpent reared up, taking my friend with it. It swayed side to side some ten feet above the ground, holding Chiyo, who hung limply in its grasp. The snake began to retreat once more, and my torch beam followed it to the cellar doors.

The heavy doors had been pushed open from within; the red snake withdrew into the darkness, taking its prey with it. I ran to the doorway and shone the beam down. It illuminated what I took to be the cellar floor. It was not earth, or wood, or tile; it was an uneven, lumpy surface, dirty-white like grave mould. It was covered in strange, squat protuberances. As I watched, it seemed that the ground was heaving in a soft, rhythmic fashion. Swinging the beam round, I saw Chiyo suspended in mid air, still in the grasp of the red snake. Something glimmered in the dark, and I lowered my torch to illuminate it; it was a golden orb the size of a beach ball, with a black disc at its centre. I saw the black disc shrink, and realised that I was looking at a huge golden eye, its pupil contracting in the light. Playing my torch across the weird, warty floor, I found a second giant eye and, below it, a great black slit from which the red snake seemed to protrude. The slit opened wider like a cavern, a foul stench billowing up. It was a mouth - a vast, lipless, drooling mouth. The 'red snake' was the tongue of some beast so enormous that it filled the whole cellar of the big house! The fungoid, warty floor was the skin on its bag-like body. Stepping back, I saw that what lay in the cellar was a toad - a toad the size of a whale. The elastic tongue flashed back into its maw ,and that predatory chasm snapped shut.

I ran and screamed out of the house, through the tatty garden to the road. I was still screaming when I reached home. There really was a red snake, only it wasn't a snake - it was a tongue, the tongue of a Kami - the tongue of Gama, the White Toad.

I've told the story again and again. People come and listen, then they go away again. I'm an old lady now; I've lived here at the hospital for decades. They never found a single trace of Chiyo, nor the great White Toad, but I heard that soon after the old house was pulled down and the cellar filled with concrete.

15. Straw Devils

"Are you sure we can trust Captain Takeda? His drinking has got much worse over the past twelve months." Mrs Maruyama of the Amainminato Women's Institute folded her arms over her ample stomach and gazed disapprovingly at the Mayor.

"Maruyama san, if you are that worried, why didn't you bring the matter up months ago, not on the night before the festival?"

"I hardly need to point that out, Kobyashi sama, that he and his drinking friends are staggering around the streets most nights."

Mayor Kobyashi rubbed his aching temples and looked out of the window into the grey December sky above the grey December sea. There was little to denote one from the other; they seemed to merge into one horrid mass that took up the horizon. He hated winter.

"I hate to think of him behind the wheel of a fishing boat," said Hara Shiro, a local businessman and head of the Amaiminato Namahage Festival Committee.

"Look, he does a good job as a fisherman. He brings in a good catch and he's never drunk at work - neither is his crew," the Mayor protested. The meeting was already giving him a headache.

"That's beside the point." Mrs. Maruyama's voice was shrill and irritating. " I don't want him near my children with his breath stinking of sake and beer."

"He's been playing the part of the chief namahage for fifteen years now, and he's never let us down; he takes the part very seriously. After such a long service, we can't just give Takeda san the push at the drop of a hat." The Mayor turned to the Shinto priest who sat politely at the end of the table.

"What do you think, O-Shin?"

The priest smiled. "Takeda san wrestles with his own daemons, but he becomes a very convincing one for one night a year."

"What if he makes a mess of it? We are beginning to attract more outsiders. People are beginning to think the festivals in the bigger towns are getting too commercial. Amaiminato is a little town in the middle of nowhere; we need the extra revenue, especially at this time of year." Hara Shiro was becoming more agitated.

Mayor Kobyashi wished he were on a beach in southern Okinawa, not in a measley fishing town on Oga Peninsula.

"It was a success last year, and I don't see why it shouldn't be an even bigger success this year. You're worrying over nothing."

Dr Uchida Isamu, who ran the town's little museum and historic society, leaned forward, whilst scratching his silver beard.

"You know, the namahage costumes were looking a little threadbare last year. The straw was falling off the raincoats and the paint was chipped."

"Well, there will be no worries on that score, Dr Uchida. I was talking with Captain Takeda and a couple of his friends just last night - he says that they all have new costumes. Apparently they have been working on them for months, without letting any one see. He says they are spectacular."

"I hope they live up to your expectations," said Dr Uchida.

The Mayor glanced back out of the window and, with falling spirits, noticed that it had started to snow.

The snowstorm that had blown in the previous day had largely subsided, but left a healthy covering on the ground. It was bitingly cold as the Mayor stood with the crowd around the bonfire in the town square. It was New Year's Eve, night of the Namahage Festival. There was a mixture of locals and interested visitors, all wrapped up against the chill wind that blew in from the Sea of Japan. O-Shin was coming to the end of his ritual and blessing. Soon Takeda and his friends would arrive in their new costumes; he hoped that his trust in them had not been misplaced.

The cold air was split by the deep, rhythmic booming of a drum. All eyes turned to the sound. There was a crunching of heavy feet on crisp virgin snow. Out of the shadows strode three towering figures; Mayor Kobyashi realised that Takeda and his companions must have been wearing some kind of built-up shoes, or small stilts. As they stepped into the dancing light of the fire, the crowd all gasped. The craftsmanship of the costumes was astounding. The traditional straw raincoats looked more like shaggy fur. The hands and feet each bore three clawed digits that must have been made from worked leather; all terminated in hooked claws. The masks were truly horrible. The man in the centre, who Kobyashi took to be Takeda, wore a blue one; on either side, his companions had red masks. They were leather-skinned and warty, with bulbous noses above loose, slavering mouths furnished with long yellow fangs and tusks. Long black tongues hung wetly down and twitched. The venal, mad eyes, the size of tennis balls, rolled grotesquely at the screaming audience. Each beast was crowned with impressive, spiralling black horns.

God, Takeda had surpassed himself. These were Hollywood-standard costumes. The blue faced Namahage held a large drum, which it beat with a wooden cudgel; the two other held aloft swords and pails.

The trio began a mad dance about the bonfire. The dancing flames made the leering grins and flashing eyes seem all the more ghastly. On occasion they would stop to slurp hungrily from the bottles of sake left out for them, or make mock charges at the audience, drawing squeals of delight and alarm. Finally the capering ceased, and the chief Namahage spoke, its voice a weird, guttural howl.

"Come my brothers - it is time that the children of Amaiminato were judged."

The crowd parted as the three strange figures stalked off in different directions. The Mayor saw Dr Uchida in the crowd and hurried over. The doctor seemed dumbfounded.

"Mayor, I'm sorry I ever doubted you. Those were the finest Namahage I have ever seen."

"I'm lost for words," said Kobyashi shaking his head. "If word of how good this is gets round, we will have thousands here in a couple of years."

"If you will excuse me, Mr. Mayor I've got to get over to my daughter's house. I can't wait to see what my grandson makes of this."

The doctor vanished into the crowd, and a bemused but rather satisfied Mayor began to stroll home.

A hammering so heavy that it rocked the whole house fell upon the Maruyama household's door. Mrs Maruyama hurried over to open it. She had been waiting with her children, six-year-old twins, a boy and a girl, all night. They were not scared of the Namahage; both knew full well it was just Captain Takeda in a mask and a straw raincoat.

As she swung the door open, the first thing that hit her was the smell. It was an animal musk, like something she had last smelled in the zoo. A three-clawed hand shoved her roughly aside as a hair-covered bulk stooped to enter the room.

Mrs Maruyama's two children stood frozen to the spot as the red-faced creature turned its horned head towards them. In a single bound, the Namahage had crossed the room and snatched up a child in each claw. Both exploded into fits of tears.

"I hate crybabies." The voice was a feral hiss that blew fetid breath into their white faces.

"Will you be good in the coming year?" He shook them both like dolls.

"Yes, yes, yes!", they both screamed.

"I can smell naughtiness. I can sniff out a naughty child from halfway round the world."

"We will be good, we promise," the children whined.

Thinking it might be time to intercede, Mrs. Maruyama rushed over with a tray of sake. The bottles and cups were shaking as she offered it speechlessly to the Namahage.

He grabbed the bottle and slurped it down greedily. The mask seemed to be stuck directly onto his face as it moulded itself around the actor's features. He slammed down the empty bottle and turned once more to the children.

"Remember - half a world away."

He sniffed like a bloodhound, then lumbered back out into the night, leaving two children with rapidly-growing damp stains on their pyjamas.

Hara Shiro hurried to open the door as it was savagely banged. His eight-year-old daughter waited in the living room, more excited than scared. A hairy bulk smelling like a wet dog barged Shiro out of the way and stepped into the light. A nasty leer played across its red face as it saw the expression on its prey's face.

"Are you a crybaby? I hate crybabies!" The Namahage spat the words out like pieces of gristle.

The girl's bottom lip was trembling. The monster lifted her up with a claw under each shoulder as she started to sob, and lifted her up so that its ugly face was inches from hers.

"Are you going to be good? I can taste naughty children." A long, slick, black tongue wriggled from between the sharp yellow teeth and lapped at the girl's face.

Mute with horror, she nodded frantically.

"At night I crawl into your bedroom and lick your sleeping face. If you have been bad, I will taste it."

Shiro ran over, brandishing a sake bottle. The Namahage dropped the girl and swiped the bottle from Shiro's hands. The liquor was drained in one long draft. As the monster turned to go, it looked back at the girl.

"Remember, child, I taste you every night - so be gooocooood!"

It bounded out through the door like a huge ape.

Dr Uchida's twelve-year-old grandson had resented been pulled away from his Playstation. He insisted that the he was too old for the festival, and that the whole event was stupid and childish; his mother and father had to more or less drag him away from the wretched machine. Dr Uchida never approved of it – 'brain-rotting garbage,' he had called it. Youngsters should be out and about in the fresh air, or reading a book.

The hammering at the door sounded like it would splinter the wood at any moment. As Dr. Uchida's daughter opened the door the thing in the shadows stooped to place its huge drum on the floor.

The rank, bestial smell filled the room as the horned, blue-faced, shaggy giant entered, steam rising from its head and shoulders. The thing's black horns almost scraped the ceiling as it stalked across to where the pouting boy stood.

"Nice costume, Dope, but you don't scare me - I'm not some stupid little kid," the youth sneered petulantly.

"Ooooh, I'm glad to hear that," the Namahage crooned in the back of its throat.

"I've seen things more scary than you on my Playstation." The boy nodded to the device in the corner of the room.

"Playstation? Play, you say?"

The Namahage pointed at the machine with a crooked talon. The gadget exploded in an arc of electricity, spitting sparks and billowing smoke.

The boy turned with a look of fury, but was stopped dead by the Namahage's own unearthly gaze. Its eyes seemed to be burning red, like glowing embers in a fire - no pupils, just a throbbing, pulsing red light.

A clawed hand grasped his neck and drew him in close.

"I can see naughtiness. I can see when naughtiness grows with age into spite and thuggery. See these eyes, boy? These eyes see into your mind and your soul. I'm watching you, boy."

It released the grip on the boy's neck and he fell gagging to the floor, the red marks of the three-fingered hand lividly visible.

"Sssssssake!" It hissed.

Dr Uchida seemed to be the only one composed enough to do anything and brought forth the liquor. The namahage sucked at the bottle with a lurid slurping sound.

"Thank you," Uchida whispered, and the creature seemed to nod. Then it lumbered away, leaving a terrified boy and a shattered Playstation in its wake.

New Year's Day was surprisingly bright. Mayor Kobyashi had a spring in his step - the Amainminato Namahage Festival had been an unprecedented success. That would shut up all the naysayers; soon the little town would really be on the map. He could see it now - TV documentary film crews, tourists from overseas - the potential was limitless. And it was Takeda and his friends he had to thank for this. He strolled along the harbourfront, enjoying the sea air. Takeda had a small house down near the little port - the Mayor just had to thank him in person. He rapped on the door.

There was a low moan and a muffled sound of movement from within the house. The door opened, and Captain Takeda stood blinking in the light. He was unshaven, his hair a mess and his tee-shirt stained. He rubbed his head.

"Oh, God, I'm so sorry, Mayor sama, I don't know what came over us! Come on in."

The Mayor stepped through into Takeda's untidy sitting room. Beer cans and liquor bottles lay strewn about, and his two friends lay insensible on the sofa.

"I just came over to thank you and your friends, Takeda san. Last night you were amazing - I've never seen a festival like it. Those costumes were astounding; they must have taken months to make. Did you use animatronics in the masks? How was old O-Shin with you using modern costumes?" The Mayor stopped his barrage of praise and questions when he saw Takeda's puzzled expression.

"I don't know what happened last night; all I know is that the three of us woke up this morning with godawful hangovers."

"Drunk or not, you did a great job. There are quite a few kids so scared that they will never be bad again in their lives, let alone for the next twelve months. Scarred for life some of them - ha, ha, ha!"

"Mayor, last night - I don't recall a thing. We must have blacked out. But the weird thing is, I don't even recall drinking a drop. We had been working on the costumes, and we had agreed not to drink at all until the festival was over."

Kobyashi was getting confused.

"Can I see the costumes?"

"Sure; shame we never had chance to use them."

Takeda led the Mayor across the litter-strewn floor, through the kitchen, to a room at the back of the house. Three suits made of straw with carved wooden masks lay on a table. They were an improvement on those used the year before to be sure, but they were nothing like the costumes of last night's performance.

"Thanks," he mumbled.

"I'm sorry Mayor," said an abashed Takeda, "I don't know what came over us."

"Forget it," said Kobyashi, and wandered out onto the seafront again in a daze.

Something caught the Mayor's notice. In the crisp snow were three sets of tracks. Each seemed deep and heavy, and each bore three claw-like toes. They led past Takeda's house, out of the little town, across the one-lane road and away into the wild hills of the Oga Peninsula.

16. I'm Behind You

There had been nothing unusual about that particular night - no bad dreams, no disturbed sleep, just a night of watching re-runs of old sitcoms on TV, a bowl of yogurt, then bed. She awoke feeling rested but lazy. Through one open eye she glanced at her tableside clock. It was 11 am; fairly late for her, but she had no assignments today. She yawned and fought the urge to go back to sleep.

She felt them before she saw them. As she drew back the crumpled sheets, her hand fell on something soft. She looked down. There were hairs on the sheets, lots of hair; long, black glossy hairs. She new instantly they were hers. They had to be - she kept no pets and no animal could have gotten into her apartment. She instinctively ran her fingers through her long hair. It seemed a little damp; she must have been sweating heavily last night. It had been hot - she had had to switch the air conditioning on. As she drew back her hand, several more hairs came with it.

She ran through into the bathroom and looked at herself in the mirror. Apart from the slight dampness and the dishevelled early-morning look that greeted her first thing every day, she seemed ok.

She showered quickly. A few more hairs fell to the floor at her feet. A few more came loose as she dried it, then combed and brushed it.

It's bound to happen sometime, she told herself, *with all the conditioners and sprays you use to keep it looking that good. Sooner or later a few hairs are going to fall out - nothing to worry about.*

She put the thoughts from her head as she opened the curtains and looked down on the sprawl of downtown Tokyo. She ate breakfast on the veranda, enjoying the cool breeze on her bare legs. She spent the day shopping, and in the evening had dinner in a restaurant with her boyfriend Akira. They took in a movie, one of the old Toho pictures they were both so fond of, *Godzilla vs. Mechagodzillia,* playing at a little retro cinema they often frequented. By the time she crawled into bed again, she had forgotten about the hair.

The alarm woke her at 7 a.m. She had to be across town for a modelling assignment. There was more hair on the bedclothes. This time she was a little more worried. Again, her locks felt damp and clammy. She tried to force the thoughts away as she began to shower. The feeling of the warm water had a lulling effect. She closed her eyes and thought about the day ahead, a photo shoot for a shampoo company. She was jolted out of her reverie as she felt something touch the small of her back. She let out a shriek and span round, dropping the soap; there was nothing save for the rapidly-steaming glass of the small cubicle. She turned off the shower and stepped out into the bathroom, looking around. It was empty and the door still locked. It was an odd habit, as she lived alone, but she always locked the bathroom door.

She shook her head and began to towel herself dry. She saw more black hairs against the white towel. She took the mobile phone from her purse and called Dr. Yakimoto.

On her journey across town, she saw her own face smiling back at her from glossy magazines in newsstands - Sasaki Chou, the face of Cherry Orchard Shampoo. *What,* she wondered, *would the company think of a model who was losing her hair?*

If the photographer or make-up artist noticed anything awry, they didn't mention it. The shoot was a pleasant one, outdoors in a field of flowers grown on a rooftop garden. Looking at the pictures, no-one would guess it was shot scant minutes outside of the city centre.

Later in the afternoon, she attended the appointment she had made that morning. It was a small, private practice, patronised mainly by the rich. Dr. Yakimoto was a thin-faced man with a sharp chin and receding hair. His gaunt appearance did not exactly advertise the picture of health, but the wall behind him was covered with framed qualifications and awards. His thin mouth smiled, showing perfect white teeth.

"Sit down, Sasaki san. What seems to be the trouble?"

She sat nervously on the edge of the seat.

"For a couple of days now I have been waking up to find that my hair has been falling out."

"We all lose a little hair from time to time." He pointed at his own receding hairline and grinned.

"No, doctor, I'm losing quite a lot. My hair is my profession - you can understand why I am worried."

He nodded. "Of course, of course. There are many things that can cause hair loss, but stress is the most common. I imagine being a model can be hectic at times."

Chou shook her head. "Not really; not for me, in any case. I'm well paid, my job is easy, and I have lots of free time and no money worries."

"Any relationship problems, or trouble with friends or family?"

"None at all. I have a lovely boyfriend and family. It must be some sickness."

"May I take a look?"

She nodded and he rose, walking around to the back of her. She felt oddly uncomfortable with him standing behind her. He ran his fingers through her hair and bent down to inspect the strands.

"The hair itself looks very healthy. It's strong, glossy and has lots of body. It is a little ragged at the ends, though."

"Doesn't cancer cause hair loss?"

Dr. Yakimoto smiled. "Yes, it can do in some cases, but I doubt you have cancer, my dear. You are the picture of health."

"Could you run some blood tests just to be sure?"

He nodded. "If you really want me to."

"I'd feel better."

"Very well." He led her through the office into the small clinic at the rear of the practice.

Chou winced slightly as the needle pricked into her arm. Yakimoto took several small syringesful.

"If you come back next week, we should have the results in. I'm sure this is nothing more than a case of split ends; something for the hairdresser, not the doctor."

She smiled weakly and said, "I hope you're right."

Chou tried to put the thoughts out of her head. She spent the night with Akira at his apartment. To her relief she found no more hairs in the morning. She spent another day on another shoot for a new line in hair conditioner. After a night spent on the town with friends, she stumbled into bed quite late and soon fell to sleep.

She awoke with a start. It was still dark, but the neon lights of the city sent beams through her half-closed blinds. She knew she was not alone - there was an overwhelming feeling of someone else in the room with her. She lay still, trying to hear movement or breathing; all she could detect was her own shallow breaths. Slowly she turned her head away from the window and towards the wall.

In the diffused light, she saw the silhouette of a man against the wall. She could pick out no facial features, but he seemed grossly obese, the head sitting on the shoulders without hint of a neck.

Screaming, she flicked on the bedside light with one hand, whilst fumbling in the drawer for something with which to defend herself. The light showed nothing. No man, obese or otherwise, stood in the room. She clutched a nail file, and then, realising what an inadequate weapon it made, picked up a vase.

She crept into the hall, flicking the light on. It was as empty as the bedroom. She moved from room to room, turning on lights and finding nothing. She checked in every closet and cupboard, but each harboured no intruder. Doors and windows were tested and found to be locked tight.

Chou slumped onto her settee and took deep breaths. She lived in an apartment 16 storeys up. There was a doorman. The chances of anyone getting into her flat were minimal. Plus, she had checked everywhere. Maybe she had dreamed the whole thing and had woken up thinking it was real. She walked back to her bedroom and her eyes fell on an untidy pile of clothes thrown on top of a set of drawers. The mass of linen had a vaguely human outline that could have easily cast a monstrous shadow on the far wall when backlit by the city light. Shaking her head, she picked up the clothes and put them into the laundry basket. She climbed back into bed and fell asleep. In the morning, there was more hair on the pillow.

Chou looked up the causes of hair loss on the internet, but stopped because she realised that she was frightening herself. During the days she tried to busy herself with work and shopping. In the evenings, she was out with Akira or her friends. Oddly, she never found fallen hairs when she stopped with Akira, or when he stopped with her, only when she slept alone in her own apartment. Chou had not mentioned her hair loss to Akira or to her friends. None had seemed to notice anything wrong.

She now noticed that each morning she slept alone, not only did she find hair, but also a wet patch, on the pillow beside her. Her hair felt clammy, sticky. She wondered if whatever malady she had caused excessive sweating from the head as well as hair loss. She visited Dr. Yakimoto once more. Beside herself with worry she awaited the results.

"According to the tests we ran on your blood sample, there is absolutely nothing wrong with you whatsoever."

"But it's getting worse, Doctor. I'm losing more hair, and each morning the pillow has a wet stain on it and my hair feels damp and sticky. There must be something wrong."

"It may not actually be an illness - as such."

Chou's confused expression showed she needed him to elucidate more.

"Tell me, Sasaki san, have you ever heard of a trichobezoar?"

She shook her head mutely.

"A trichobezoar is the correct name for a hairball."

"You mean like what cats cough up."

"Yes, but they are not limited to cats; many mammals have trichobezoars. Cows can get huge, compact balls of fur as hard as stone in their intestines from licking themselves, for example."

"What has this got to do with me?"

"Well, trichobezoars are not unknown in humans. A girl in Canada had one weighing five pounds removed from her stomach. It was the size of a grapefruit. The ingestion of hair has even being given a name, the Rapunzel Syndrome, after the German fairytale of the girl with the long hair which she hangs from a tower so her lover can climb up to be with her."

"How do they come about?"

"They are caused by the swallowing of one's own hair. We all swallow some hair by accident, but a trichobezoar is formed by a large mass that collects in the intestine when a person has the habit of chewing or eating their own hair. Hair is indigestible to humans, and it can form a compact mass inside you. It can interfere with digestion and, in some extreme cases, prove fatal."

Chou shook her head again. "I've never chewed my hair. My hair is my living - it would be insane to do that."

Yakimoto smiled softly. "Maybe not consciously, but there have been cases of people chewing their hair in their sleep. It's rare, but not unknown."

"My appetite is fine and I don't suffer from any stomach pains."

"These masses take a long while to form. If I'm correct, then we will have probably caught it before a trichobezoar has had chance to form. Do you mind if I take a closer look?"

"No, go ahead."

"Very well; please hitch up your blouse."

Chou pulled up her blouse, exposing her midriff. The doctor pressed his hands against her stomach in several areas. His hands felt rough, like old worn leather. The fingers pressed deeply.

"Feels fine; I can't detect anything." He took a stethoscope from a drawer. The cold of the metal against her skin almost made her cry out. Dr.Yakimoto shook his head.

"Sounds in good order, too. I can book you in for an x-ray just to be sure if you like."

"Yes, please, Doctor. I'd rather be safe than sorry."

She left the practice feeling worse than when she had come in. She ate lunch at an internet café whilst looking up trichobezoars; they were both appalling and fascinating. They came in a variety of shapes and sizes, from hard, smooth, spheres that looked like organic bowling balls, to marrow-shaped masses of frightening size. There were graphic pictures of specimens being removed from human intestines (which made her question the wisdom of eating lunch whilst looking up this subject), and Victorian trichobezoars kept as curiosities by amateur naturalists. Some resembled headless rats in size and shape. Chou felt sure that if one of these horrors were growing inside of her, she would have known about it.

That night she stood at her apartment window overlooking the Tokyo cityscape. Neon vistas were stretching off as far as the eye could see. She would do this from time to time - sit with the lights off and just look at the spectacular view of the city at night. The buildings reminded her of deep-sea organisms flashing and twinkling in bioluminescent displays; after a while, they had an almost hypnotic effect.

Chou had no idea how long she had sat there, gazing at the lights. Her eyes refocused from the distant buildings to the glass she was looking through and to her own reflection, and the reflection of the person behind her - bulky and looming, its indistinct form seemed to swallow hers, almost.

Screaming, she span round to find nothing, just a darkened room. A flick of the light switch showed nothing. It had been an optical illusion, her mind playing tricks after being in an altered state from gazing out of the window so long at those flashing lights; nevertheless, she slept with the lights on that night.

Chou spent the weekend with Akira. They travelled down to the coast and stayed in a bed and breakfast. Away from the apartment, Chou felt better than she had in days. The sun and the sea air, and her boyfriend's company, made her forget her worries for a time. Late on Sunday night, when she returned, the apartment felt heavy and oppressive. Once more she slept with the lights on. There was a feeling that permeated the place, a feeling as if someone were standing right behind her. Each time she turned there was, of course, no-one, but the feeling was so palpable that it made her skin crawl.

The worst occurrence was one evening after she had taken a shower. The feeling of something standing just inches behind her was overwhelming. She hardly dared to look up into the mirror for fear of what she might see. The rational part of her mind won through, and she forced herself to look. Of course, there was nothing behind her; yet, when she looked down at the damp, tiled floor there was a horridly-suggestive mark. *Was that.. could it be... a footprint?* It certainly wasn't a human footprint; it was large, rounded and broad like that of some hefty creature, such as an elephant or rhinoceros. It must be a simulacrum, a random shape in the condensation on the tiles. She exited the bathroom quickly.

She threw herself into her work, taking any excuse to stay late. She began eating out most nights - anything to stay out of the apartment. Chou began looking for other places to live, browsing through the property pages of Tokyo newspapers.

The day of her hospital appointment came round, but Chou was not nervous. After the x-rays were carried out she awaited the results at the hospital rather than returning home. She ate in the soulless cafeteria and read magazines in the lounge - several of them featured her smiling face and flowing black hair.

The x-rays showed nothing wrong with her digestive system - no blockage, no ominous dark patch. She had suspected they would show nothing; in a way this was worse. It gave credence to an idea that was growing inside her, that the whole thing was psychological.

That evening, after showering, she wrapped her hair in a towel and sat in her living room in nothing but a nightgown. *Destroy All Monsters* was playing on a late-night slot on one of the many satellite channels. As she watched the atomic monsters smash their way through a plaster and plywood city, she felt something at her bare neck. It was brief but unmistakeable - the feeling of lips on her neck, fat and wet.

That night Chou did not sleep at all. At first light she thumbed through a phone book, looking for the number of a psychiatrist.

Dr Watanabe Haruna was a short woman with greying, bobbed hair and a lined face. She sat impassively as Chou told her story. On occasion she would nod her head in a way that Chou thought made her look like a puppet.

The diminutive psychiatrist waited a while and seemed to be thinking.

"It is strange," she said, "the way in which we define ourselves by our hair. Pharmaceutical companies make millions each year by selling quack cures for baldness. How many hair-related products are there? Hundreds, I would say. And then all the glossy magazine ads and the TV adverts - but you would know more about this than me, eh?"

Chou nodded.

"You know, this obsession goes back centuries. In China men used to wear their hair in a plaited ponytail in the belief that their god would lift them up to heaven by it. Here in Nippon, we had hair-cutting demons, spectres that supposedly snipped off the hair of unsuspecting passersby. My point is that our hair has been held to be of the utmost importance since time immemorial. You, Sasaki san, are one of the country's top hair models. You are a household name; that is a lot to be on the shoulders of a lady so young, if you will forgive the pun."

Chou forced a weak smile.

"Despite all your success, it is my belief that subconsciously you worry about your hair because so many people, a whole nation, are looking at it. Not a hair can be out of place; it must be perfect 24/7, or so your mind tells you. We are apt to externalise our fears. The idea that there is someone in the apartment with you, watching you, is closer to the truth than you would like to admit. You see people are watching you all the time on television and in magazines - these worries, this pressure, even though you may not realise it, is causing you to lose your hair. It's very common, hair loss through worry - even subconscious worry."

"What do you suggest?", asked Chou.

"A long holiday. I'm sure you make enough money to afford some time off. Maybe somewhere abroad where you are unknown. The famous oftentimes crave anonymity. When you are a stranger, no-one will be looking at your hair."

The more Chou thought about it, the more it made sense.

"I think you might be right. I've always wanted to see Europe. Sometimes I think Tokyo is stifling me."

She rang Akira and suggested a long holiday together. He arranged to meet her that night to discuss it over dinner.

Chou dropped by the internet café again rather than going back home. She was going to look up some European destinations, but instead found herself typing 'hair-cutting daemon' into the search engine.

She found a number of pages on the subject. It seemed to have been some kind of mass hallucination or delusion. The author of one website described it as an urban panic. Beginning in Nanjing in May 1876, invisible and uncatchable assailants were cutting off people's pigtails. So swift and silent were the attacks that the victim usually did not notice that their hair was gone. The panic spread to Shanghai and Hangzhou during the summer, and men in Shanghai, fearing attack from the rear, held their pigtails in front of them. Doctors offered charms, and soldiers were stationed on the streets.

In Japan it had been particularly prevalent near the end of the Tokugawa period in Tokyo, or Edo as it was back then. One story related to a geisha girl called Hanakichi and her lover, both of whom had their hair cropped by an unseen assailant as they walked through the city streets at night. One website drew comparisons with Spring-Heeled Jack in London in the 1830s, and the Mad Gasser of Mattoon in Illinois in the 1940s.

There were pictures of hair-cutting daemons, or Kami-kiri. They were grotesque monsters with bird-like heads, furnished with long beaks and yellow eyes. Their bodies looked like shrivelled little men's, save for that, in place of hands, they had sharp pincers.

During the Meiji era, Kami-kiri attacks even made it into the newspapers. It was thought that the Kami-kiri attacked people in order to punish them for vanity.

Worse still was the Kurokamikiri, or 'black hair cutter'. The thing's appearance was truly disturbing. It had a bloated body with chubby arms and legs, and no neck, but a bulbous head. Its skin was deepest black and the only features visible on its face were a wide mouth with a slug-like tongue, huge flat teeth, and two tiny, evil yellow eyes spaced far apart on its dark visage. Kurokamikiri was said to creep up behind its victims and bite off their hair.

There were a number of historic accounts of the thing. In the beginning of the Genroku Emperor's time, around 1688, people reported that their hair had been bitten off whilst they walked the streets. The thing did its deed at around midnight. Often the victim did not notice that their hair was missing until they reached home.

During the Edo period, a woman had her hair bitten in this manner whilst on her way home from a cutlery shop. She fainted during the attack.

On April 20th, 1810 in Edoshimota, a servant in the household of a man named Tomigoro Kojima was attacked in such a manner. As she opened her door in the morning, she felt a weight upon her head and saw her severed locks fall to the floor. One year before, a person was attacked in a household called Kohinatashikenyashiki; the victim reported feeling drowsy at the time of the attack. These events were written in an Edo period book called Hanjitsukanwa. The thing was said to make a "mogaaaaa!"sound.

A picture accompanied the description, by the artist Utagawa Yoshifuji. It depicted three guards; one with a lantern, rushing to help a woman who was being attacked by the Kurokamikiri. It was shown as a coal-black beast as large as a bear. It had a weirdly-outsized cranium and a gaping mouth that was greedily devouring the terrified woman's hair.

Chou wished she had never bothered to look. The creatures seemed to be the products of diseased minds. She quickly switched to tourist websites and began looking at European holiday destinations.

Chou and Akira ate in an upmarket restaurant and talked over where they would like to go - Prague, London, Paris, Venice, Berlin. Akira would take most of his annual leave in one go, and they would take a grand tour. Both had been working too hard of late. They spent the night together in an undisturbed sleep.

They booked the tickets and made the arrangements online over the next few days. Chou had one modelling assignment left. It would only take her a week, then she and Akira would be free to get away from the city.

After a particularly long day on a photoshoot at Ueno-Koen Park, where she had to pout and shake her hair whilst on noisy fairground rides, Chou ate a quick supper and tumbled into bed, exhausted.

She felt the tugging in her scalp; not violent but a rhythmic series of jerks, as if something were pulling her hair. She became aware that her long hair was being held out at an angle of nearly 45 degrees from the bed. The rhythm of the pulling was accompanied by a grinding, slopping sound. Chou realised that something was chewing her hair.

Her scream resounded round the flat as she sat bolt upright and switched on the bedside lamp in one movement. There was nothing in the room. Her hair fell around her shoulders - it felt wet and sticky. As her fingers touched it, she found that the ends were ragged.

She grabbed some clothes and left the building. Even though it was 4 a.m., she stood outside 'til she could hail a cab, then took it straight to a hotel. She sat awake until first light, thinking. Maybe she was mad; certainly she needed to see Dr. Watanabe again - she must have been right. Subconscious pressure, always having to have immaculate hair; it was manifesting in unhealthy ways. The websites about hair-eating monsters she had visited only focused her illness into something more tangible. Her resentment had taken a form in her mind. She herself must be pulling and biting at her own hair in her sleep, like a somnambulist unwittingly walks into danger.

Time to see what damage she had done. With the sun beginning to rise on the Tokyo cityscape, she walked into the bathroom to examine her hair. As she looked in the mirror she saw it behind her - black as midnight, bigger than a bear, no neck, and a bulging cranium with flabby, rubbery skin. Its eyes were two beads of yellow in a featureless void bisected by the absurd mouth; it had square, yellow horse teeth, and a fat red tongue festooned with drool.

"Mogaaaaa!" it said.

* * * * *

The papers had been full of her mental breakdown, of how Sasaki Chou, famous hair model, had been found wandering the streets screaming and screaming. Columns were full of speculation as to what had caused it. Drugs? Work pressure? Some inherited condition rearing its ugly head? The covers all showed the same picture - Chou's head crudely shaven bald.

17. Brother on the Hill

The disappearance of Dr. Oka Akio in a remote part of the Shiretoko Peninsula in northeast Hokkaido has never been explained satisfactorily. Dr. Oka, an anthropologist from the University of Hokkaido in Sapporo, was known to have been conducting a study of the Ainu people in the rural areas of Okhotsk Sub prefecture. It is believed that Dr. Oka entered the Shiretoko Peninsula illegally in the summer of 1988. The Peninsula is strictly closed to the public, as it is home to a large population of brown bears; the official line is that Dr Oka was probably killed and eaten by one of these animals. As a close personal friend, much of his papers came into my possession. Reading through his notes, I have reason to doubt that he was killed by a bear.

I present Dr. Oka's notes here without comment. I leave it for the reader to decide what they make of Dr. Oka's findings and his ultimate fate.

* * * * *

"Even in the remotest Ainu villages, the influence of 'civilisation' is now felt. There are precious few full-blooded Ainu left. Many have intermarried. Only a hundred individuals know the Ainu tongue now; the culture and the language are dying out. It is as if these people are fading before my eyes. I am recording all I can, but in another hundred years, I believe that they will be just a memory.

I have read of this happening to other aboriginal peoples. No one passes down the lore or the rites, and they are forgotten. I'm thankful I began this project when I did - I may be able to record *something* for posterity. I think the time has come once more to visit my old friend Turushno.

I first met this hermit four years ago, when villagers told me of an old man who lived in the wilds of the Peninsula far beyond the remotest Ainu habitation. He was apparently a skilled hunter and trapper, and on occasion would travel down to some of the villages or kotans to trade; I had been lucky enough to be in one of the villages when he visited with his pelts. The headman introduced us. Turushno was an old man who still wore the traditional Ainu garb of the attusi robe, woven from the inner bark of elm trees, and deerskin leggings. He was heavily bearded, even for an Ainu - his mighty beard fell down as far as his waist. He was hairy and heavy-browed, with dark eyes and thick, bushy eyebrows. His skin was weather-beaten, like old leather.

Turushno and I liked one another straightaway. He, like I, was worried about his people's vanishing way of life - he thought my work would help to preserve it. I didn't tell him that I thought he was being insanely optimistic. He had a liking for chocolate, which is hard to come by so far into the wilderness; I happily gave him the couple of bars I had.

I knew in this man I had a link to generations past and information soon to be lost. He was, in essence, a living time machine. When Turushno asked me to be his guest for a few days at his remote mountain hut, I jumped at the chance.

He took me on a long and torturous trip back into the mountains of the Shiretoko Peninsula, up through the dank forests of Mongolian oak and Sakhalin fir. I knew there were bears in the area; several times I came across their vast paw prints in the soft earth, claws showing like knives. I asked the old man if he feared living cheek-in-jowl with such beasts; he told me that he had never had any problems with bears in the many years that he had been living in the wilderness.

It took us all day to reach his hut, and the sun was beginning to set when we arrived. Turushno's domicile was a rude shack of reeds and thatch. It had a single door and three shuttered windows. Outside in a pen of bamboo, a number of chickens scratched and pecked. Fish were drying on a wooden rack.

Once inside, he lit a fire in the fire hole, and illuminated a step back in time. The floor was matted with rushes. There were no chairs, but only mats on which to sit. The beds were rough wooden pallets covered with reeds and cloth. Crudely-carved figures of animals and men stood on the wooden shelves.

We dined on fish with rice and herbs, washed down with home-brewed sake. We talked all night by the firelight, and I recorded everything he said on my dictaphone.

That first time, I spent three days with the old man listening to Ainu folktales and legends, accounts of his youth, fishing and hunting trips, bear worship and the slow-but-sure fragmentation of his culture; that, he said, was why he had retreated to the mountains - after the death of his wife many years ago, he felt more at home in the vastness of the Peninsula.

And so it was that I began to pay old Turushno regular visits, bringing him the odd little comfort. He eschewed most of the trappings of modernity, but retained his love of chocolate. He also like to read, so I would bring him up books from the city.

I travelled up again in the spring of 1988. I reached the Ainu kotan fine, and early on a beautiful morning in April. I paid some of the fishermen to row me along the coast to a small bay. I discovered this route some time ago, and it cuts hours from my journey if I can travel by boat part of the way.

After a long climb through the forested woodland, I finally found the path that led me to Turushno's hut. I found the old man sitting outside. He did not stand and greet me as usual; he seemed taciturn and distracted.

"Turushno, how are you?", I asked.

"Chickens," came his cryptic reply.

"Chickens?", I repeated.

He shook his woolly head. "All gone in the night. Must have been a bear."

Now I understood the reason for the old man's poor spirits - the eggs his chickens laid were a major part of his diet. "I thought you said they never bothered you?"

"They never have 'til last night. One came and ate all of them." He gestured to the empty coop, the bamboo door wide open.

I walked over and looked at it. There were no claw marks. "How do you know it was a bear?"

"I've lived up here for years; nothing else would have been strong enough to force the door open."

I looked around, but could see no footprints in the grass around the coop. Turushno continued.

"Tanuki, kitsuni - neither are strong enough to force the door. It must have been a bear. No matter, to us the bear is the kami of the mountain; he will take what he wants."

I had brought Turushno more chocolate and books. He brightened a little when he saw this. I promised I would buy him some new chickens from the nearest kotan and pay someone to bring them up to him, but he refused, saying that he had a number of fine pelts to trade and he would be going back down to the village in a few days - he would pick up more chickens then.

We ate together and he talked more about his past and his late wife. His two sons had grown tired of the Ainu way of life and had left for the city; he had not heard from them in years. In the afternoon he showed me the river in which he had set eel traps. That evening we dined on a fat eel with yam and dried berries, and drank beer as he told me old Ainu folktales of giant octopus, shape-shifting rats, and dragon kings. As usual, I recorded the tales.

Later we retired, and I crawled beneath the woven blankets on the surprisingly- comfortable bed. Almost as soon as my head touched the straw-stuffed pillow, I was asleep.

It was still dark when I awoke with a start. I could hear Turushno snoring at the other side of the hut - but there was another, softer noise intermingled with it. I strained my ears, suddenly alert that something was not right. The sound was a subtle fumbling at the door of the hut, as if something were trying to gain entrance. Fortunately, the bolt held fast, and whatever was outside seemed to retreat.

I found myself doubting that a bear would behave in such a manner; surely it would have just smashed the door in to gain entrance. As I sat up in bed ,I heard whatever it was return. It seemed to be furtively skirting the hut. I heard something scratch at the wooden shutter on one of the windows; then, with a terrific bound, whatever it was leapt onto the thatched roof. I could hear it scuttle to and fro. I could have sworn it was a monkey, but there are none on Hokkaido, and whoever heard of a monkey moving around in the middle of the night?

Finally it dropped down to the ground again, and I heard it scurry off into the forest. I lay awake 'til the dawn rays crept under the shutters. I decided not to mention our nocturnal visitor to my host as we ate millet porridge for breakfast.

Turushno had spoken before of the remains of an old Ainu village deep in the forest. He had always promised to take me there, so I was delighted that he suggested that we visit the place. He had reset all his snares and traps, and could afford a little time to indulge me.

We wandered away from the little valley his hut stood in, which afforded it some degree of respite from the elements. It never failed to amaze me how Turushno could find his way through the dense thicket like a man navigating a familiar city street; I would have become lost quickly in the impenetrable morass were it not for my elderly guide. I was also acutely aware that, should something befall him, I would be totally at the mercy of the wilderness.

It began to drizzle slightly, and I was glad I had brought a rainproof coat. It didn't seem to bother Turushno in the slightest.

We reached what was left of the village; the forest was reclaiming it already. The place had been abandoned some thirty years ago, before Turushno had come to the hills. He knew nothing of the tribe who lived here, or what had happened to them.

"I suppose the advantages of living in a modern town were too much to resist," he commented wistfully.

Most of the huts had collapsed, the reed and thatch rotting and becoming mulch. There must have been around eight huts with small outbuildings, such as latrines and animal pens, as equally tumbledown as the huts. Some even had trees growing up through them.

"It rots away just as we shall rot away, forgotten by time." The old man shook his head.

I walked around, taking pictures with my camera. Only one hut still had the remnants of a roof. I wandered inside. The rush matting had long since rotted. The shelves were bare and the fire pit was bereft of even the traces of ash. I found myself wondering about the people who had lived there and their reason for abandoning their home. I imagined children playing by the hearth, old women gossiping, and hunters arriving back from the forest. A wave of melancholy swept over me, and I felt I had to leave the decaying hut.

As I walked out of the door, I noticed something in the damp earth - it was a bare footprint. The print was no longer than my own foot, but a fair bit wider. It sunk deep into the earth, indicating its owner must have been a heavy person. It seemed human, with five toes, but something about the print seemed odd. Perhaps it was the width or the fact that the big toe seemed - unusually - widely separated from the others.

I bent down and took a couple of shots of it before calling Turushno over. "Look," I said, "who would be running around up here barefoot?"

Turushno looked as puzzled as I did.

"I am the only person up here. The other Ainu are long gone."

"Maybe it's another hermit like you?"

"If anyone else was living in these hills, I'd know about it. I would have smelled their campfires, found their traps. No, I am the only man up here."

"Well, who made those tracks?" I asked.

"I do not know," he mumbled, and a vaguely worried look came across his face.

There were more of the tracks in the moist ground. They led away from the old village and were lost in the forest.

"Come," said Turushno, "it is time for us to go. It is a long walk home." With that, he set off at a brisk pace.

Back at the hut, Turushno seemed oddly quiet. He busied himself preparing a meal, and was not as talkative that night.

The next couple of days passed without incident. The old trapper caught fish and smoked them. He brightened up when he saw one of his snares had caught a deer. Soon I had to leave for Sapporo, and he guided me down the mountain paths that lead to the little Ainu village. He brought with him animal pelts to trade, and seemed in good spirits when I left him.

It was six weeks before I travelled up to the Shiretoko Peninsula to see my friend again. I found him smoking fish on a rack outside of his hut. He greeted me warmly, and we were soon catching up again. He had sold his pelts and deerskins, and bought more chickens, which he proudly displayed. He invited me inside for some millet dumplings and fish.

I was keen to return to the old village at some point, but Turushno did not seem keen on going back. He made excuses about being busy with other things, but after some badgering he said he would lead me there again - but not today.

We drank well into the night, sitting beside the fire hole in the centre of the hut. The grey spectre of the smoke coiled up and crept across the ceiling, exiting in the hole in the angle of the roof. It must have been close to midnight when we first heard it - my first thought was that it was a woman screaming. Turushno and I were jerked out of our near soporific state, and leapt to our feet. It sounded as if some woman were screaming in terror - then I realized that Turushno and I were probably the only two people on the whole of the Shiretoko Peninsula.

The sound came again, and it gradually dawned on me that this was not being caused by any human vocal chords. The long, shrill shriek came again, closer this time. I saw Turushno's face by the dying light of the embers. His expression said it all; he was as confused as I was.

"What is that?", I whispered.

"I have never heard an animal make a noise like that in all my time in the hills."

Slipping from the bed, I crossed to the window and peered through a crack in the shutters. The moonlight gave me reasonable vision. For a third time, that awful cry rang out in the darkness. It seemed that whatever was making it was just inside the tree line. Then, briefly, something crossed my field of vision where there was a gap in the trees. Its silhouette was visible for a split second; whatever it was seemed to be walking on two legs, like a man.

I fumbled for my torch and dictaphone in the backpack I had brought. Running back to the window, I threw open the shutters and waited with the dictaphone switched on. Luckily, the animal called again, its eerie scream making my flesh crawl - at least I had caught a recording of the noise. I shone the torch's beam out towards the trees in the direction the vocalisation had come from - it illuminated nothing but bark, leaves and branches. I heard the sound of something retreating deeper into the forest.

Later I played the recording back, and Turushno and I stared mutely at each other. Neither of us slept for the rest of the night.

In the morning we searched the area, but found no tracks. The chickens and the rack of fish were undisturbed. The old man had his own ideas about what had made the noise.

"My grandparents spoke of 'mountain devils,' spirits that dwelt in the remote hills. They came down to steal livestock and crops. My grandfather told me how he had seen them as a boy. He said they walked like men, on two legs, but they were covered with hair, like a wild beast. They had faces like monkeys and were stronger than any man."

"Was he talking about monkeys?", I asked. "There are none on Hokkaido."

My host shook his head. "No, they had faces like monkeys, but they stood and walked upright like men. They had no fire, but they used clubs and rocks as weapons. They came down from the mountains and the deepest forests. They were here long before the first Ainu set foot in Japan."

"You have never spoken of this before in all the time you have been telling me Ainu folktales," I said.

"This is no folktale, my friend. My grandfather recalled them from his youth. Sometimes they would band together to attack our village - that was much further down, closer to the villages you know now. They became such a pest that the tribe decided to deal with them. Some men followed a few of them up to a cave. There was a whole group of them up there. The chief formed a plan. He had barrels of sake brought up and left outside of the cave. The mountain devils got so drunk on it that they fell asleep in their cave, then the village men blocked up the entrance with straw, wood and reeds and set fire to it. The creatures were smoked to death as they slept. Afterwards, their rotting corpses caused a stench for miles around, and attracted a swarm of flies so large they blocked out the sun like a thundercloud."

"And this really happened?"

"Oh, yes; my grandfather helped carry up bundles of straw. But it was said that some of the mountain devils escaped into the forest and bred. Hunters would occasionally glimpse one in the remotest areas, but never again did they come down to attack the villagers."

I was frantically scribbling down notes - it was an amazing story. If the events were based on something real, I worked out they would have happened around 1870, taking into account Turushno's age. The old man seemed to believe that the animal we had heard last night was one of these 'mountain devils.' Whatever it was, with its strange cry I could well believe it could generate such weird tales.

When we left for the village, Turushno took with him his hatchet, knife and an antiquated rifle - I had never seen him so nervous before. He left me at the ruins, saying that he had to check up on his snares; I knew full well that he had done this the day before. It was simply that the place made him nervous.

Turushno quickly left, promising to be back within the hour. I began to search the area for any artefacts. I came upon a few old arrowheads and some broken pottery. As the noon sun got hotter, I decided to make for the shade of the last standing hut to relax a while. I drank some tea from my flask and began to examine the scant relics I had found.

I heard footsteps approaching, and thought it must be Turushno back from 'checking his snares,' doubtless wanting to go back home. As a shadow fell across the doorway, I looked up and saw it.

It was a creature about my own height, five feet six inches. It was covered in dirty grey hair about four inches long, save for the face, hands and chest, which were bare. The hair was longer on the arms, hanging down in untidy strands. On the thing's head, the hair formed a mane that ran down to its shoulders. It was barrel-chested and its long arms reached its knees. The face was the most disturbing thing about it; the thick brow, wide, thin-lipped mouth and flat, broad nose were simian, and in stark contrast to the eyes, which looked startlingly human.

The creature seemed as surprised by me as I was by it. It halted in the doorway, staring at me. The flask slipped from my hands and hit the floor. The sharp sound seemed to break the spell, and the creature turned and fled. I ran after it, but it moved so fast that it had vanished into the bush by the time I had reached the doorway. All that it left behind was a vile odour, like that of rotting cabbage.

I realised in anger that I had my camera in the chest pocket of my shirt. A whole range of emotions ran through me in quick succession - fear, confusion, amazement, disbelief. I looked down and saw the thing's tracks in the dirt. I photographed them before looking for hairs; I found none. I resisted the urge to go further into the forest; I knew the way up from the little cove on the coast to Turushno's hut, but I would soon become lost in the deep forest. I had no other choice but to wait for his return. I found myself being both horrified and excited at the thought of the thing's return.

What was it I had seen? It was certainly no monkey. It looked more like some kind of ape, but it walked upright like a man. I concluded that it was nothing known to science. The implications of what I had found were staggering - a new species of ape living in one of the world's most populous and advanced nations!

When I heard footsteps returning I had my camera ready, but it was just Turushno. I told him what I had seen.

"It was a mountain devil, like my grandfather told me about. They have returned from the deep forest. We cannot stay here." He insisted that we go back to the hut immediately. He was visibly upset by what I had told him.

"But the creature did me no harm; it didn't seem aggressive."

"My grandfather said that they would come in groups to attack. They were strong and cunning. The only thing they feared was fire."

Turushno seemed on edge for the rest of my stay. He carried his gun wherever he went, and usually insisted that I come with him when he checked his traps and snares, or when he went picking edible plants and berries. Nothing further happened, no screams in the night or scratchings at the door. When the time came for me to leave, he accompanied me down to the Ainu kotan. He said he wanted to buy more bullets for his rifle. Before I left, I heard him speak to some of the villagers about the 'mountain devils;' none seemed to believe him.

Back at Sapporo, I had the pictures of the footprints developed. Thankfully they are quite clear. I have not mentioned my sighting to anybody except Turushno - my peers would think me utterly insane. I must collect more evidence - a picture, hair, bones, anything.

I have been leafing through books on apes, and the creature I saw does not really fit any of the known ape species. The closest approximation I could get to it was in a book on the evolution of man - the thing I saw most closely recalled the hominid *Autralopithecus robustus*, yet this was an African species that died out 1.2 million years ago. The creature I saw was taller and the hair was longer than the artistic reconstruction in the book, but the face was very like it. The 'mountain devils' must be some branch of late surviving Australopithecines that migrated out of Africa and moved across Asia long before the first wave of *Homo erectus*.

How did they get here? Nippon has been an island chain since the formation of the Perouse Strait 11,000 years ago cut Hokkaido off from the mainland. This was the last land bridge to mainland Asia - it is possible they entered Nippon long before this.

The creatures must have retreated into the mountains when the ancestors of the Ainu arrived on Japan, entering into folklore. The modern Nipponese have ape-like monsters in their folklore. I have become quite obsessed by the subject. The Satori was a beast like a huge monkey said to be able to read the thoughts of humans. The Yamachichi was a silvery-haired ape that sucked the breath and life from sleeping victims.

As recently as the 1970s and early '80s a creature resembling the one I saw was reported around Mount Hiba in Hiroshima Prefecture. The media dubbed the creature Hibagon. It was described as being around five-feet tall, upright and black or brown in colour. It had an odour like decaying flesh, and was reported to have used primitive tools. The face was said by witnesses to be ape-like, but with strikingly human eyes. The last known sighting was in 1982.

Could these creatures have survived in small relic populations in several areas of Nippon? Hiroshima Prefecture is far less wild than the Shiretoko Peninsula. If the creatures could have survived there, then it begs the question where else could they be today? So much of our nation is mountainous and poorly populated.

It scarcely seems believable, one of the ancestors of man, or at least a close relation to it alive and well in 20th Century Japan! This discovery will grant me scientific immortality, but I must proceed with caution and gather more evidence before I reveal my findings.

In mid-July I returned to the Peninsula. Long before I reached the little valley where my friend's hut stood I could detect the smell of woodsmoke. I became alarmed and hurried along the trail to his abode.

Thankfully both he and his hut were fine; the smell had come from a bonfire he had lit outside of the hut and near to the entrance to the tiny valley. The old man himself looked grubbier than usual, his hair and beard blackened by woodsmoke. He ran over to me, looking this way and that with furtive eyes.

"The forest devils returned, Oka; I knew they would."

"They?"

"Yes, a whole group of them. They stole my chickens and my fish. They were banging on the doors and the walls, apes that walked like men. Fire from my fire pit scared them away. Now I build a great fire outside each night, and they have not entered the valley again."

In the hut, Turushno described the beasts; it was clear he was talking about creatures of the same kind as the one I had seen. "There were old and young, male and female. It was the males who did most of the attacking." He pointed to some large round rock the size of a football.

"They threw these like a normal man throws a pebble. I think they were after food, but they fled from the fire."

"When was this?", I asked.

"Three nights ago. They have not been back since."

The old man seemed glad I was there with him. As night fell, I helped him heap wood onto the bonfire until the flames rose high, illuminating the little valley. Turushno gazed out into the dancing shadows beyond the flames. "The mountain devils will never force me to leave my home. I built it with my own hands; I will not surrender it to these monkey men."

We retired fairly early. Turushno kept the fire in the fire hole burning, as well as the bonfire outside. I lay awake in the dark, the camera still about my neck. I prayed I could get a second chance at seeing one of the creatures and photographing it.

In the early hours of the morning, when the flames in the fire pit had fallen low, something struck the roof. There was a dull thud on the thick thatch. I sat up and saw that Turushno was also awake. After a pregnant silence that seemed to last forever, there was another sound of something heavy hitting the roof.

Turushno motioned for silence and crept to the shutters. I followed. He gingerly drew them back. The flames were still fairly high. Beyond their light was darkness, in which nothing moved.

A fist-sized rock flew down and struck the earth in front of the hut - then it struck me. The creatures were on the cliff above the valley, hurling down rocks. I grabbed my torch and ran to the door as more rocks were hurled down. Turushno tried to stop me drawing back the bolt, but I managed to scramble outside. Several rocks narrowly missed me and I looked up onto the clifftop some hundred feet above us.

There, on the edge, stood at least ten of the creatures. On seeing me, they began to screech and wail, gesticulating wildly. I fired off several shots from my camera. The flash made them shrink back, covering eyes that seemed to glow in the light. A number of them stooped to pick up more ammunition. I shone the torch up and along the cliff in a sweeping arc, and the ape-things dropped their rocks and scattered back into the shadows.

I heard a noise behind me, and turned to see several more of the creatures behind the bonfire. They were wielding primitive clubs that were little more than tree branches. The creatures seemed loath to move past the fire, but one hurled the thick stick it was carrying. It only just missed my head and crashed into the wall of the hut.

I ran back inside and slammed the door behind me, pulling the bolt across it. I made sure that the shutters were bolted, too. Turushno was loading his old hunting rifle, a grim look on his face.

Outside the animalistic vocalisation rose again. I switched on my dictaphone. In the chilling screams and guttural cackles, I thought I could detect some primitive ancestor to language. My thoughts were interrupted as the rocks began to fall again with renewed violence. One rock tumbled down the chimney hole in a cloud of dust.

There was the sound of something heavier still landing on the roof, followed by a scurrying sound. It dawned on me that the creatures must have climbed down the cliff face, and now one of them was on the roof.

Turushno raised his gun and shot through the thatch at the man-ape. He evidently missed, as it continued moving. Another of the creatures jumped down onto the roof from some vine or ledge. At the same time, the first one bounded down off the house and began pounding at the walls.

Again and again Turushno's gun sounded, but he was shooting blind. One of the creatures was rattling the door. I crossed the room to see if I could secure it more firmly. As I passed one of the shuttered windows, the wood was smashed and a hairy arm intruded through, looping about my neck. I struggled, but the thing had an iron grip many times stronger than a modern man's. The coarse brown hair of its arm was in my mouth, nose and eyes. The stench of it was over-powering. I was almost yanked off my feet as it tried to pull me through the window. I swung my camera up and fired off the flash directly into the thing's face from point-blank range.

For a second I saw its ghastly visage in the light, the face of a crazed ape with sickeningly-human eyes. It jabbered and retreated, dropping me to the floor as it pulled its long, muscular arm back through the window. I found I was clutching a hand full of its rank hair; I quickly shoved it into my pocket.

The front door was bowing inwards as one of the hominids pushed at it with inhuman power. Turushno raised his gun and shot at the man-ape through the wood, splintering a large hole. The thing bounded away, but more stones and sticks began to strike the hut.

"I am running out of bullets," the old man said desperately.

"We need to make a run for it before they get in."

Turushno shook his head. "I will not leave my home!"

"We can come back with men from the village, but we need to get out now, while we still can. I can hold them off with my torch."

Not allowing time for argument, I opened the front door and shone the torch beam out. Several hairy figures recoiled back into the dark. I grabbed the old man and ran. As we passed the bonfire, he stooped to snatch up a burning brand. He waved it at the creatures as they cringed back from the flames. One of the beasts leapt out in front of me, swinging a gnarled club. It dashed the camera from my hands, smashing it to pieces.

Turushno thrust the burning brand into the hominid's face. It leapt away screaming, its singed hair smouldering.

We ran for the path through the forest. Thankfully, most of the hominids seemed to be most interested in getting into Turushno's hut to steal his food supplies. A handful pursued us, but backed off from the torch beam. We fled through the night with fear-spurred stamina. Hours later we stumbled into the Ainu village, ragged, bleeding, filthy and exhausted.

Turushno collapsed and was taken into one of the villager's huts. He was in a fever and raving. I stayed with him for several days before his fever broke. He vowed to return to his hut when he was strong enough. I left for Sapporo the next day.

My camera had been destroyed, but I still had the hair in my pocket that I had pulled from the hominid's arm as I struggled with it. I have sent this to Professor Yoshida Aki, Head of the Zoology department at Hokkaido University. I have not mentioned the back-story, but just asked him if he could identify what animal it came from. As for myself, I have bought a new camera and a sturdy handgun. I plan to return to the peninsula in August to finally secure the proof I need that mankind's older brother is living in 20th-century Japan."

* * * * *

Here Dr Oka Akio's notes end. He is known to have left Sapporo for the Shiretoko Peninsula on August 3rd, 1988; he was never seen again. Enquiries at the Ainu villages close to the area confirmed that an old man called Turushno had indeed come down from the mountains raving about monsters. He died before he could return to his remote abode. A search of the Shiretoko Peninsula found no sign of Dr. Oka Akio. In newspaper reports, his strange story of a battle with ape-men was not mentioned.

The hair sent to Professor Yoshida Aki contained no follicles. and hence no DNA could be extracted; however, the Professor made a study of the scale arrangement and medulla. His conclusion was that they were 'near human.'

18. A Damp Patch on the Ceiling

I was ten years old when my family moved from Tokyo to Yokohama. It was 1963 and, as I recall, a hot summer when we moved. My father was being transferred by the company he worked for. It was an exciting time for the family. My father had been promoted to shop foreman at a transistor radio factory in Naka Ward. The job came with a nice house on the outskirts of the city in Aoba Ward. Father commuted to work each day; sometimes he was gone for long periods.

The house was a large old one with a big, somewhat-overgrown garden. My sister and I used to play hide-and-seek in it. My new school was fine. I've always made new friends easily, and I fitted in well. Everything was fine until one morning my mother noticed something on the kitchen ceiling.

"Look, there is a wet patch on the ceiling." She pointed up, and all four of us saw a damp, dark stain about the size of bathroom towel.

"A pipe must have burst. Can you check it, darling?"

My father nodded and ran upstairs. The room immediately above the kitchen was a spare room that we had been using to store things in, like books and bits of furniture we had brought with us from Tokyo.

Dad came back downstairs, looking puzzled.

"Well, the carpet in the spare room is as dry as a bone. I moved some stuff and rolled it back, but the floorboards underneath were dry, too. I'll take them up and look at the pipes when I get back home from work." He kissed my mother and then trotted off to catch his train.

I didn't think anymore about it whilst I was at school, but when my sister and I got home, we both noticed it again as we were getting snacks from the fridge.

"I wonder what causes it?", my sister said.

"Do you think we should have a closer look?", I asked. My sister nodded, and I ran off to fetch dad's stepladder.

I climbed up to the top step, but I still had to stretch out and stand on tiptoe to reach the stain. The ground floor had a ceiling that was very high, and I was only little. I ran my fingers over the stain and quickly drew them back. It did not feel like water; it felt warm and thick. The texture was repellent, like the slime trail of a slug. I nearly fell backwards off the stepladder. The substance was tacky, and had the consistency of the paper paste used in art at school.

I quickly climbed down and showed my sister.

"Eeew!", she said upon touching it.

I washed my hands quickly.

When dad got home from work, he took up the floorboards in the spare room. He found that there were no pipes anywhere near the wet patch below. Also, it was bone dry below the boards, so whatever it was, the liquid was on the surface of the kitchen ceiling, not dripping down from above. Dad touched the stuff too.

"Yuck, it doesn't seem to be water," he said. "It's some sort of goo, all thick and warm." He brought his fingers up to his nose and sniffed it. "Doesn't smell of much."

"Maybe it's rising damp?", suggested mum.

"I think you might be right," dad said. "I'll call someone out to have a look.

That night I woke up and heard a strange sound. It seemed to be coming from the floor below. It was an odd, wet noise; a sort of sucking, slurping sound. It reminded me a little of a big dog drinking water, but somehow 'heavier.' We had no pets at the time, and I wondered what could be making the noise. Finally it stopped and I dropped off back to sleep.

The next day a man came and looked at the damp patch. He said it wasn't rising damp, as that goes up from the floor of a house towards the ceiling, and this was just a wet stain in the middle of the ceiling. He thought that it might be some kind of fungus. He took a sample, then sprayed the ceiling with some fungicide. He promised to have the sample analysed and get back to us.

It was a few days later when I awoke again in the night. Once more, I heard the heavy, wet, sucking noise from downstairs. Somehow I just *knew* that the noise had something to do with the damp patch. Strangely, I felt no fear at the time, just curiosity. I decided to investigate.

I slipped out of bed and across the landing, past the rooms of my sleeping sister and parents. I climbed down, taking care not to make a sound. The moon was full and I could see clearly. The kitchen door was slightly ajar and I could plainly hear the sound, louder now and wetter. Still I felt no fear; I just wondered what was making the noise. I pushed the kitchen door open.

There was some kind of animal standing in the kitchen. I had never seen anything like it in a book or on television. It was a pale, hairless, pinkish thing. Its arms and legs seemed to be analogous to those of a human, but stretched out to unnatural proportions. It had a wizened torso that reminded me of an old man, and an elongate neck. The head resembled that of a horse more than anything else, but instead of a mane of hair, masses of ruffled skin hung about its neck. From between wide, yellow teeth protruded an absurdly-long tongue of a livid pink hue, with which it licked ardently at the ceiling.

The thing seemed to notice me; it withdrew its saliva-coated tongue and turned to regard me as I stood in the doorway. It gave me a wide, horsey smile. The last thing I recall before I passed out was screaming.

I came to with mum gently pouring water onto my face. I remembered the dripping saliva and screamed again. She and dad both had to hold me down as I panicked. I babbled about monsters and horse faces and long, long tongues like a lunatic. Finally, I calmed down enough to tell them what I had seen. They both tried to comfort me, telling me I had been sleepwalking and had a nightmare - but I saw mum glance up at the damp patch. It seemed to have grown bigger.

Mum kept me from school for a couple of days and sent for a doctor, who told her there was absolutely nothing wrong with me. Both mum and dad kept telling me it was only a bad dream, reciting the words like a mantra. Then dad got a telephone call from the man who had inspected the house for rising damp. I was in the living room at the time and the telephone was in the hall, but the doors were open and I could hear the conversation. I think mum and dad would not have liked it if they knew I was listening.

The man told dad that the stuff from the kitchen ceiling was saliva, animal saliva. They didn't know what kind of animal it was, but the damp patch was certainly a patch of saliva.

The subject was not mentioned again. Everyone seemed to just clam up. Sometimes at night I would hear the noise of the thing as it licked the ceiling - sometimes slowly with long, languid laps, or sometimes fast, with an eager slurping. The damp patch grew wider.

Soon after, dad had to work a later shift at the factory. He would come in late at night and creep upstairs so as not to awaken us. One night he did wake us, with wild screams.

We ran down stairs to find him shaking with fear on the floor, pointing into the kitchen. We looked but there was nothing there, save for the damp patch that had grown some more. He sat in the living room, drinking brandy and shivering. He described exactly the same creature that I had seen. We all knew now that it was not a dream. That night we all slept in the same room.

In the morning dad rang into work sick, something he had never done in his 25 years with the company. He left the house early and came back within the hour. He had a Shinto priest with him.

Between us we told him our story, and a look of recognition crossed his face.

"Ah, yes, this is a Tenjōname."

We all gave him blank, worried looks.

The Tenjōname is a yokai, a spirit animal. They have been written of for centuries. They are usually found in old houses with high ceilings. This house is fairly new; it must have been the high ceiling that attracted it."

"Can you get rid of it?" asked dad.

"Of course," the priest said.

He lit incense and carried it from room to room, then he began chanting prayers. I can't recall what he said, but he made complex hand movements. It lasted for about an hour. Afterward, the priest looked very tired.

We never saw the Tenjōname again after that. The wet patch vanished. In time, the family got over the events and moved on. Dad was more successful than ever in his work. But I did not forget; questions still lingered in my mind. Why has the Tenjōname come? Why did it lick the ceiling?

I began to research in the many libraries of Yokohama. Over the school holidays I spent hours looking through old books on folklore whilst my friends were out playing in the hot sun. I found out more about the Tenjōname; I also found out that it is sometimes better to let things alone.

It seemed that these creatures haunted old mansions, houses and temples with high ceilings. The dark, damp patches were all thought to be the creature's work. No-one seemed to know where they came from. The Tenjōname did not seem to be aggressive or cause any harm. They licked at the ceiling to keep it damp. It seemed that the creatures all suffered from an irrational fear that the building they inhabited would catch on fire; their constant licking dampened the wood of the house to prevent this. Why they thought this was never explained - maybe the reason is lost to history.

It was faulty wiring that caused the fire in our house. It happened in early September, weeks after the Tenjōname had vanished. Sparks caught onto the carpet in the living room in the early hours of the morning. The place went up like kindling. Thankfully, mum and dad managed to grab my sister and escape by the back door. None of it would have happened if we had just left the old Tenjōname be. Looking back now, I don't understand why we were so scared of it; it had never done us any harm. In fact, in its own strange way it was helping us.

But that was years ago. The old house is just a shell now. The building was never pulled down or built upon - it was just left. I suppose it got round that our house had a funny reputation. What's left of it is still standing. There is nobody there now, except for me. Mum and dad tried hard to save me, but I had inhaled too much smoke. Of course, the Tenjōname is long gone. Now there is just a sad, blackened little shade wandering a soot-caked ruin.

19. Wandering Eye

"Forgive my Wandering eye. I cannot explain it, I cannot contain it."

– Savlonic: *Wandering Eye*

The air was heavy with the scent of incense. Candlelight danced, sending fantastical shapes across the far wall. Outside cymbals clashed, prayer wheels span, and voices chanted in unison. The old abbot lay on the bed, his saffron robes hanging down over the sides. He feebly raised a claw-like had and beckoned the high priest over.

"I am dying," he wheezed. "I have no fear of this transition, but I have not broken the wheel of re-birth yet."

The high priest shook his head.

"Sensei, you have lived a pure and blameless life. If anyone...,"

The abbot raised his hand again to silence his colleague.

"No, no. When I was a youth, I was quite different. I need to tell you something; it is something I have never shared with anyone, not even the other monks, not even my own teachers when I took up the vows."

The ancient cleric motioned for the priest to sit down. The younger man dragged a stool closer.

"I grew up in a village some miles outside of Kumamoto. In my teenaged years I was a thief and a rogue. I would pickpocket in the city, and when I was not doing that, I would roam the hills of Higo stealing livestock. I was lucky never to have been caught. My parents despaired of me. I spent my money drinking sake and whoring in Kumamoto.

"One day I was walking in the hills searching for some small farmstead from which I might steal chickens or ducks. I was in an area I had never been to before. It was further away from my village, but it was a fine summer's day and I had no worries. As I was walking across a patch of ground covered with small, loose rocks, the earth beneath me

161

seemed to give way. At first I thought it was an earthquake. The ground opened up and I fell.

"I awoke with a sore head and a covering of dirt and stones. I had not been badly hurt, just a little dazed. It dawned on me that I had fallen down into a cave, the roof having eroded, then given way under my weight. The pit in which I lay was about seven feet deep. I was more cross than worried; the mass of earth that had fallen into the hole would make it easy for me to climb out again. Light was streaming in from above and I could see quite clearly. As I rose to clamber out, I turned to see that a passage ran off into the dark. The walls of the passage looked too smooth to be a natural formation. I decided to look closer, and found that the walls of the passage were indeed manmade, and of cut stone. My first thought was that I may have stumbled upon a tomb of some description, a tomb that may contain treasure. I walked for a little way along the tunnel, but it swiftly became too dark to see. I had neither lamp nor candle to light my way. I did once think I saw something briefly glint in the darkness further on. My mind was full of images of coins and gems. I thought also that I heard the faintest rustle.

"I decided that I needed to return with my friends and some light. I ran back along the passage, and scrambled up the fallen rocks and earth. I covered over the hole with branches and leaves, then set off home."

At this point the abbot broke off, coughing violently. The high priest brought a flask of water and waited until he had recovered.

"Do not try to talk; you are too weak," the priest advised.

The abbot shook his head. "This is my last and only chance to say what has to be said."

It was evident that the old man needed to tell someone this story before he died.

Eventually he continued. "Back in the village my friends needed little persuasion to return with me the following day. There were four of us - Kenta, Takuya, Kazuki and myself. I recall our excited talk about what might lie below the ground. Was it the tomb of some rich merchant or nobleman? We all thought we could get rich from the discovery.

I soon retraced my steps, and within a couple of hours we had reached the place where I had my adventure the day before. We moved the branches and then, one by one, slid down into the hole. We lit our candles and began to slowly creep down the smooth-walled passage in single file.

The tunnel led for perhaps one hundred feet until it reached a larger, central chamber. Here we all stood and gaped - nothing in our dull little imaginations could compare with this. There was a great pile of riches heaped up in the middle of the chamber - jade carvings, gold statues, jewel-encrusted necklaces and bangles, and great earthenware pots spewing out gold coins and rubies, emeralds and sapphires. In the midst of it all sat who I took to be the tomb's owner. In a lifelike, upright pose was a body in samurai armour.

"As a boy, I had taken an interest in the samurai. I even harboured a foolish idea that I could, one day, become one. I recognised the style immediately. It was the heavy ō-yoroi armour that had not been used for several hundred years. The iron mengu facial mask was of a sardonically-grinning man. By candlelight, he looked positively evil. His studded kabuto helmet was decorated with great horns like some awful Oni, and in the flickering light it gave an eerie impression. Bulky shoulder guards jutted out above the breastplate and arm guards. The lamellar plates and scales of the suit looked as if they had been created the day before, so perfect was their preservation. His leg plates and sealskin boots seemed hardly touched by time. His right hand still gripped the long-shafted Tsuki nari yari, a spear with a crescent-shaped blade at the tip; it still looked sharp.

"Several more passages led off from the main chamber. I knew the samurai had to be high-ranking, due to the quality of his armour. Its dated design would have put it in the period of the Genpei War. Why he was placed in the tomb in the sitting position I have never understood; however, what was apparent was that the tomb must, at some point, have been buried, perhaps by some earthquake or landslide.

"Our awed gaping was swiftly replaced when greed broke its spell. We ran forward and began to scoop up handfuls of treasure into the sacks we had brought with us. We intended to take as much as we could carry, then come back for the rest, bit by bit, until we had it all.

"It was I who heard it first; the others were too intent on the booty. It was a sort of dragging noise that seemed to come from one of the passages that led off the main chamber. My first thought was that it was another robber who had beaten us to the tomb. I prised the crescent-bladed spear from the centuries-old dead grasp of the samurai, and turned to look at the tunnel from which the dragging sound emanated.

"Something waddled slowly into the wan light our four candles were producing. It was not a tomb robber. It was not a man. It stood perhaps eight feet tall on fat, ungainly legs. I would say that it was waving its arms, if it had arms; they looked to me more like flabby flippers ending in tiny hands. The head and body were one single mass of glistening obesity; rolls of loose, grey-green skin. Worse than this were the eyes. The creature had no face as such, but out from beneath the sac-like rolls of skin hundreds of large, round eyes peered.

"I dropped the spear and the others looked up to see the thing slowly shuffling toward us; then, with an audible 'pop,' one of the eyes detached itself from the mass. It hung in midair like some kind of flying jellyfish. Tendrils hung down from beneath it. Another fist-sized orbit oozed out of the fatty flesh and floated beside its brother. More and more detached themselves, moving independently of their owner - then those unblinking, wet eyes began to drift forward.

"We all ran back along the passage. I heard Kazuki cry out. Turning back, I saw that one of the eyes had attached itself to his left arm. The hanging members were now burrowing into his flesh as he flailed wildly in an attempt to rid himself of the ghastly organ. Even as he thrashed, another of the glistening orbs fastened itself to Kenta, forcing itself beneath his tunic and sending its vein-like roots into his chest as he clawed wildly at it.

"Takuya and I had seen enough. We ran, scrambling for the light, with several of the flying eyes in pursuit. As soon as we reached the shaft of light at the end of the tunnel, the eyes drew back as if the brightness hurt them. Takuya and I clambered out of the hole and ran on. We heard the others behind us and eventually they caught up. Kenta and Kazuki were hysterical, screaming and weeping. They pulled at the eyes with no effect. The eyes had dug deep into the flesh in an oddly-bloodless and - painless way. Now they rested in my two friends as they had done in the thing that had sent them.

"Somehow we made it back to the village, and each went our separate ways without speaking. Amazingly, each of us still clutched a sack of treasure from the tomb.

"I did not tell my mother and father where I had been that day. They tended not to ask too many questions; we were a poor family, and I brought back money and food - that was good enough. I hid the sack under my bed, then ate supper in silence. I retired early and swiftly fell asleep.

"I awoke in the night to a soft pattering sound. It was coming from the shutters, and I wondered if it was one of my friends come to see me or to ask for help. I whispered softly at the shutters, asking who was there. No reply came save for the slight noise, as if something were pawing softly outside. Gingerly I opened the shutters.

"There in the night air floated an eye. It had tracked me back all this way from the tomb, having waited for nightfall. Before I could slam the shutters again, it had darted through into my room. Choking back a scream, I snatched up a stool and tried to bludgeon the flying eye. It moved as fast as a fly on the wing and, before I knew it, the thing had wrapped its tendrils around my right arm. They burrowed deep into my skin. Strangely, there was no pain. The flesh itself moulded around the eye.

"I looked down at it, and it looked up at me. I could not see through it, and it rolled around independently of any will from me. My skin had formed lids over it and it blinked. I picked up a small knife and tried to cut the alien eye from out of my flesh; it was excruciating, like stabbing your own eye. The thing seemed independent of my brain, but its nerves were linked to my own. As I looked the wounded eye healed, reforming at an unnatural rate.

"It was the same with the others. Takuya had a visitation in the night, and now he had an eye on his shoulder. All three had tried, as I had, to cut the parasitic eyes out - all had suffered the same consequences.

"We decided that the thing, whatever it was, was some sort of guardian. The eyes it sent after us were punishment for stealing from the samurai's tomb. We all agreed to put the treasure back, every last coin and every last gem. We returned with the sacks and, despite being sick with fear, we climbed down into the hole and walked along the passage once more. The creature was nowhere to be seen. We emptied our sacks back onto the great pile of riches. I even returned the spear to the long-dead warrior's hand.

"We all got out as quickly as possible and returned home. It did no good; the eyes remained. By day they would stay tightly shut - at night they would open and gaze accusingly at us. We all took to covering up our affected parts. From that day on, I always wore garments with long sleeves, even in the heat of summer.

"I think the thing wanted to mark us out as thieves. I also think that the eyes were sent to watch us for the rest of our days. My friends moved away after that. I heard that Kenta hanged himself; what became of the other two, I do not know.

"It was shortly after these events that I took up holy orders and became a monk. I did not speak to anyone about what had happened, but years later I found a picture of the creature we saw in an old book. It was called a Hyakume. My friends and I were correct - it is a guardian of tombs. It is a spirit of yokai raised for that purpose. It grows many eyes in its flesh that relentlessly pursue robbers and attach themselves to the bodies of their prey, marking them for life as thieves."

The abbot reached for the water once more and took a swig.

"I can see by your expression that you doubt my story. It matters little now, as this body is not long for this world. I will show it to you now, this thing, this curse, this watcher that has been with me for so long. Never, ever have I shown it to another."

The old man rolled up the right sleeve of his saffron robe. Deep in the flesh of his upper arm was an eye - an eye as large as a persimmon, and as green as grass. It swivelled in its fleshy socket to look at the high priest. The iris widened as it regarded the man. The priest screamed and ran from the room.

It was hours before he had the nerve to return. The old abbot lay prone on his bed. A quick examination from the priest confirmed that he was dead. Where the eye had once been was just a strange, bloodless hole in the old man's arm.

The high priest heard a soft noise behind him. A cold terror crawled through his stomach as he slowly turned to see the eye, floating in mid air, clumsily fumbling at the latch on shutters with its horridly-motile, root-like tendrils. The latch fell away and the shutters swung wide open, then the horror was out and flying away into the night. The priest watched as the pale orb receded into the darkness and was finally lost.

"Back to its master," he mumbled under his breath.

20. The Night Driver

He could never live in the city - all that noise, the polluted air and, worst of all, the lack of space. If there was one thing he hated, it was being crowded. Perhaps it was all down to being brought up in a small country village. As a boy, the fields, woods and mountains were his playground. He didn't even like being shut indoors. A roof and four walls seemed to get claustrophobic after a time.

Kinjo Nao worked in a small firm of solicitors in the city of Towada, Amori Prefecture. It was an awful job for someone who loved to be outdoors - long hours shut in a stuffy office, reams of paperwork and a view from his window that showed nothing but the straight lines and greyness of a human environment. He could have taken a job with the parks department, the forestry commission or even the national parks, but the pay would have been less than half he got in his current job; it weighed out in the end. In this occupation, he could afford to live in the country, miles from anywhere. Once the working day was over, he could return to rural solitude and breathe fresh air. On the wages of a worker in the parks department he would be forced to live in cheap, nasty accommodation in the city, and that he could not bear. He lived for the weekends and long walks in the forests and hills. Most of his co-workers were pasty-faced; not so Nao - he had the ruddy cheeks of an outdoorsman. To look at him, a strapping, round-faced man, the last thing you would think he would be was a solicitor.

The job did demand long hours and, as he was fairly senior in the firm, he often found himself working into the night. His house was on a rural road some twenty miles northeast of the city. He would drive a few miles along the busy National Route 4 before taking a side road left that led off to several smaller back roads leading into the hills. Even during the day these roads were quiet, and at night he was often alone. There was one long, straight stretch of road that always seemed strange to Nao. On the map it could not have been longer than five miles, but it always seemed to take longer than it should to drive down it. It also seemed to be unnaturally straight, quite at odds with the other winding little back roads that all seemed to lead off into nowhere. Nao vaguely recalled hearing about the road being an accident hot spot, though he dismissed the idea as nonsense because so few drivers ever used it.

It was on one bright October night that he first saw it. Work had caused him to tarry after hours in the office; it was eight before he left, and half past eight by the time he had navigated his way through the traffic and out of the city. The rush hour was long gone, and National Route 4 was fairly empty. He took the turn off left and soon was driving along the dark, twisting, little roads towards his isolated home.

By and by he reached the straight stretch, as he had done countless times before. He found his thoughts taking strange paths; he as a little fleshy parcel inside his hard metal casing, moving so fast in a little world of its own, a motor bubble. The trees and bushes blurred as he passed, seeming to be little more than flickering shadows in his peripheral vision. The white road markings seemed hypnotic, flickering black and white like a zoetrope.

Then, to his left, he noticed something in a meadow. It was some kind of animal, loping on all fours and keeping level with his car. It was distant, but he could make it out in the clear night. Was it a dog? There were no farms in the area and he was the only resident for miles around. It kept with him until he turned off the road and onto the next one. Nao thought it was a little odd, but by the time he had reached his home he had forgotten all about it.

The following night he saw it again, and was somewhat surprised at its reappearance. At exactly the same place, it emerged from the shadows and ran across the meadow. Looking as close he could whilst driving, he became sure it was large dog. He felt it was somewhat closer this time; it was almost as if it had been waiting for him. He wondered if it was a stray.

Again, he thought little more of the animal once he had reached his home. The next day at work, however, he found his thoughts straying back to the creature and wondering if he would see it again that night. Sure enough, it was there, bounding across the meadow, seemingly marginally closer again. He toyed with the idea of stopping and trying to get a closer look, but instead he kept on driving.

The following day was a Saturday. After breakfast, Nao decided to walk down to the meadow and see if he could find any tracks. He was surprised at how long the grass was and how much taller than the bushes it was. The dog must be a big one, something like a Great Dane, but who would let a prize animal run around off the leash like that a night, and in the middle of nowhere? Could the animal have been something else? Was it an escaped exotic? There were no zoos for miles around. He had heard of large exotic cats turning up in Europe, America and Australia; they were supposed to be the descendants of big cats kept as pets and ultimately released into the wild. Could the animal he saw be something akin to them? It was dark-furred, long-legged and long-tailed. The head was rounded, but he had never got a good look at it. It was too small for a bear, and not bulky enough. Nao thought it *might* have been a big cat, but it seemed to move much more like a huge dog with that distinct, loping gait.

The ground was fairly hard, and there was no trace of any tracks. There were indeed a number of paths beaten through the vegetation, but they could have been made by anything from badgers to deer.

He spent the rest of the weekend relaxing, and the strange animal did not prey on his thoughts again until he was packing his briefcase that evening. He had a strange conviction it would be there again, almost as if it were waiting for him, almost as if it knew what time he would drive along that particular stretch of road. Sure enough, the animal was there again, and once more it seemed slightly closer than before. It seemed to be able to keep pace with his car effortlessly. Still, the head seemed unclear; it seemed rounded and quite flat, like that of a bullmastiff.

Oddly, the animal was never there in the mornings as he drove to work, despite it still being fairly dark.

By way of an experiment, he decided to drive home at a later hour than usual the next evening. He left work and went to a restaurant he knew in town. It was a pleasant change of pace not having to cook for himself after a long day in the office. It was well past ten o'clock by the time he reached the familiar little road.

It seemed to melt out of the darkness. This was a cloudy and dark night, but the dog, if that's what it was, seemed so much blacker than its surroundings - it stood out against the night itself. Nao thought he could see the muscles at work under its pitch fur as it ran. It was closer still, now half-way between the far edge of the meadow and the road itself. It followed him until he turned off. For the first time since he first saw the creature, Nao felt scared. He had an eerie feeling that it was following his car. The flesh on his back and neck crawled. He glanced in his rear view mirror several times; of course, there was nothing on the road behind him. When he was back at his house, he parked the car and ran as fast as he could into the house, locking the door behind him. He found himself peering out of the bedroom window along the road. Nothing came.

The following evening he decided to take a different route home. He followed another back road in a circular route home. It added almost another ten miles onto his journey. On the way, he nervously glanced out of the side windows, half-expecting a huge canine shape to be pacing his car. He saw nothing save for a solitary owl.

For the rest of the working week he took this far road home. His journeys were unremarkable, a fact that relieved him no end, but he knew that he couldn't continue this way habitually. For one thing, it took far more time to get home, and for another it put up the cost of running his car.

Over the weekend he plucked up courage to drive along the straight stretch in daylight. He slowed down and drove up and down it twice. At one point something big moved in the undergrowth, and Nao's heart leapt into his throat. The creature emerged, revealing itself to be nothing more than a deer.

On Monday night, as sure as the rising and setting of the sun, the dog was there once more. This time it was so close there was no doubt; it was a colossal black dog; still, its head was hard to make out. The face seemed pale. The thing had him shaken. Nao found he was losing concentration at work. He decided to take the long route home again for the rest of the week.

The strategy worked. Without his mind on the black dog, his work improved again. By the weekend, he was feeling fine. On Saturday morning he woke early, intending to go for a walk. As he opened the front door, something stopped him - great paw prints in the mud running up the path and stopping at the door. They were the prints of a dog, a huge dog. Nao knew to which dog they belonged.

The tracks must have been made in the night, though he had heard nothing. They ran around the house as if looking for an entrance. Abandoning the walk, he locked himself in the house and began to question his sanity. Trying to think straight, he toyed with the idea of the whole thing being some kind of mental aberration, something repressed in the subconscious, manifesting as a hallucination. Perhaps it was just as simple as overwork. The idea of visiting a psychiatrist repelled him; he always held the profession in contempt as so much quackery.

Gaining composure, he took a camera and photographed the tracks. They appeared on both the camera and his computer as he downloaded them. The prints were recorded by two machines. *Machines don't suffer from hallucinations; the tracks, and whatever made them, are real.*

Again, Nao rationalised. It was a dog - a big one, but just a dog. Dogs chase cars. It just happened to turn up at his house last night. It was probably feral. It would have approached the house looking for bins to rifle through. Nevertheless, he thought a holiday was long overdue, and on Monday he booked one. In the intervening days he took the long way home.

Nao had two weeks in sunny Okinawa. He had never felt better, and returned to work invigorated and faintly embarrassed at his own stupidity. At his first day back in the office, his co-workers commented on how well he looked, what a nice tan he had, and the fact that he had not looked so well in weeks.

On the straight stretch, the dog was waiting for him. No longer in the meadow, it paced the car at the side of the road. In panic, Nao accelerated, but the hound moved just as fast. Then, impossibly, it was in the car with him. No pawing at the door - it was just there on the passenger seat beside him. It turned to look at him as he screamed. For the first time he saw its face. The dog had a human face, the rosy-cheeked, well-tanned face of an outdoorsman - it had *his* face.

21. Sharpened Senses

"Thank you for granting me this interview, Dr. Ajibana."

"Oh, not at all." The older psychologist smiled at his colleague as they walked across the immaculate lawn of the hospital. "Your paper on masked withdrawal syndrome was ground-breaking, Dr. Jumoni. I am only too glad to help you with your new work."

The two men paused beneath a cherry tree in blossom and looked up at the hospital. It was not a new, clinical building of steel, concrete and glass as one would see in a city; the country retreat was a converted manor house built in the late Meiji Period in the 1890s. The western influence was clearly visible in the architecture. One could have believed that this was England, and the building a late Victorian country retreat.

"Thank you," the younger man bowed politely. "It was my work on that paper which gave me the idea for my book. The human mind is an endlessly-fascinating phenomenon; it is little more than a network of electro-chemical impulses, yet it has tamed fire, built the pyramids, split the atom and put men on the moon. Study of its illnesses is my life's work and, in particular, the study of the arcane maladies of the mind; hence, I found the case here quite intriguing."

"You read the report in detail, then?" asked Dr. Ajibana.

Dr Jumoni nodded.

"Miss Ebisawa's case is totally unique. She has been with us for eighteen months now, and is still suffering from the same delusion."

"But, Dr. Ajibana, how much of this could be physical, stemming directly from her medical condition rather than from the mind?"

"An interesting question; as you know, she is a tetrachromat - her eyes contain four kinds of cone cells rather than three. She can perceive ninety-nine million more colours than those of an average person. Obviously, the possession of these extra cone cells is a physical condition.

Her mental condition may have arisen as a direct result of her super sense."

Dr Jumoni looked up at the pink cherry blossoms and wondered what Miss Ebisawa saw when she looked at them, then he remembered that she had seen very little in nearly two years.

"You would think that if she had this condition since birth, it would seem normal to her."

The older man nodded and frowned. "Yes, you would, and this makes the case all the more strange. It seems she lead a perfectly normal life until the age of twenty-five."

"Do you suppose the whole thing could be a mental breakdown from living in a world tailored to people with normal vision?"

"It's a possibility, Dr. Jumoni, but if that's the case, why did she crack when she did? What pushed her over the edge?"

"And any idea why we have we had no other cases like this in other tetrachromats?" Dr Jumoni added.

"I'll take you up to see her now, but remember, stand behind her at all times. She becomes hysterical at the sight of colour. Her room is whitewashed. Her furniture is white. Her food and drink are dyed with white colouring, and she eats it off a white plate with white plastic cutlery. She wears white clothes and, on the rare occasions she leaves her room, she has a heavy blindfold. Her room is scrubbed daily to eliminate all traces of dirt. Of course, there are no windows in her room."

"It sounds like hell."

"Miss Ebisawa says it is the only way she can find peace."

The two men walked towards the looming hulk of the hospital. Dr Jumoni knocked at the large, white-painted oak door and from inside heard a soft voice bidding him to enter. The room was surprisingly large, and totally devoid of colour. The windowless walls were white, as was the ceiling and tiled floor. The bed and chairs were white, as was the radio that sat on a white table. There were no mirrors in the room.

Miss Ebisawa sat in a white chair facing away from the white door. She wore a white gown with white gloves. Her hair was dyed white. She seemed small, almost doll- like. Of course, Dr Jumoni could not see her face.

He entered gingerly and carefully closed the door behind him.

"Thank you for seeing me, Miss Ebisawa."

"Oh, I won't be *seeing* you; at least, I hope not."

"I understand that colours make you..."

"No, Dr. Jumoni, you do not understand. Colours do not make me afraid; it is what I can see in them."

"The monsters?"

"Call them that if you will."

"And you, because of your condition - you can see them?"

"Condition? I can see ninety-nine million times as many colours as you, Dr. Jumoni. Ninety-nine million; have you any idea what that means?"

The psychologist shifted nervously from foot to foot. She had not asked him to sit.

"Well, I suppose...."

"Do not ask me to describe what my vision is like - it would be like asking you to describe colours to a person who has been blind from birth. My vision is more akin to that of birds. Not only does it allow me to see colours and shades beyond the ken of other people, it allows me to see into both the infrared and ultraviolet spectra. I might as well be a different species than you, Doctor."

"And did this feeling of difference alienate you, make you feel alone?"

The slight figure in the chair laughed, throwing back her head.

"As a girl I thought that everyone saw the way I do! No, I had a normal, happy childhood. I found out that I was different as I entered secondary school, but I never thought of myself as a freak. I thought that what I had was a gift, a talent. I felt like one of the X-Men!" She laughed again.

"I think anyone would consider such ability a great gift," said the doctor.

"If you had seen what I have seen, then you would think it a curse."

"So, when did you first see these 'monsters?'"

"Soon after my twenty-fifth birthday. I recall that day as if it were yesterday. I had visited Mount Osore in Amomori."

Dr Jumoni was familiar with the area, an axe-shaped peninsula in northern Honshu. The mountain itself was volcanic and was surrounded by a wasteland of barren rocks, sulphur pits and Lake Usoriyama, with its poisoned waters. Small wonder that the place had so many legends attached to it.

"Our ancestors used to think that Mount Osore was the gateway to Hell," he said.

"Perhaps they were correct. I was there to see the Osorezan Taisai Festival. I had an interest in anthropology back then; it has somewhat waned since. At the festival there were a number of itako - blind women, mediums who are supposed to be able to speak with the dead."

"You were trying to contact a relative who had passed on?"

Miss Ebisawa shook her head.

"No, no, I was just there to observe; I had no belief in such things. My interest was purely academic - I was an observer. One of the old itako grabbed hold of me. She said that she had been blind from birth, but could see in 'other ways,' just as I saw in other ways. We had never met before; don't ask me how she knew. She told me that I was in danger here, that there were *things* that I could see that no-one was supposed to see - things that did not like to been seen. I thanked her and walked away."

"You thought she was mad?"

"Quite mad, but I know differently now. I was stopping in the Bodaiji Temple near Lake Usoriyama. The smell of sulphur from the lake can be quite trying at times. I went out for a walk along the Sanzu River. Do you know it, Doctor?"

"Yes; it was once thought that souls crossed the red bridge there to escape from the underworld."

"Yes, and I saw them there - on that day, on the bridge. At first I thought they were some kind of firefly, but as I drew closer I saw that they looked like nothing so much as floating jellyfish. They pulsated many different colours - of the ones you would be able to see, blue - many shades predominated. I had no idea what they were. I returned to the temple and put the whole thing down to a trick of my super sense.

"I returned home. I worked as a secretary in the Ikebukuro district of Tokyo. The office I worked in had an amazing view and opposite it was the Sunshine high-rise block. One day, about a week after I had returned to work, I noticed colourful blobs moving around outside the Sunshine Tower. At first I thought that they were balloons, until I saw that they seemed to be moving of their own accord against the wind; so I looked closer, and I could see they were the same jellyfish-shaped lights that I had seen back in Amomori. I realised then that the things were some kind of life that, due to my condition, only I could see."

"And were you afraid of them?", asked the doctor.

"Oh, no, they had done me no harm. Are you familiar with the works of Trevor James Constable, Dr. Jumoni?"

The doctor shook his head and then, feeling somewhat foolish at forgetting she could not see him, said that he was not.

"He is an American author who believed that the phenomena we call UFOs were, in fact, living organisms. He theorised that large amoeba-like creatures lived in the atmosphere of earth. They were generally invisible to most humans, as they spent most of their time in a low-density state that was reflective only to infrared radiation. He claimed to have even photographed specimens using infrared cameras. I looked at the images he claimed were these creatures, and some of them looked passably like what I had seen.

"I began to see these things more often; as I was walking down the street, in the park. They didn't bother me until I saw a painted image of one in a book. The painting was over 300 years old. It called the jellyfish thing a 'Hito-dama;' these are ghost lights, the spirits of the newly-dead, according to legend."

"So you were able to see ghosts?"

"I didn't think they were ghosts. I reasoned that in the past there had been other people with my condition, people who could see these life forms and thought that they were ghosts - but then I began to see other things.

"I had begun to notice a strange smell, like rotting fish, in my flat. It had been there for several days and I couldn't find a source. Then I awoke one night in my apartment to see something squatting at the edge of my futon. It was about the size of a chimpanzee. It had an ape-like body covered in damp brown hair. The worst thing about it was the face - it had the, hairless, wrinkled face of an old man. The thing was chewing on a dead fish with sharp little teeth in a wide mouth. It made an awful crunching sound. I think it realised I was awake and noticed that I could see it. It turned its yellow eyes on me with a look of surprise, then disgust. It just sat there and glared at me. I was too afraid to move, or even scream. I lived alone and my apartment door was locked. Even if I could summon help, by the time they got in the thing would have had its teeth buried in my throat."

"So what did you do?"

"I just lay there, looking back at it all night, until the first rays of dawn, then it scuttled out of the door and vanished. I could find no trace of it. I tried to convince myself it was a bad dream, but that ghastly fishy smell persisted.

"It was back again the next night, and the night after that. It never did anything except squat there, looking at me, but I got such a feeling of disgust from it that it was almost as bad as a physical attack. I resented the fact that I could see it and it hated me."

"Did you know what it was?"

"I found its picture online. It was a Hyosube, a water-dwelling imp. It dawned on me that my vision now allowed me to see spirits and monsters invisible to others, but it seemed that now they had noticed that I could see them and were showing an interest in me.

"I visited a monastery to ask for advice; I was never a religious person and it felt silly. On the monk's suggestion I burned some incense and said some prayers, but it did no good - the Hyosube was there again in the night, watching me. Then the monks wrote out sutras for me to hang about the flat. It seemed to work, for a while at least - the creature vanished. But outside the apartment I could still see yokai. The city was crawling with them.

"On my way to work I would see Kitsune and Tanuki walking upright, like men. Along the canals, I saw Kappa lurking in the water, unseen by passers-by, and Gaki, hungry ghosts, scavenging around bins, eating filth. I began to research these things... yokai, like some kind of ghoulish, terrified birdwatcher.

"Back in my flat, creatures of sterner stuff than the water imp had breeched the protection of the sutras. I found my dresses in shreds, and in my cupboard a weird creature with a head like a bird, pincers like a crab, and a body like an elongate lobster. It was busy ripping every item of clothing I had to bits. I recognised it from my online searches as an Ami-kiri. It reared up, trying to snap at my face with its pincers. I tried to beat it way with a broom, but its pincers splintered the wood to matchsticks and it ran from my flat.

"I stayed in a hotel that night as I tried to think of something I could do. At around 1 a.m. I heard something bumping softly at the window of my hotel room. Drawing back the sash, I saw a human head floating in mid-air. The room was ten storeys up! The head had no body attached; it was just a man's head looking in at me with an expression of longing. It was bumping the window softly and licking at the glass. I saw it had sharp teeth. I knew it was a Nukekubi, a weird kind of vampire unique to Nippon. By day they look and act like normal humans, but at night their heads detach from their bodies and fly about, attacking people and drinking their blood. I felt I was being hunted, and it was all because my vision allowed me to see them.

"I reasoned that, if I could not see them, they would no longer wish to harm me. I consulted with the monks again. The abbot told me that he could tattoo my whole body, including my head, after shaving, with sutras that would render me invisible to yokai. I told him that I would never consent to such a thing. He gave me a charm to wear about my neck and sent several monks to bless my apartment and perform rites. Other residents noticed and stories began to circulate."

"What sort of stories?"

"About my apartment being haunted."

"I take it these rites failed again?"

"Once more there was a quiet period when nothing happened. In a weird way, I was adapting to my new condition. I was getting used to seeing horrors slithering and hopping the streets every day. Nothing could get into my flat, or at least that's what I thought. I began to feel safe again."

"What happened?"

"Something further up the yokai food chain than water imps and vampire heads noticed me."

"What kind of something?"

"I visited the Hie-Jinja Shrine at Chiyoda. I felt safer in crowds, and I knew the shrine would be thronging with tourists. As you may know, you have to walk up through a tunnel of torii gates. Sitting on top of that tunnel of gates was an Otoroshi."

"A what?"

"An Otoroshi, the guardian of the torii. It is written in legend that they destroyed anyone impure they detected as they walked through the luminal space of the gate from the profane to the sacred. I saw this thing sitting there - a mass of shaggy, dangling hair over a vaguely-man-like shape. Bigger than a gorilla, it had massive hooked claws. I could make out little of the face because of the hair, save for curving tusks; I am profoundly glad of that fact. But I knew it could see me quite clearly.

"It leapt down from the torii gates and came bounding towards me on all fours, like some insane ape. I screamed and ran. I'm sure those around me thought I was insane. It was almost at my back as I barged through crowds of tourists. I lost it when I ran out into the road - I was almost hit by a car."

The doctor walked over to where Miss Ebisawa sat.

"If these things you see are really there, and not just manifestations of your mind, then why is it that no other tetrachromats report them?"

"I don't know. Maybe they do and people take no notice. Perhaps something triggered it in me at Mount Osore. Maybe other tetrachromats who see these things go missing. Have you thought to ever cross-check with the police what percentage of missing people are tetrachromats?"

"No, it never occurred to me."

"Maybe you should. Anyhow, I knew I couldn't keep on living the way I was."

"And that's when you checked yourself in here?"

"Yes. Now I have peace. I wear a blindfold most of the time. On the rare occasions I take it off,I make sure that I am looking at blank white surfaces."

"After seeing in so many colours, isn't that difficult?"

"It is a blessed relief. I am free of the horrors that tormented me. This room is not a prison, doctor, it is a stronghold. I am perfectly sane, but I do not mind living here, in a madhouse; it is preferable to death."

The doctor walked back to the door.

"Thank you for taking time to see me, Miss Ebisawa. Our talk has been most enlightening. May I come and speak with you again?"

"Certainly, doctor. Your conversation is far more stimulating than that of the orderlies."

Back in the garden, the two doctors walked over towards the car park.

"Well what did you make of her?" asked Dr. Ajibana.

"She has the most detailed delusion I have ever come across. It's early days yet, but I'd like to make a detailed study of her, if she will let me."

The older man nodded in agreement.

"Yes, yes, of course. We may be on the brink of discovering a whole new mental state. To my knowledge, no person with her condition has ever been examined from a psychological viewpoint."

The two men shook hands as Dr Jumoni climbed into his car.

"Let me know how she gets on," he said as he drove away.

Miss Ebisawa's words played on Dr Jumoni's mind. In the following weeks, he contacted a number of police departments around the country, explaining his research; most were happy to help. A startling pattern emerged - a significant percentage of missing people were tetrachromats, as high as 10% in some areas. Given how rare the condition was, this was clearly significant. He needed to talk with Miss Ebisawa again.

Before he had the chance, Dr. Ajibana contacted him with an alarming e-mail.

```
Dear Dr Jumoni,

     A terrible event has occurred at the
hospital. A nurse visiting Miss Ebisawa this
morning found her missing from her room.
There was a quantity of blood in the room,
but no sign of Miss Ebisawa herself. A closer
examination turned up a horrific clue - a
pair of human eyes, presumably Miss
Ebisawa's, were found in a corner of the
room. They appear to have been gouged out.
The police were called and discovered what
looked like deep gouge marks in the walls of
her room. They currently have no idea what
made them. A search of the grounds and an
examination of security tapes have proved
fruitless. The police are now searching a
wider area.
```

Miss Ebisawa had been complaining lately of seeing colours even when her eyes are closed, and behind her blindfold. She said she was seeing colours triggered off by her own brain activity, and that she was now seeing monsters in those colours. She told me she thought an Oni was stalking her.

I will, of course, keep you posted on any further details.

Yours,

Dr Ajibana.

* * * * *

In the temple at Mount Osore there was a new Itako, one younger than the others. Like her sisters, she was blind; and, like her sisters, she now saw more than she had ever seen.

22. Juggernaut of Hunger

The crowds and the accompanying noise seemed odd to Wakai Aguri; he was used to the park being empty. For three years he had been working here on location as the chief designer of the rides and attractions. The noise of construction was one thing, but the screams of excited children were a different kind of sound altogether, one he would have to get used to. After three years of seeing no one but construction workers and technicians, he would have to mentally adjust to this horde of 'outsiders.' He checked himself. It was a stupid attitude; this was a theme park, and theme parks were created for the public - that's how they earned money.

Aguri always felt like this when a park opened. He had worked on dozens of them across Nippon for the past thirty years, swiftly becoming the leader in his field, but this park was different - this park was his brainchild, and it was unlike any other in the world. Aguri had always loved the ghost train as a child, and the hall of mirrors - the stranger, less visited attractions. He hated the saccharin of Disneyland and its imitators. Reading up on the history of fairs and sideshows in Nippon, he discovered a rich tradition of the ghoulish.

Many of the old fairs of the Edo period featured 'haunted houses' with mocked-up ghosts and monsters; this had given him the spark of an idea. It took years of planning, of course, and he had to find financial backers. Many were initially skeptical of his idea, but some businessmen had the imagination to share in his vision. This was the culmination of all of those long hard years - Yokai World.

The company backing Aguri had bought 300 acres of land just outside of the city of Fuchū in Hiroshima Prefecture, and turned it into a wonderland of horror. Yokai World was a celebration of the ghosts, monsters and strange creatures of Nippon's ancient legends. Where Disneyland had hired hands wandering around dressed as Mickey Mouse, Donald Duck or Goofy, Yokai World had its staff dressed as Kappas,

Tengus and Onis. The rides were all yokai-based - the Yakashi rollercoaster shaped like a giant slimy eel, and the Itsumaden death flight, where children were swung around at great speed inside of ghastly phantom birds suspended on wire. There was also the Tsuchigumo big wheel, shaped like a vast web with the monstrous Earth Spider squatting in the centre, and the house of the Tsukumogami, where inanimate household objects were given creepy life by animatronics.

Of course there was a haunted house full of groaning Yurei ghosts, faceless Noppera-bo, and savage phantom Inu-gami hounds. Even the food was yokai themed. There was a Yuki-onna ice-cream parlour, where 101 varieties of ice cream were being sold by beautiful girls all dressed as the legendary snow woman. The many eateries had suitably morbid names for the foods on offer - fish made to look like grotesque Ningyo mermaids with ape-like faces, and beef served up as Hakutaku, the man-faced ox of legend. The waitresses were dressed as Futa-kuchi-onna, complete with false mouths in the back of their heads; and, of course, the souvenir shops were overflowing with cuddly Tanukis (complete with huge testicles) and inanely-grinning Kijimuna dolls.

Yet all of this paled in comparison with what stood at the centre of the park - Aguri's finest work, his pride and joy, the creation he looked upon as his child, A ninety-foot-tall robotic skeleton with burning red eyes - Gashadokuro, the Juggernaut of Hunger. In myth, it was said to be a kind of colonial ghost organism, a giant skeleton made from the souls of famine victims who died en masse. The skeletal giant was supposed to roam around, continually trying to slake its hunger by biting off and eating human heads. It was one of the grimmest legends of Nippon, and a firm favourite with Aguri.

Gashadokuro was a miracle of robotics; even he had to admit that. A couple of decades ago, it was virtually impossible to create a bipedal, walking robot. The balance of human feet and legs, with their millions of sensory nerve endings and the workings of the inner ear, were impossible to regulate. How times had changed! Gashadokuro could move and walk with perfect poise and balance, despite its 200-ton bulk; the key was its brain.

It could be argued that Gashadokuro was not a robot, but a cyborg. Its brain contained organic matter. As well as electric circuits, an efficient biological network was housed in the brain made from the slime mould *Physarum polycephalum*. The idea had been pioneered years before in England, where simple robots had been driven by the autonomous oscillatory activity of the slime mould. In Gashadokuro, the same organism had created an intricate neural net. Aguri found it amusing that once a week he had to sprinkle oatmeal into the giant steel skull to feed the organic component. *A cyborg whose brain was powered by porridge - priceless!*

Strange as it seemed, the plasmodium brain linked to the millions of sensors inside the giant cyborg's body gave the titanic construction perfect balance, enabling it to walk about like an outsized man.

Aguri had seen it perform dozens of times during the tests; he never failed to be impressed. A ninety-foot walking steel skeleton - that would scare any kid. Ever the perfectionist, Aguri had researched the legends well. In ancient tales, the coming of a Gashadokuro was heralded by a ringing in the ears. Aguri had fitted resonators into his creation that transmitted infrasound at 19 Hertz, creating a vague ringing in the ears of anyone near it, as well as a sense of unease.

And now he stood with Mr. Yakimoto, his chief backer, and Chikamatsu Sachi, the mayoress of Fuchū, surrounded by television crews and members of the press. The park was already swarming with people, and he was about to flick the switch which gave Gashadokuro life.

With an uncanny smoothness, the steel skeleton rose from its crouching position. The red lights in its eye sockets flickered into life. The head, the size of a small bungalow, swivelled as if looking for prey. There were gasps from the crouds, both the media and public.

"Gatchi-gatchi," it said as it ground its metallic teeth together. The arms, as long as pines, swung up, and the skeletal hands began clutching with an ardent longing. As programmed, it strode towards the Ayakashi rollercoaster in order to thrill those riding upon it.

The rollercoaster had been designed so that, rather than sitting in cars on the tracks, the riders were suspended in harnesses below, giving them the feeling of flight. As the Gashadokuro lumbered towards them, they screamed in delighted excitement.

The giant paused, watching the tiny patrons whizz by as it repeated to itself "gatchi-gatchi". The infrasound ossilations only added to the thrill.

"This is amazing, Aguri san!", exclaimed the mayoress. "The monster is so life-like - better than anything from Hollywood!"

Aguri bowed and smiled, knowing that she spoke the truth.

"Sachi san, the Gashadokuro is the culmination of years of work. I am very proud of him; he is my baby!"

The mayoress laughed. "I hope he doesn't give anyone a heart attack."

The film crews and reporters all had their cameras trained on the huge cyborg as it stood swaying by the rollercoaster. Suddenly one of the great hands swept up and snatched at the passing riders. They were plucked from their moving harnesses like fruit from the branches of a tree. The excited cries of the onlookers turned into screams of horror as the metal monster transferred the still-living people into its huge jaws and began to chew.

The masticated flesh fell in rills of gore from the lower jaw as the the horror tried to swallow its prey without dint of a throat. It grabbed more victims as the crowds looked on in mute astonishment; again, they were tossed into the steel maw, which bit down greedily.

Someone had managed to switch off the Ayakashi rollercoaster. It ground to a shuddering, halt but it had left a number of park visitors hanging in mid-air, like cherries from a branch. Gashadokuro lost no time in plucking the hapless families from the ride and transferring them into its mouth for processing. More pulped human flesh fell through the bottom jaw, splattering onto the neck vertebra and rib bones. The crunching was clearly audible above the panicked screams of the public.

Chikamatsu Sachi had fallen in a dead faint beside him, and Aguri was vaguely aware of someone shouting at him. He turned and saw Mr Yakimoto yelling, half in rage and half in terror. "Aguri, switch the damn thing off!"

Aguri was furiously pressing buttons on his control unit, to no avail. "I don't understand! He's only programmed to go through a pre-determined set of actions. I can get it back under control."

Yakimoto looked sick. "You realise that you have ruined my company. The families of those people will sue; you and I will be charged with manslaughter!"

"I've switched off the power, but it's still moving."

"God, man, didn't you test the damn thing?"

"You know I did - again and again. You were here yourself for most of the tests."

Gashadokuro raised its steel fists and smashed through the rollercoaster, shattering the tracks and supports. It lumbered across the park looking for food, crashing through another section of the rollercoaster. The panicked crowds were rushing for the exits, many being trampled underfoot by their terrified fellow patrons.

"Gatchi-gatchi," the cannibal giant said, as it scooped up handfuls of the fleeing and fallen, and began its gleeful chewing and pointless swallowing.

Aguri found a microphome and a TV camera shoved into his face as he realised that one of the film crews had turned their attention to him.

"Wakai san, can you tell us what is happening? Can you bring the Gashadokuro back under control?"

Aguri shoved them out of his way.

"Where are you running to?" shouted Yakimoto.

"The main control tower. There is another control unit for the cyborg in there; this was just a mobile one I used for the show."

Yakimoto stooped to pick up the still-prone Sachi before she was crushed by the barging crowd.

Aguri scrambled up the stairs, not trusting the lift in case whatever electronic malady had infected his creation had spread elsewere. At the top of the hundred-foot tower, he began a total shutdown of the park. From his viewpoint, Aguri could see hideous destruction being wreaked upon the park. His dream was being destroyed by the greatest and most valuable attraction there.

Gashadokuro had wrenched loose a fifty-foot section of support from the remains of the rollercoaster, and was using it to skewer fleeing humans with horrid accuracy. Several dozen were impaled on the steel spike like a human shish kebab. The ravenous giant paused to bite away at the corpses. When it had picked the support clean, it tossed it across the park.

Aguri realised that the events must have been captured on hundreds of mobile phones and cameras, as well as by the TV crews - people would be screaming for his blood. Now all the park rides had been shut off, and the whole of Yokai World was without power. He knew that Gashadakuro had batteries as backups, but these would only last so long. He prayed that the titan could be held in the park until all its power had run out, yet still he could not fathom how it had gotten away from manual control and had broken its programme. It had to be something to do with the organic component in the brain. The slime mould must have grown new networks he had not seen, networks that were acting as new neural pathways, creating new behaviour patterns that no-one could have predicted. The cyborg replica was acting exactly like the legendary creature that it was based on!

Aguri peered out of the control tower window once more. His 'child' was continuing its reign of terror, turning its attention to the big wheel. It grasped the spider's-web-shaped structure and violently shook it. The people in the cradles were jerked loose and fell. The monster caught a number of them and devoured them. Ripping the big wheel free of its moorings, it sent the ferris rolling across the park, smashing into other rides, several of which burst into flame.

Striding over to the haunted house, constructed to resemble a pagoda of the Asuka period, Gashadokuro ripped the larch and pine roof. Fleeing patrons had crammed into the five-storey structure and were hiding from the nightmare outside. The nightmare now reached in and withdrew its hand, clutching a mass of hapless victims. Again and again the arm reached down and the hand transferred the flesh to the mouth, like a greedy child at a chocolate box. Finally, Gashadokuro simply pushed the pagoda over, sending it crashing down in a cloud of splintered wood and dust.

Aguri heard the distant sound of police sirens. Looking over to the car park, he saw chaos where panicking families desperately trying to exit the park had crashed. Some cars had overturned; others had jack-knifed. The exits were blocked. A number of police cars had pulled up outside of the exit, but were unable to enter the park. Swarms of people were escaping on foot, scrambling over the cars or clambering over the fences. It looked as if the police were trying to question them, with little luck.

Gashadokuro had heard the noise and turned its vast head. Aguri guessed that the ossilators that created its infrasound effect could now also pick up sound and direct it to the brain. Leaving the ruined pagoda, it ran over to the car park. Its massive, skeletal feet crushed cars like pop cans. It reached down and lifted a car up, biting into it. The police seemed to be calling for backup. What good extra police cars would do against a ninety-foot-tall, steel cyborg skeleton, he could not guess.

Several of the police had drawn their guns and were firing at Gashadokuro as it stooped to grab another car. The cyborg did not even register such pinpricks. Flinging the car down, it strode over to the park's entrance gates in pursuit of the fleeing masses. Aguri's hope that it could be contained in the park had been shattered. Most of the fleeing people were running back towards the city of Fuchū, barely three miles away. He knew that the monster would be there in no time, and winced at the thought of the carnage it would wreak. Hundreds upon hundreds of deaths would be upon his hands.

Aguri descended from the tower and walked through the ruins of his dream. Fires were still blazing. Body parts were strewn about like ghastly bunting. The park was empty, the people had fled, and the horror he had created had pursued them. His only hope was that the back-up battery cells in the giant cyborg would run out quickly; the monster had been performing far more energetic acts than it was programmed for.

On reaching the gate and squeezing past the wreckage of mangled cars, he saw a police car still *in situ.* An officer was speaking into a police radio; he looked pale and shaken. Aguri approached him.

"Officer?"

The man looked up. "Do you know what the hell went on in there? What was that … that THING?"

His voice sounded shaky; Aguri could understand. Feelings of unreality and mental detachment were already beginning to blanket him; he suspected it was some kind of inner defence mechanism.

"I'm the man who built it." Aguri fumbled for his park ID card.

"Get in," said the officer, opening the door.

As they drove, Aguri tried his best to explain what had happened.

"Best leave it 'til we get to town. The Special Assault Team will be there - you can tell everything you know to the Inspector. This is beyond me, or any of my team."

As they drove closer to Fuchū, the trail of destruction became apparent. The roads were littered with crashed cars. A coach had been overturned and its roof ripped off. The motorway was jammed with the vehicles of those fleeing the city.

The officer pulled over and used his radio to ask for advice. He turned with a grim look to Aguri.

"It's reached the city. The SAT is trying to contain it."

The officer drove like a madman through the city suburbs, swerving wildly to avoid cars and fleeing people. Fuchū was a small city with little skyline; it didn't take them long to find the Gashadokuro or the SAT.

The cyborg was at Fuchū Station. The SAT was peppering it with fire from sub-machine guns, which it was ignoring. The giant had already ripped up a lamppost from outside the station, and was using it to bludgeon the building. The station was swiftly becoming rubble.

One of the SAT team in a flak jacket and mask barked at the officer, "What's that civilian doing here?"

Above the chatter of gunfire and the crashes of falling bricks, the officer answered. "This is Wakai Aguri. He built the damn thing!"

The SAT officer looked surprised momentarily, then ran, head-down, to another team member, who returned with him, an older man with white-streaked hair.

"I'm Inspecter Cino of the Special Assault Team. This man tells me you are responsible for this thing?"

"Well, yes - I designed and built it."

"Then how do we stop it man?!"

Aguri shook his head. "It was built as an attraction at the theme park, but it's out of control."

"That's putting it mildly."

"It won't respond to remote control. It's broken its programming and gone wild. Bullets won't stop it; the frame is constructed from tungsten steel. It's built to support 200 tons."

A look of exasperation flickered across Inspector Cino's face. "We have informed central government. The defence minister thought it was some kind of joke at first. The Air Self Defence Force from Tsuiki Airbase have been scrambled; they are sending Mitsubishi F-2 fighters. They think they can take the thing down with sidewinder missiles if they can get it out in the open, away from civilians. Trouble is, they won't get here for nearly an hour yet, and the thing is in the middle of the damn city. The Central Army have been informed, but they will take even longer to get here. This toy of yours could kill hundreds of people by then. For now it's just us and it, and we are not equipped to deal with this thing."

Aguri was thinking fast. "Inspector, it is on auxiliary power. Its battery cells can't last forever. If we can keep it busy, it may run out of power."

"We are created to deal with terrorism, not fight some mekka escapee from a manga."

The Gashadokuro had turned its attention back to the men who were peppering its steel frame with bullets. It hurled the lamppost at the them, scattering the ranks.

"Pull back!" shouted the Inspector, and the men obeyed.

Aguri, the police officer and Inspector Cino ran down a side street, then around the back of a block of flats where the SAT was regrouping. Some of them had pulled out heavier artillery - shoulder-mounted rocket launchers. Others were priming them.

As the glittering giant came into view around the side of the building, the inspector gave the order to fire. The M9 bazookas spat their deadly payload. Flowers of fire blossomed around the torso of the steel giant. It stopped in its tracks, rocked backward, and then lumbered forward again. As the smoke cleared, it became apparent that the bazookas had done little more damage than the machine guns; the metal ribcage hardly seemed dented.

"Split up! Confuse it!", the inspector shouted. The men scattered down side streets like mice. The Gashadokuro swung its head from side to side as it murmured, "gatchi-gatchi."

The strategy had bought them time as the monster had trailed some of the other men, who lost it in a network of back streets. It was now ripping the roofs off houses and searching for victims inside.

"Any idea why this thing went AWOL?", asked Inspector Cino.

"Its brain has an organic component - slime mould."

"You mean it has fungus for a brain?" said the police officer, who thought it was safest to stay close to heavily-armed men.

"No," Aguri replied. "A slime mould is not a fungus; it's much more complicated than that. Look, inside that monster's head it's not just circuits, there is a network of protoplasmic veins, and many nuclei formed by a *Physarum polycephalum* in the plasmodium stage."

Both the Inspector and the officer said "What?" at the same time.

"I'll put it in layman's terms. Think of a slime mould as a collection of cells that can move and act as one organism. It is linked in with the manmade computer components in the cyborg's brain; however, the organism has mutated, causing a primitive thought pattern in the cyborg and making it act against its programming. Do you understand? It has grown in a way we could not foresee."

"Well, I can just about get the basics of it," said the Inspector, "but what I want to know is how to take it down."

"Is there any way of damaging the brain?", asked the police officer, whose name Aguri had not got around to asking.

"It's encased in a skull made of foot-thick steel. Bullets won't do any good, that's for sure."

The officer scratched his chin. "You said that slime moulds are not really fungi, despite the name?"

"Yes, they are a colony of amoeba that act together as one organism. They may act like fungi at times."

"Can't they be killed with fungicide?"

Aguri grabbed the officer by the shoulders. "Christ, man, you may be onto something! Yes, certain copper-based fungicides can kill slime mould - something like Dithane or Manzeb."

"How would we get it into the brain through that steel skull?", asked Cino.

"The skull has cooling vents on each side of it. They pass air over the brain to keep it from overheating. If we can get the fungicide into one of the vents, it will be drawn into the brain and poison the slime mould. In effect, it would act like an aneuyrism."

"I could get one of the tech boys to take the explosive charge out of some of the bazooka shells. We could fire them up at the thing's head," said the inspector.

"It's as good an idea as any," replied Aguri.

"I know where there is a hardware and garden store," said the officer. "It's in a mall a couple of blocks from here."

They followed the officer through the streets to the mall. There were crowds of people hiding inside. On seeing Cino's uniform, many ran over.

"What's happening?"

"Is that thing still outside?"

"Are you with the army?"

"Have the army stopped it?"

The panicked questions came thick and fast.

Cino raised his arms for silence. "I am Inspector Cino of the Special Assault Team. My men are tackling the menace as we speak. My colleagues and I need to collect something from the mall that will help us neutralise it."

He pushed his way through the crowd as the officer pointed out the way to the garden store.

"But just what is it?" a woman asked.

"A fairground attraction gone insane," said Aguri.

Once in the shop, Aguri swiftly located a number of large plastic jars of Manzeb.

"Powdered form," he whispered. "Excellent."

Between them the three carried as much of the fungicide as they could hold and ran back out into the street. If any of the crowd wondered how they were going to fight a ninety-foot-tall cyborg skeleton with fungicide, no one asked.

The sound of battle drew them back to the monster's location. It was still in a built-up area of business and residential blocks. The team had re-grouped and were peppering the monster with bazooka shots. They leaned out from corners and shot before retreating again. The creature occasionally hurled a car at the SAT, but otherwise paid more attention to ripping off the sides of buildings and reaching in after its prey.

Cino raced over to a small bunch of his men who had taken cover behind an overturned lorry. They spoke briefly and then rushed over to where Aguri and the police officer waited.

"We can open the shell, remove some explosive, and fill the main body with powder. The remaining explosive should be enough to crack the shell open and scatter the fungicide powder."

"You will need to aim for the side of the head. Imagine you were shooting at the ears, if it had any," said Aguri.

Several men busied themselves with the shells, gutting them swiftly and filling the insides with Manzeb powder.

From around the corner came a crash; as they looked up they saw a blazing car come crashing down barely fifty feet away. A number of men ran across the street opposite, and the Gashadokuro lumbered in pursuit, following them off down another street.

"Damn!" snapped Cino. "I was hoping they could hold it."

When the men had finished adapting the shells, the group followed the monster's trail.

"You need to get up high. Get a clear head shot from the same level," said Aguri.

The inspector nodded. "I'll try to get into one of the tower blocks."

At the far end of the street, ignoring the SAT attacks, the Gashadokuro was busy poking its huge metal fingers through the windows of a block of flats. It was feeling around for prey.

Aguri, the officer, and Cino barged through the doors of an office block on the opposite side of the road. They bounded up the stairs to the tenth floor, ignoring the confused looks of the few people hiding beneath desks. Cino carried the bazooka, and the others several more doctored shells. Cino kicked open a door and ran across the office. He had a perfect view of the Gashadokuro as it plucked a wriggling, screaming victim from a flat and dropped him into its snapping steel jaws. "Gatchi-gatichi." It seemed to moan in delight.

Aguri opened the window and Inspector Cino shouldered the bazooka.

"Stand back," he said.

The officer and Aguri backed off, and Cino took aim. He squeezed the trigger, and the weapon roared and spat its payload. The shell tore across the gap between the buildings. Cino's aim was true, and the shell struck the giant skull, exploding in a cloud of fungicidal powder. The cooling system in the skull sucked the cloud in like an extractor fan.

Gashadokuro ceased its gleeful groping and stood. It turned to look at the office block, the camera eyes sending images to its visual circuits.

Cino lowered the bazooka and began to reload, doing what was supposed to be a two-man job. The monster crossed the street in two strides, its ghastly steel-skull face now level with the office window. It peered in with an awful fixed leer. The massive metal teeth and jaws were befouled with human gore that was beginning to stink.

The infrasound rung in the men's ears, turning guts to jelly. "Gatchi-gatchi," the hellish giant muttered.

Cino backed away from the window. "It's facing us directly - I can't get a shot at the side of the head."

Aguri grabbed a chair and ran across the office, hurling it at the next window along. As the glass shattered, the Gashadokuro turned its massive head. Cino fired again, almost at point-blank range. He instantly dropped to the floor to avoid the flying shards of casing as the shell exploded on the side of the metal skull in another cloud of Manzeb powder.

Turning back, the Gashadokuro smashed its hand through the window and began groping with long, spidery, metal fingers. Cino rolled out of the way as they ran along the office floor, ripping up the carpet as they drew back.

All three men backed up against the far wall. The Gashadokuro withdrew its hand. They made a dash for the office door and were barely through it when the steel talons reached in again, scratching at the far wall and splintering the door.

In seconds they were on the stairs and scrambling down.

"Two direct hits," gasped Cino.

"I hope that's enough," said the officer. "How long does this stuff take to work?"

"I've no idea," answered Aguri. "There was a whole jarful in each shell, so it's a massive dose. I only hope it works."

As they reached the bottom of the stairs, Cino paused to reload. They ran across the reception and out through the doors. Looking up, they saw the huge cyborg looking down at them. It bent down, the huge skull moving closer to its tiny prey. As it did so, Cino fired the third shell directly into its face. The exploding shell coated the cameras in its eye sockets with Manzeb powder.

The monster withdrew, shaking its huge head from side to side. The three men turned and ran as fast as they could back up the street. Thunderous footseps behind them indicated that the Gashadokuro had wiped the powder from its electronic eyes and had set off after them.

Behind them, they heard the awful "gatchi-gatchi" of the flesh-eating horror. Turning a corner, they found themselves close to a small city park. They made a run for a copse of trees in the park.

The Gashadokuro thundered after them. As they dodged between the trunks of the trees, their towering pursuer began to tear at the canopy with steel claws, ripping away branches like twigs.

"Gatchi-gatchi," it cried again, but this time the roar sounded quieter, less powerful. The giant backed away from the trees and clutched its head. It began clumsily stamping about the park in what looked like some kind of slow-motion, demented dance.

"It's working!" shouted Aguri.

All three men slipped out from their hiding places to watch the bizzare spectacle. The Gashadokuro was waving its arms in the air wildly as it staggered to and fro. It would stop to claw at its own skull and violently shake its head. The red lights in its eyes were flickering as it let out inarticulate groans; then, with a creaking of tortured metal that set the teeth on edge, the Gashadokuro toppled. All ninety feet and 200 tons came crashing down face-first across the park. The great skeleton shuddered once, then lay still.

"Is it dead?", asked the officer, as they gingerly approached.

"I sincerely hope so," said Aguri.

A yellow slime was oozing from its eye sockets and out through the tiny ventilation holes in the sides of its head.

"The slime mould, I take it?" Cino crouched to look closer at the smouldering organic goo.

"The cause of all this," Aguri said.

Above them, several F-2 fighters streaked across the sky.

"You're too late, guys," mumbled the officer.

Cino shook his head. "You know, I'm sure the army will want to have a look at this. Think of the military implications. Imagine a whole army of these things striding across a battlefield!"

"There is still something I don't understand," said Aguri. "Why did the brain take on the characteristics and the behaviour of the legendary Gashadokuro?"

"You didn't programme it that way?", said the officer.

"God, no. It's programme only allowed it to do a number of simple actions."

Cino chipped in. "I recall the story; my father told it to me as a boy. The Gashadokuro was a giant skeleton made from the souls of hundreds of dead famine victims. It craved human flesh to sate the hunger of the ghosts that made it. One of them was supposed to have turned up in the old Bingo Province hundreds of years back."

The officer looked up. "Bingo Province used to be in what is now eastern Horishima Prefecture - just where your park was built."

Some horrible thought was creeping into Aguri's head.

"When we first started building the park we came across human skeletons, hundreds of them - all ancient. We knew if we told anybody the development would be delayed, or even stopped. The whole area would be deemed an important archaeological site. Millions and millions of yen down the drain."

"What did you do?" asked Inspector Cino.

"We destroyed them. All of them. Hundreds of them. We had them ground up into powder."

Cino looked back at the metal giant. "Perhaps they all died of starvation."

Aguri said no more, and all three walked briskly away into the coming dusk.

23. Witchcraft of the Venomous Rats

The Kyushu summer was hot and muggy. The Hita district sat in a natural basin surrounded by mountains. It caught the heat and held it; even after dark, it could be uncomfortable.

The little, shabby inn up a side street in the town of Ōyama was overcrowded, and the heat was making the patrons irritable and argumentative. The wandering rōnin Ryuu had left his heavy armour in his room. He sat in a light shirt and knee-length trousers. On his feet were comfortable sandals. His meal had been surprisingly good for such a tatty little inn; now he was enjoying a bowl of sake.

His wandering had taken him all the way up from Kagoshima in search of a new master. Here and there he found small jobs dealing with brigands and protecting merchants on lonely roads, but nothing lasting.

Ryuu had sat himself in the corner. Several fights had already broken out in the hot, overcrowded inn - he wanted no part of it. He was only interested in fighting if he was being paid.

A burly, drunken man barged into Ryuu, knocking the sake from his hands.

"Out of the way, filth," spat the man.

Ryuu felt the fury rise inside him, but kept calm. Another man, more scrawny than the first, appeared behind him.

"This weasel causing you trouble?", he sneered.

The first man nodded. "The stranger was in my way."

"The stranger needs to be taught a lesson," said the first man, reaching into one of his sleeves. His larger friend followed suit, reaching down into his pocket. By the time both men had drawn dirty-looking knives, Ryuu had whipped his shōtō up from his side, and slit the throat of

---

the first and the belly of the second. Both fell back, gurgling and screaming respectively, in two fountains of red.

The noise of the inn ceased instantly as all eyes fell on the rōnin and the dying thugs.

"Oh no, just look at the mess," shouted the landlord, as he rushed over red-faced and flustered.

"Don't worry about it. I'm sure this pair have enough stolen coins on them to cover any inconvenience."

The landlord was not so easily placated. "But my reputation! You have just killed two men in cold blood in my inn!"

Ryuu stifled a laugh. "Your reputation? I've been here less than a week and I've seen ten fights and two murders. Besides, it was not in cold blood - these two drew knives on me. You know as well as I do they were troublemakers."

The landlord, seeing he was beaten on all counts, shook his head and shouted for assistance. Two men from the kitchen emerged.

"Take this pair outside. Dump them at the end of the street."

Without batting an eyelid, the men dragged the still-twitching corpses out of the inn.

"And when you get back, mop up the blood," shouted the landlord.

It seemed to Ryuu that both the landlord and staff were used to such events. He began to clean the blood off his shōtō.

"That was impressive."

Ryuu looked up to see a smartly-dressed, middle-aged man standing before him.

"Not really, they were a pair of drunken peasant brigands - hardly a real threat."

The man smiled. "You do yourself a disservice, san. You obviously have training."

Ryuu nodded and continued to clean his short sword.

"Excuse me for being so forward, san, but I am looking for a warrior."

Ryuu looked up again. "Why?"

"My master is Oshiro Akako. I am his retainer, Honda Goro." He gave a bow before continuing.

"Oshiro sama is a very old and very rich man. He believes that his life is under threat and wants a bodyguard. He is willing to pay handsomely."

"And who does he think is trying to kill him?"

Goro frowned. "It is not a person, as such. It may be easier for my master to explain in person."

Ryuu looked around at the shabby lodgings and nodded. "Very well, let me collect my things. will be with you soon."

So it was that Ryuu, with his simple backpack, found himself walking the night time streets of Ōyama with the retainer of an elderly eccentric.

"Your master's name seems familiar."

Goro smiled. "He was a well-known noh actor in his younger days, one of the most celebrated in all Kyushu. You may have seen him on stage or read about his performances."

Ryuu nodded. "Yes, that's it. I think I may have seen him perform when I was a boy."

"After the death of his parents many years ago. he retreated to the house. My master never married or had any children."

"He lives alone, then?"

"No, he has younger siblings - a sister, Akene, and twin brothers, Mceta and Hayate. Then there is the old priest he now has living with him, Yasuhiro."

"A priest?"

"Yes, he thinks the old man's mummery will protect him."

"From what?"

"It is best that he tells you himself."

The Oshiro house was set in several acres of wooded parkland in one of the better areas of Ōyama. It was an old, large house, several storeys high. It had seen better days, but Ryuu was sure that with a little attention it could be quite grand again. An outer wall surrounded the grounds.

Goro produced a large key and opened the outer gate. They walked through the ornate gardens to the door of the house and entered. In the hall Ryuu noticed an odd, disagreeable smell, despite the superficially-clean appearance. Goro led him through into the living room.

The Oshiro family, minus Akako, were all sat around on fine, if ageing, furniture. It was the sister that commanded attention first -Akene, who despite being at least 70, was dressed in the manner of a geisha. The porcelain-white lead face paint that would look so lovely on a young woman was cracking due to her wrinkles. Her hair was obviously dyed black, and pulled back tight in a Shimada knot at the base of her tortoise-like neck. An ornate Kanzashi nestled in her hair. She wore a long kimono with a decorative obi. The old woman lay stretched out on an overstuffed couch. Upon her lap a fat, bob-tailed cat sat. It was white with untidy patches of yellow and black. It eyed Ryuu as he entered the room. He noted that the cat had one blue eye and one yellow.

Moeta and Hayate were busy at some card game. Beside them was a large bottle of sake and two cups. Both men were considerably younger than their sister, being perhaps in their mid-fifties. They were startlingly alike, even for twins. They had thin, hollow-cheeked faces and small, active hands. They looked slender - almost feminine.

On a stool beside the fire sat Yasuhiro. The old priest was squat and shaven, save for the iron-coloured bristles sprouting from his chin. His robes looked faded. Ryuu could have imagined him more as some kind of vagrant than a holy man. He seemed to be pawing over some ancient books.

The old woman spoke first. "So you found someone to protect the fool?"

"This is Ryuu - he is a rōnin. I have seen his skill with a sword," said Goro.

"And where did you find him?", asked Hayate, without looking up from his game.

"At an inn in the town. He slew two ruffians who attacked him."

"So you brought a killer into the house from some grubby little hostel?" asked Moeta, as he reached for the sake.

"What's to stop him gutting us all in our beds and running off with our money?", added his brother.

"Such as we have," said Akene, with a barely-concealed bitterness.

"Please," Ryuu said, "I have taken the vow of a samurai and trained for many years. I served a master loyally until his old age took him. Since then I have been searching for a new master. I hope I have found that master in Akako san."

"Neither the sharpest sword nor the strongest arm will protect Akako san from what he fears." Yasuhiro looked up from his books. "Only my prayers and the sutras I hang about his doors will stop what wants his blood."

"And just what is it that Akako san fears so greatly?"

At the rōnin's question, the priest looked down again. It was clearly not his place to say.

"Our dear brother thinks he is haunted," piped up Moeta

"Haunted?"

"Oh, yes - hasn't Goro told you?", sneered Hayate. "Ordinary ghosts are not good enough for him."

"I don't understand."

"Akako fears he is being haunted by monster rats," laughed Moeta.

"Rats?"

"If there were any rats in this house, my darling Chkia would have killed them, wouldn't you?" Akene stroked the cat, which began to purr. Ryuu thought it looked too idle to stand up, let alone kill a rat.

Hayate slurped more sake noisily.

"Come," said Goro, "my master will explain things to you himself."

Goro led Ryuu along a corridor and up two flights of stairs to the old man's bedroom. Sutras written on scrolls were pinned to his door; he was clearly trying to keep something out. Goro knocked and a frail voice bade him enter.

The room was lit by wan candlelight. Rather than a futon, the old man had a bed on wooden legs. Ryuu guessed that the occupant might find getting up from the floor too hard. Down among the folds and creases of the sheets there was a wrinkled face; it seemed like some puppet made of weathered leather with a thinning top of grey hair.

"Akako san, I have brought you a protector, as you asked. This is Ryuu. He is a rōnin and a fine warrior."

The old man struggled to sit up and squinted at Ryuu. "Come closer, my boy."

Ryuu stepped forward.

"You are young and strong - that is good. Your blade will protect me from them."

"I understand you have a problem with rats, Akako san."

"Indeed I do. Tell me, what do you know of rats?"

"Very little san, other than that they are brothers to mice, they spread disease, and follow man wherever he goes."

"Rats are truly remarkable creatures, my boy. You should never underestimate rats. You know there are *hundreds* of rats here."

"Why do you not just lay traps and poison, san?"

"Rats grow immune to poison and wise to traps. Rats are the most adaptable of all creatures. They are found from the jungles and deserts to the frozen wastes of the far north. They live wherever man can live, and plenty of places he cannot. They are social and clever; they even have kings. Rats can eat almost anything. Rats can use tools. Rats can learn fast and multiply just as fast. Rats are survivors."

"You sound like you admire them, san."

"Oh, but I do, Ryuu, I do. But you see. these are no ordinary rats. Tell me what do you know of the history of Mii-Dera Temple?"

"Nothing."

"It is quite a story. Back in the days of Emperor Shirakawa, there was a great rivalry between the monks of Mii-Dera and the warrior monks of Enriyaku-ji. Mii-Dera was burnt to the ground four times. Ah … we humans, even our holy men make war. Anyhow, the Emperor wanted a son to succeed him. He asked a monk called Ragio of Mii-Dera to pray on his behalf for a strong son. In return the Emperor would grant the monk a favour of his choosing.

Ragio prayed long and hard, and eventually the Emperor's wife gave birth to a boy, Prince Taurhito. The Emperor was delighted and returned to Mii-Dera to ask what boon Ragio would ask of him. The pious man said that he wanted but one thing - his own monastery, where he could train new novices who were taking up holy orders. The Emperor duly agreed.

"However, when this news fell upon the ears of the warrior monks of Enriyaku-ji, they became furious. These monks had much military and political power. It was said that there were three things Emperor Shirakawa could not control: the blowing of the winds, the roll of dice and the warrior monks of Enriyaku-ji. They put pressure on the Emperor, who went back on his promise to Ragio. Outraged, the monk starved himself to death in protest.

"Ragio was reborn as a horrid yokai known as Tesso, the Iron Rat. Tesso was a creature, part-man and part-rat, with iron teeth and claws. He fell upon the temple of Enriyaku-ji, leading an army of huge, savage, cunning rats. They swept through the temple ripping the monks' precious, irreplaceable scrolls to shreds. They devoured books and relics, and scattered the monks to the four winds.

"Tesso and his rat army terrorised the area until they were finally destroyed, and their carcasses cast into a huge pit somewhere in Ōyama."

"And you believe that Tesso and his horde of rats have returned to haunt you?"

The old man nodded solemnly.

"But why would he choose to haunt *you*? You have no connection to the monks of Enriyaku-ji, or Emperor Shirakawa."

"That is true. But last year I had a summerhouse built in the garden. When the men were digging the foundations they found the skulls of rats - huge rats - hundreds of them. They had stumbled on the grave of Tesso and his minions. By disturbing the pit, he set their spirits free; now they haunt me. I hear them at night, their furtive scrabbling in the walls and in the rafters. At night, always at night, they come scampering in the dark with their sharp teeth and long, naked tails and poison in their drool. Each night they draw closer. I can almost feel their teeth in my flesh, gnawing at my old frail bones. They come in their hundreds and at their helm is Tesso, the man-rat, the Iron Rat of Mii-Dera!"

Akako's eyes had taken on a strange lustre, and he sat up in bed looking about him, clutching the covers and staring into the shadows. The old man seemed to strain as if to catch some sound.

"Cannot you hear their scratching in the walls?"

"I cannot, Akako san; but my blades are here to fall upon anything that threatens you."

And so it was. By night Ryuu stood on guard outside his master's door; by day he ate and slept in a humble room. To be sure it was a strange job, guarding an old man from his own fears, but he was paid amply and it felt good to have a master once more, even if he were not a nobleman.

A number of days passed with no event save the old man's ever-more-paranoid ramblings about huge rats with venomous saliva. Then one day, a week or so after he had taken up his position, Ryuu heard a commotion in the garden, a woman's hysterical screaming. It could only be Akene. Ryuu hesitated, loath to leave his position, but his honour won through. The old man's fears were clearly in his head, but his sister was in distress.

Ryuu ran out into the twilight. The twins and the priest were already standing around the prone body of the woman. She lay near a rhododendron bush. Some smaller distorted object lay close by her prostrate form.

"She has merely fainted." Yasuhiro had been crouching beside Akene and now stood up. "It must have been the shock of finding her cat."

Ryuu looked down and saw Chkia, or what was left of her. The cat had been attacked and killed. Whatever had done it had eaten most of the body; only the head and some of the skin from the back and flanks remained.

"She has been torn to ribbons," squeaked Moeta. "What could have done that?"

"A wolf?" said his brother.

"Not so close to town. Wolves stay in the mountains and forests." Ryuu bent down to look more closely at the remains. "A fox, perhaps?"

"Or rats," mumbled Yasuhiro.

"Aren't cats supposed to kill rats?" asked Hayate.

"Not these kind, they aren't," whispered the priest, clutching at the charms about his neck.

Ryuu lifted up Akene, whose limp body was surprisingly heavy. "Never mind, we need to get Akene back inside. We can deal with this later."

Ryuu carried her into the house and laid her out on the couch. Hayate made tea whilst Yasuhiro gently tried to rouse her.

She awoke with a start and immediately began to screech and cry. Her tears made the white face paint run, dripping down onto her silk kimono.

"Oh, my little Chkia. My darling baby. What could have done that to her?"

"We think maybe a fox got into the garden," said Ryuu.

"A fox? A fox here? Go, take your sword; search the grounds and kill it!"

She was near hysterical. Ryuu thought it would be best for her nerves if he did as she asked, though he did not expect to find anything. Leaving the shrieking woman, he took up a lantern and went back out into the garden. It was becoming darker,and the shadows of the trees and bushes grew deeper, like ebony pool. Ryuu made a circuit of the grounds, shining his lamp into each and every shadow. He found nothing, but a fox could have easily scaled the wall or ran up a tree. The animal was probably miles away by now.

By the time he returned to the house, the others had put Akene to bed. Ryuu returned to his post, but heard his master calling him from inside his room.

"What is the matter, Ryuu? I heard my sister screaming."

"Akako san, she found her pet cat dead in the garden. It had been killed and eaten by some kind of animal. I am inclined to think it was a fox."

"It was no fox that killed Chkia - you mark me. The hordes of Tesso are growing bolder. Today they dine on cat flesh; tomorrow it will be man flesh."

"No rat shall pass through this door, Akako san."

The following day Goro went into town and came back with poison from the apocethary. He liberally scattered poisoned meat and grain about the garden. By morning the poisoned bait had gone, but there were no dead rats to be found.

Akene insisted that Yasuhiro perform a Buddhist ceremony over the body of the cat; it was then burned and the ashes collected in an urn that was placed in the garden. Afterwards Akene confined herself to her room, refusing to come out. Food and drink were brought in to her. Akako had Ryuu nail his shutters closed and secure them further with planks. The old priest pinned up more charms and sutras about his door and window. He too seldom left his room. The twins seemed not as worried as the others, and continued their lives as before - talk of monster rats and a ghostly rat man from Yasuhiro or Akako brought nothing but derisive laughter.

Again things seemed to slip back to normality, or the closest thing that the Oshiro household ever came to it. Occasionally Ryuu thought he could hear movements in the darkness, but he could never be sure. The strange old house and its queer inhabitants could have been affecting his imagination.

It was two weeks later when the next incident occurred. This time it was the dead of night when Akene's screams rang through the house. When Ryuu arrived at her door, Goro and Yasuhiro were already trying to force the door.

"It's locked from the inside," said Goro, who was ineffectually trying to put his shoulder to the wood. The old woman's screams had ceased and, worryingly, no sound issued from the room.

"Here, let me try." Ryuu, who had been trained in martial arts, tried forcing the door with his shoulder, but it held fast. Stepping back, he sent a blindingly-fast kick at the door. There was a sound of wood snapping. He kicked again and the door swung open.

The room was in darkness, the lamp having been blown out. The shutters at the window were open. Goro quickly relit the lamp from his candle. Akene lay upon the floor in her nightgown. Her hands seemed to be clutching at her chest, and upon her face was an expression of unutterable horror.

At that moment the twins arrived. "What has happened now? Why is she screaming again?" Moeta's eyes fell on his sister and his mouth abruptly closed.

Ryuu had seen death so often that he didn't need to check for a pulse, but he did anyway - the old woman was dead.

"Is she... ?", stammered Hayate.

Ryuu nodded gravely, and Yasuhiro bent over the body, mumbling prayers.

"Her face - it's horrid." Hayate could hardly choke out his words.

"What did this?" asked Moeta. "She looks terrified."

"Scared to death," Yasuhiro whispered as he fumbled with his charms and stared about the room.

"We will need to bring a doctor from the town. I will go now. Ryuu tell Akako san his sister is dead."

As Ryuu stood up, he saw something in the corner of his eye - just for an instant he saw something move near the windowsill.

"There!" he pointed, and they all looked as one but saw nothing.

"What?" asked Goro.

"I thought I saw something move by the window." In an instant Ryuu had snatched up the lamp and was peering down into the garden. He thought he heard a rustling in the creepers that ran up the side of the house, but, when he swung his lamp up, nothing was there. He went downstairs and into the grounds. Once more a thorough check of the grounds showed nothing untoward. As Goro left for the town, Ryuu returned to his master's room.

"Akako san, it is my sad duty to inform you that your sister has passed away."

The old man sat up in his bed. He looked sad but unsurprised. "I knew they would come for her, as they will come for us all."

"We do not know what she died of, master."

"I know. The rats have gotten to her - the rats of Tesso."

"Her body was unmarked as far as I could see, master."

"They have many ways to kill. But they'll not get me - oh, no. Not whilst you are here. Not whilst your blade is keen."

"Goro has sent for a doctor from the town."

"Yes, he is a good man. Yasuhiro will make the arrangements, no doubt. I am too old and ill. She will be laid with our ancestors in the family tomb. At least the rats did not worry her like they did her cat."

Goro returned with a physician from the town, a thin, worried little man with hair like threadbare thatch. The doctor seemed irritated to have been called out at such an hour. He busily examined the body for the better part of half-an-hour. When he was done, he addressed all assembled.

There are no marks or signs of violence save for a slight bruising where the lady tumbled from her bed. It would appear that she died of heart failure; however, never in my fifty years of practicing medicine have

I seen such a look upon the face of a deceased person. I would say that the heart failure I mention had been precipitated by the lady having been severely shocked by something immediately before death."

"You mean she was scared to death?" asked Hayate.

"You may say that."

The doctor proceeded to fill out paperwork, and then Goro escorted him home again.

Yasuhiro and the priest of a nearby temple presided over the ceremony. Akene was dressed in her finest kimono and made up like she was attending some grand ball. Her body was interred in the Oshiro family tomb alongside her mother and father. There were few mourners. The twins seemed to take it the worst, wailing like women. Akako was dressed in his best clothes, and yet, despite his smart appearance, he seemed disturbed, looking about him and jumping at the slightest noise. The old man was glad when he could return home to the safety of his increasingly-more-fortress-like room.

It seemed that the whole house was now in shutdown. The old man never left his room, and the twins were now being infected by the same reclusiveness as their brother. Goro did what he had to - cooking, running errands and so forth - but even he seemed withdrawn. Only old Yasuhiro was active, pacing up and down as he chanted, ringing bells and burning incense. All his mummery did no good; it was less than a week until the next incident.

Ryuu was disturbed at his post one night as Moeta came rushing along the corridor in his nightgown, screaming. He was clutching at his neck, and his gown was spattered with red.

"My neck - it bit my neck."

"What?" Ryuu ran forward to try to calm him before he woke Akako.

"A rat; it must have been a rat!"

"Did you see it?"

"No, it was dark. Something fell on me in the night. I felt its fur. It bit my neck. I threw it off and it escaped. It must have come through the window."

Ryuu moved the panicking man's hand. The bite was not deep, but was bleeding. It looked raw and swollen.

"I will rouse Yasuhiro; he knows a little medicine. Then I will search your room."

"It felt so big and heavy, larger than any rat I have ever known."

Ryuu awoke the old priest, whose eyes widened at the sight of Moeta's neck.

"They have struck again. We must bathe that wound and get ointment on it. I will prepare some charms for your room to guard against the beasts."

Ryuu ran to Moeta's room. Furniture was scattered and the dishevelled futon was speckled with blood. The shutters were open. Peering out, he could see that the sill was in leaping distance of the branches of one of the trees in the garden. He lifted a lamp to illuminate the tree, but could see nothing in its thick vegetation. He shut and bolted the shutters, then searched the room, but found no sign of the attacker.

In the morning Moeta was feverish. He sweated profusely and complained of a splitting headache. By the afternoon, he was vomiting and had diarrhoea. Goro when into town for a doctor.

The same little man as before returned. He looked at the bite mark and said it had become infected, leading to the fever. He left some tablets, handmade at his shop, telling Moeta to take two every four hours with water. He gave instructions for the patient to be kept warm and given plenty to drink.

That evening Moeta complained of stomach cramps. Later in the night he said his vision was blurring, and finally that he could not see. His brother sat with him and made sure he took the tablets the physician had left.

Hayate's wailing awoke everyone the next morning. Moeta lay pale and dead on his futon. Greenish vomit covered his nightgown. The doctor was summoned again. He examined the body and made a pronouncement.

"This man died of arsenic poisoning."

"What!" shouted Hayate. "He was bitten by a rat."

"Quite so," the doctor continued. "The bite on his neck was consistent with a rat's incisors, so I treated him for fever brought on by a rat bite; however, this is something different. Arsenic has been added to the wound and entered the bloodstream. See the discolouration of his fingernails and hair? This is indicative of arsenic in the blood."

Hayate turned to Yasuhiro. "You - you, priest, you put ointment on his bite. It must have had poison in it."

Yasuhiro looked horrified. "It was just ointment, a balm to stop the swelling."

Hayate would not be placated. "You are only here because Akako believes in your superstitious nonsense. He pays you. It's in your interest to keep his insane fantasies alive."

"But you heard him yourself, Hayate - he said he was attacked by a huge rat."

"He didn't actually see it; he just felt it in the dark. It could have been you attacking him with a poison blade. I'm fetching the town guard."

Hayate rushed out before anyone could stop him. Ryuu went to tell his master.

"I warned them all," the old man said, "yet none would listen. Tesso's grip grows tighter. You must be vigilant, young man."

Hayate returned with several burly-looking men from the city guard. They searched Yasuhiro's quarters, insisting the doctor came too so he could look at whatever potions the priest had. The old man had a few herbs and ointments. The doctor examined each, often smelling the contents of jars.

"There is no arsenic I can detect here," he declared.

"Is it possible the rat was infected with the stuff?" asked Ryuu.

"Someone might have been using arsenic to poison rats and this one had it on its teeth when it bit the victim, but the arsenic would be just as lethal to the rat as to the man."

"I put down rat poison I bought in town, but that was a week ago. The rats should have all been long dead by now. Besides, I don't think it was arsenic."

"It's a large town," said the doctor. "There are many rats. Maybe one of your neighbours poisoned some of them with arsenic, and one came here before it died, perhaps driven mad by the poison."

The guard, who had seemed to show little interest, seemed satisfied with the doctor's explanation. The doctor wrote Moeta's death certificate.

"I have medicine that is of use against arsenic poisoning – a combination of potash and garlic extracts. Come by my practice tomorrow and I will have some ready. There may be more of these poisoned rodents at large." With that, he turned and left.

Hayate was still suspicious of Yasuhiro. He took Goro and Ryuu to one side.

"That priest could have hidden arsenic anywhere. It wouldn't surprise me if he wanted to kill us all; then, when the old man dies, he will leave his house and grounds to the temple."

"You forget, Akako san was worried about the rats before Yasuhiro was here. He brought the priest in to protect him with his prayers, just like he brought in Ryuu to protect him with his sword," said Goro.

"That's a point," Hayate murmured. "These deaths started not long after you came here, Ryuu."

"Ryuu came on the night your sister died," said Goro. "He had to kick the door down. She was dead before we entered the room."

"It seems like someone wants just about everyone in this house dead," hissed Hayate, and stormed off.

Once more a funeral was held, and once more the body was placed in the family tomb; the only difference was that there were now fewer mourners.

"They will come for us all in the end," Akako whispered to Ryuu, as he and Goro helped the old man hobble back through the streets to his home.

Summer faded into autumn, but the cooler weather had not yet extended down into Kyushu. As the leaden pall that hung over the Oshiro household continued, Hayate was the next to be attacked. His feminine screams brought Ryuu to his door. Hayate was on a chair, shaking with fear. Both his legs had been bitten. Ryuu noticed that the shutters were closed. Drawing his sword, he crept into the room, closing the door behind him.

"It attacked me in the night. I will die like my brother," sobbed Hayate.

Ryuu ignored him and lifted up Hayate's bedside lamp to search the flickering shadows of the room. He heard a furtive scrabbling, sharp nails on wooden floorboards. A dark shape sprang from a corner of the room with a shrill squeak. The rōnin's katana was out of its sheath in an eyeblink, carving a deadly arc that met the assailant in midair. The shape it met was severed in twain in an explosion of red. The larger half fell, twitching at Ryuu's feet. It was the body of a rat, but what a rat - it was larger than the biggest cat he had ever seen. Even without the head, the tail and body must have measured almost three feet. It was dirty brown with a long, nude tail that even now twitched in its death throes like some ghastly grave worm.

The head had rolled away to the wall and was looking up at them with a maniacal fixed grin, the yellow incisors glistening wetly. Like the body, there was still movement in the head. Even as the eyes faded, the long whiskers danced with the spasmodic movement of the lips and snout.

Goro and Yasuhiro were horrified at the sight of the slain creature.

"Is… is that a *rat*?" Goro gasped, incredulous at the size of the dead rodent.

Ryuu nodded. "And what's more the shutters were fast. The rats have found another way into the house. Where are the tablets you picked up from the doctor?"

"They are in the kitchen. I will fetch then now."

As Goro vanished, Yasuhiro and Ryuu did their best to calm the hysterical Hayate down. They staunched the bleeding and the priest bandaged his legs. He was put shaking into his futon as Goro arrived with the tablets. Hayate snatched a handful and gulped them down with a jug of water.

"It's strange how these things could get into the house and not be seen," said Goro. "And nothing has been taken from the food stores. It is as if the rat came here specifically to attack humans."

"Remember what the doctor said - the last one had been driven mad by arsenic poisoning," Ryuu answered.

"Two mad rats with arsenic on their teeth in the same house? I think not."

"The rats of Tesso are venomous - so it is written. My prayers go unanswered and my charms cannot stop them. I fear the witchcraft of the venomous rats is too powerful for me." Yasuhiro collapsed into a chair shaking his head.

"Witchcraft be damned, this thing fell to my blade. It is a mortal creature, not a spirit." Ryuu brandished the huge rodent's body before the priest. "I'm going to show Akako san that his fears are unfounded. These rats are huge, these rats are mad - but they are not yokai."

Ryuu returned to Akako's room. The old man was sitting up in his bed.

"I heard screams again...."

His words stopped dead when he saw the creature Ryuu held up before him.

"Your blade cut down one of the children of Tesso. Thank the gods."

"These rats of yours - they exist. They are big and aggressive. We think they may have been driven mad by arsenic poisoning, but they are not ghosts. My sword killed this one. Ghosts are not noted for their vulnerability to swords."

"Thank you, young man. You are brave indeed, and a fine protector - but you do not understand. Tesso can possess living rats. He can make them grow huge and savage. He can control them. They are his eyes, ears, and hands. Even now, hordes of them may be tunnelling beneath this mansion awaiting the Iron Rat's signal to attack. Oh, yes, Ryuu, I need you now more than ever."

The gleam of madness shone in the old man's eyes, and Ryuu knew it would be pointless to argue. Yasuhiro took the carcass, claiming that he may be able to fashion it into more powerful charms to keep Tesso at bay.

Goro sat all night with Hayate. His sleep was dream-haunted and feverish, but by the morning his fever had broken. He ate more of the doctor's potash and garlic tablets as if he were a child gobbling up sweets.

Yasuhiro was now parading about with the rat's head on a necklace. He seemed emboldened by the death of the rat. If a sword could stop them, then so could his prayers and charms - this had been a sign.

Goro bought savage-looking traps and placed them around the gardens and the, narrowly missing the iron jaws snapping down on his foot. After a week with no luck, he threw the traps away.

Hayate had been a little unsteady, but he seemed to get over the attack and the poison. He took to walking with a stick. This was not so much to steady himself as to use as a weapon should another of the freakishly-large rats put in an appearance. He also began drinking again, with gusto. Perhaps because of the loss of his twin brother, or perhaps because of his brush with death, Hayate was drinking far more than he had before.

When Goro found him one morning at the bottom of the stairs, head at a peculiar angle, he assumed Hayate had drunkenly fallen down the stairs. Ryuu had other ideas; he imagined the drunkard tripped over a sleek, scurrying shape that ran between his legs at the top of the stairs.

Another funeral, another body in the tomb, fewer people attending. On the streets of Ōyama, tongues began to wag; three deaths in one house in a few months. It got about that the Oshiro mansion was cursed. People avoided the place.

Akako now never set foot out of his room. His meals were brought to him. He ranted far less, but somehow his silence was worse, as if he had resigned himself to his fate. His eyes were forever darting about and his complexion had become sallow and waxy.

Yasuhiro was now crazed, walking the house night and day, ringing bells, making complex hand gestures, chanting and spinning the prayer wheels. He believed himself to be in a constant spiritual battle with the rat daemon.

Goro was the only sane person left that Ryuu could talk to. Ryuu was impressed by his fidelity to his transparently-insane master.

"Other servants would have long left Goro. After the deaths, and with the obsessions of Akako san and now his priest, it is a wonder you stay on."

"I knew Akako san when he was still performing noh. I have been in his service since I was a boy; I could never leave. It is a tragedy that his final years have been blighted like this. To tell you the truth, I never liked his sister and brothers. They were a mean, petty lot - not like Akako san."

Several more weeks passed without incident, then one night Goro came running along the corridor to where Ryuu stood on guard.

"Ryuu come quickly - it's Yasuhiro. He is fighting with... something."

As they ran towards the priest's quarters, Ryuu asked, "What kind of something?"

"Not a rat, but some - some creature. Like a man, but with the face and tail of a rat."

"Tesso?"

"I don't know. The old man is using his staff but the beast is besting him. It just came out of nowhere as he was at prayer."

The little temple that Yasuhiro kept was in disarray, with scrolls ripped, books torn, and the altar toppled. By the dancing candlelight, a ghastly scene met their eyes. Yasuhiro lay on the floor, his eyes wide and staring. His face and throat had been worried, as if by the teeth and claws of some huge beast. Squatting on the dead priest's chest was a creature of nightmares. It resembled a small man, but it had the face, paws and tail of a giant rat. It wore some kind of habit, caked with filth and grave mould. Its claws and incisors were red with the old man's blood. About it on the temple floor scurried titan rats, several of which had begun to gnaw at the still-warm corpse.

As the pair entered, the creature looked up, regarding them with chillingly-human eyes. The thing had a long, rodent muzzle with skin like old leather. The teeth had a metallic gleam under the blood. The creature sprang off its victim, raking with sharp claws as Ryuu's katana flew up to meet them. There was a metallic clash as the beast fell back, spitting and screeching.

"Iron - its teeth and claws are iron!" exclaimed Ryuu.

Goro had picked up the old priest's staff and was fending off a number of the huge rats.

The man rat span gracefully round and leapt again, its snapping teeth aiming for Ryuu's face. The rōnin, with a move almost like a dance step, dodged to one side and twirled his blade. The rat thing only half-avoided the deadly arc, and was caught a raking blow across the chest. It collapsed to the floor, blood leaking as it sprawled.

Ryuu bounded over and caught the creature by the lank hair on its head. He pulled and seemed to wrench the very head off the beast.

Their master defeated, the rats drew back. Ryuu looked down at his fist and saw that it clutched an exquisitely-crafted mask of leather and real hair. Sharp iron teeth furnished the jaws.

On the floor before him lay Akako. On his hands were leather gloves armed with iron claws. A tail fashioned of leather trailed down from under his wretched habit.

"Master...?", began Goro.

The old man rolled onto his back, and grinned despite his wound.

"Ah, my dear Goro, you were the only one true to me. I would never have harmed you."

"What is this madness?", demanded Ryuu.

"My rats - my rats have killed them all. Do you recall, rōnin, when we first met? I told you of how special rats were? I have been breeding rats in the tunnels under this house for years. I have selected them for size and cunning. Rats can be trained, you know, like dogs."

Akako reached into the folds of his robe and produced a thin whistle. He blew feebly into it. Neither Ryuu or Goro could hear a sound, but in an instant all the rats retreated, returning to Akako's side.

"I fed them tiny portions of arsenic until they grew immune to it, then I painted their teeth with the stuff and sent them out to kill. The mere sight of one of my rats was enough to kill my dear sister."

"Why, master - why did you do this?", asked Goro.

"My siblings wanted my house and my money. I amassed a small fortune as an actor, and when I retired I hid it here in this house. My sister and brothers were waiting for me to die; I was fitter than they were, though. They were plotting to kill me and take what was mine, so I acted first. The legend of Tesso was a perfect story to use to my end, my greatest part to date. I gained many skills in the noh theatre besides acting. Costume design was among them, stage design another. Before my wretched family moved in, I had secret passages made all through the building that linked up with the tunnels below. I bred and trained my rats and then placed them wherever I wanted them - and all the time, Ryuu, you thought I was sound asleep in my room. Once they were all dead, I could leave in peace with just my faithful servant."

"But why kill Yasuhiro? You employed him to save you from Tesso's curse!"

Ryuu tossed the mask down at the actor's feet.

"Yes, I employed him like I employed you, to make the others believe I was serious about the curse and that I genuinely feared it. But he was too good; he became obsessed. He was talking of bringing dozens of priests here to do a mass exorcism. They would have found me out - so Tesso himself had to put in an appearance."

It seemed like Akako was going to say more, but a noise interrupted him. There was a scratching, scrabbling sound from one of the wooden panels in the wall. It grew in intensity, and all three men looked over at it. The rats at their feet seemed to grow excited. Suddenly there was a rending of the wood. The panel splintered open, and a living carpet of rats oozed into the temple.

"My children, I did not call you!" Akako looked confused.

From the darkness of the tunnel behind the shredded panel came an eerie, drawn-out screech. The rats in the temple all as one stood up and squeaked in unison. Akako blew his whistle again, but this time the rodents ignored him. Something rose up from the unwholesome passage and stood at the once-secret entrance to the temple.

At first Ryuu and Goro thought it was a giant rat, massively larger even than the horrors Akako had bred in his insane playpen beneath the mansion; then the thing stepped into the room, and the watchers realised that they were wrong.

The creature was well over six feet tall, even in its weirdly-hunched posture. It was covered in greyish-brown hair and was vaguely man-shaped. The legs, arms, hands and torso resembled those of a large, distorted man, but there the similarity ended. Its head was the head of a rat - black eyes, twitching whiskers and nose, saliva running from great yellow incisors. A naked tail almost as long as the body swept the floor behind it. The thing paused and sniffed the air. The horde of rats seem to gaze adoringly at it.

"No, no, no!" screamed Akako. "It's just a story. It's just something I used to scare them. It's not real, it...."

He was cut short as the ratman fell upon him, sinking its two-inch teeth into his neck. Goro made to raise the staff and help his stricken master, but Ryuu held him back. Now the other rats turned on the faux Tesso, ripping into him with hundreds of sharp teeth. Akako could not scream, only gurgle, as the real Tesso ripped at his windpipe.

Then the Iron Rat began to drag its imitator back across the temple floor and into the passage. The horde of rats helped their master haul their prey into the tunnel. They swiftly vanished back into the dark, leaving only a trail of mud and earth.

"The spirit of Ragio must have been offended by Akako's mockery, and returned in the form of Tesso to destroy him." The rōnin slowly returned his katana to its sheath.

"I don't believe what I have just seen," mumbled Goro.

"In my travels I have seen many strange things. I have learnt that the world is not the place we think it is."

Ryuu led Goro out of the room. "It is best we leave."

"How about Akako's money? He said it was hidden here somewhere."

The warrior shook his head. "He was mad. There may never even have been any money and, even if there was, do you fancy going down into those tunnels and searching for it?"

Goro shook his head.

The two men collected what little possessions they had in backpacks and left the Oshiro mansion for good.

As they wandered through the streets, Goro said, "We are both unemployed now."

"Never mind", said the rōnin, "let's see what the road has to offer us."

24. The Art of Monsters

The Kappa's monkey face was set in a fixed grin, its glass eyes looking down at the cucumber it clutched. Simian arms and legs, dyed a suitable green, protruded from the turtle carapace. A section of the monkey skull had been removed to facilitate the cavity where the legendary beast was said to keep the liquid that gave it such uncanny strength. The carapace and plastron were taken from a loggerhead turtle, the head and limbs were from a Japanese macaque. The taxidermied chimera sat in a glass case.

Next to the Kappa was a Tanuki, or raccoon dog. It had been stuffed in an upright, human-like pose. It wore a traditional coolie hat on its head. The most arresting thing about it was its outsized testicles; in legend, the Tanuki used them as weapons. The stuffed specimen had been endowed with the genitals of a bull, which it was swinging gleefully.

The Tanuki's neighbours were a trio of stuffed weasels. The fiercely-grimacing little animals had each had been given the single sickle-like talon of an eagle on each of their front paws. The preserved mustilids represented the Kamaitachi, blood-drinking yokai weasels that slashed at their victims with outsized claws.

In the next display case was a Nigyo, the mermaid of Nippon. Unlike its Western counterpart, it was an ugly creature. The upper half had been created from a monkey. The creature had been shaved, apart from the head. The lower half of the beast was formed from the rear portion of a blackfin tuna. The whole creation had a shrivelled and somewhat antique look about it. In legend, it was said that eating the flesh of a Nigyo could expand a human life span to 500 years. The creature behind the glass looked anything but palatable; it seemed to be reaching out pleadingly with desiccated hands and arms.

Beside the Nigyo was a Kitsune. The fox was, like several other of the yokai on display, standing on two legs like a man. Its front paws were postured as if in prayer; it was, in fact, in supplication to the Dog Star. Upon its head, it wore a hat of water lilies. The fox had two tails, a sign of the dangerous, shape-shifting Kitsune that could take on human form to cause its mischief.

The neighbouring case held an Aka-name, a yokai that used its long tongue to lap up filth from poorly-kept public baths and unclean toilets. Once again, a shaved monkey formed the basis for its humanoid body, but the head had been replaced by that of a giant African goliath frog. Some of the monkey's hair had been attached to the huge frog's head. From the wide batrachian mouth protruded a blue tongue some 18 inches in length; it had once belonged to a giraffe. The head and hairless body had been dyed red.

An impressive Ushi-oni towered over the smaller yokai in their glass cases. The marine ox daemon of the western coast of Nippon was a startling creation; it was made from a huge specimen of the Japanese spider crab. Its carapace was a foot and a half across, and the spindly legs spanned 12 feet. The elongate pincers were held out in front of it like some strange surgical tools. To the central carapace the head of a calf had been attached. The head had been made to look more fearsome by grafting goat horns to it and furnishing the mouth with dog's teeth. The glass eyes did not resemble a cow's, but were modelled on a leopard's predatory orbs. The creation had a metal framework inside of the crab's exo-skeleton to support the outlandish bio-sculpture.

Hanging from the branches of a small dead tree in the display was a Sagari, one of the strangest of all yokai. The Sagari was the disembodied head of a horse that hung from nettle trees in Fukuoka and Kumamoto prefectures on the island of Kyūshū, and caused disease with its baleful neighs and whinnies. Here it was represented by the stuffed head of a real horse attached to the tree via its mane. It dangled like some ghastly fruit, and a tiny microphone inside it played distorted horse vocalisations

The centrepiece was the most spectacular of the patchwork horrors. It was a Tatsu, a Japanese dragon. The body was that of a 25-foot reticulated python. The head had been replaced by that of a Nile crocodile, its toothy maw agape. Stag's antlers had been attached to the crocodile head to represent the dragon's horns. The four legs were those of a Komodo dragon, and the wings that sprouted just behind the front legs once belonged to a giant golden-crowned flying fox.

The monsters were not alone - the gallery thronged with the great and good of the Tokyo art scene. The room was lit by the flashes of cameras, the chink of champagne glasses, and the murmur of approval.

Koizumi Naoko's latest exhibition at the Hara Museum of Contemporary Art was an overwhelming success. Naoko was the current apple of the Nipponese art world's eye. She had come from relative obscurity, graduating from Tokyo University of the Arts just a year before. She grabbed the critic's attention with her stuffed animals posed in scenes that satirised politics, modern life and even art itself; this, however, was a new move, resurrecting the creatures of Nippon's ancient myth and legend by cherry-picking parts from dead animals and then stitching them together like an arty Victor Frankenstein. The stuffed creations were so expertly created that the stitches were invisible, save to x-ray.

Naoko had already done over fifty interviews with TV crews, newspapers and magazines, some from as far afield as North America, Europe and Australia. Now the experts were admiring her work in between slurping champagne and wolfing down canapés. Their exclamations were those of the impressed - there seemed to be no dissenting voice among them. She listened to snatches of conversation and smiled.

"She is like a modern-day Toriyama Sekien - in a different medium, of course."

"They look life-like enough to bite you!"

"A whole new branch of art, that's what she has created here."

"Introducing our folklore to a new generation in such a novel manner."

One of the visitors seemed like a new face. Naoko thought she recognised everyone in the art scene. The man stood a good head taller than the other people in the gallery. This, together with his somewhat florid complexion and rather long, beaky nose, made her think he might be a Westerner. The tall man beamed and walked over.

"A triumph, Naoko san. Seldom have I seen folklore brought to such vibrant life."

He bowed - a little exaggeratedly, she thought.

"Why thank you, er...."

"You may call me Mr. Karasu."

"Thank you, Karasu san. Have we met?"

There was something about him that made Naoko feel uneasy. She was glad that they were in a room full of people.

"Tell me," the tall man continued, "where do you get all the specimens and body parts?"

Naoko's heart leapt into her throat. She tried to control herself. He could not possibly know about her new commission.

"Well, they are all gained in a one-hundred-percent-legal and cruelty-free manner. The more exotic parts are from zoo animals that died of natural causes. Others are from road kill. No animals were killed to produce this work."

"I'm very glad to hear it," said Mr Karasu. "I would hate to think any animals had suffered, even for such exquisite art, now or in the future."

What did he mean 'in the future?' Was he with some environmental agency? Had they tracked the animals for the new commission from their various countries?

"Oh, no, Karasu san, I could never condone the killing of animals for art. The very thought horrifies me. I want only to educate and entertain."

The tall stranger smiled. "I am so very glad to hear that. Keep up the good work."

He turned and strode off into the crowd again. Naoko talked briefly to another guest, and when she turned back again Karusu had gone. She tried to find out who he was by mingling with the other visitors, casually asking if he had been a critic or a reporter. Strangely none of the others seemed to recall anyone of that description. Naoko thought he had stuck out like a sore thumb.

After the party, she returned to her studio across town. The tall man was still playing on her mind. She hoped to God he didn't know about the secret project. She had too much money riding on it - a hundred and twenty five thousand yen, to be precise.

The big man in the black suit had enquired about a private commission. He had seen her work (it was plastered all over newspapers and magazines) and had been impressed. He told her that he worked for a man who also liked her work and wanted a piece of his own for a private art collection. Yamaguchi Mikio was the man's name. He had a lot of money and, it seemed, a lot of influence. He could get just about anything. Naoko suspected him of being Yakuza, but was too sensible to ask. His boss may well have been someone high on the organisation's hierarchy. Mikio's boss wanted a nue created for him. Naoko knew this beast well from the stories her grandfather had told her as a girl. The nue was hybrid monster, sometimes compared to the chimera of Greek myth. The beast had the head of a monkey, the body of a Tanuki, the legs of a tiger and the tail of a snake. It could manifest as a black cloud and cause nightmares. In the summer of 1153 one of these creatures had haunted the Emperor Konoe, manifesting on the roof of the Kyoto Palace each morning at 2 a.m. to create bad dreams in the Emperor's sleep. The monster was eventually slain by the samurai Minamoto no Yorimasa.

Mikio had said that he would provide the raw materials, and that under no circumstances was she to talk about the commission to anybody else. He would collect the nue at an agreed time. His offered price made the commission irresistible to Naoko. Mikio had left no contact number but said that he would be in touch. The next evening he arrived in a van with several other black-suited men. They carried large crates into Naoko's studio. These turned out to be the raw materials, the carcasses of a mountain gorilla, a Bengal tiger and an amethystine python. What looked like bullet holes in the bodies made it unlikely that these were zoo specimens that had died of natural causes. It was obvious these animals had been poached to order for Naoko to create a taxidermied nue. The money was too much to refuse so she has asked no questions and carried on with the work as ordered.

She used the head of the gorilla, the body of the tiger, and the bottom half of the python to create a tail. She started by skinning the three creatures with the utmost care and skill, using her specialised tools. Tail strippers, fleshing pliers and scalpels were all employed in the job. The skins were salted to draw out moisture and treated with Stop Rot to prevent decomposition.

She measured the skull of the gorilla, and the leg bones of the tiger to use them in creating the mannequin that would form the body of the nue. It was to be formed in the traditional manner, from wood wool with a wire framework.

The following day Mikio dropped in to see how things were going. He seemed pleased with the progress, and said that his boss would be happy she was working so quickly. The big man had taken the unwanted remains of the process away for, she assumed, incineration.

She already had suitably-fierce-looking glass eyes in her collection. Now she set to work on the creation of the frame.

Naoko often slept in her studio. She had a spartan flat adjoining it, and when she was working on something major she would often not leave the building for days. She had been working on the frame all day and was exhausted when she finally tumbled into bed.

It was still dark when Naoko awoke, but light from a street lamp was shining through the slats of the blind on her window. Looking across the little bedroom she saw what looked like black smoke coiling under the door. Her first thought was 'fire!' Jumping out of bed, she opened the door. More of the black smoke was hanging around in wisps close to the floor. She ran down the corridor to the studio with visions of her hundred and twenty-five thousand yen work going up in flames. When she opened the door to the studio she was greeted by a choking cloud of blackness, and felt her head swimming.

* * * * *

She awoke to the smell of damp woodland. It reminded her of the mountain walks she had as a child when her farther had taken her deep into the forests. Looking down she saw damp substrate beneath her feet. Her feet? She could feel the damp forest floor on them, but her feet were black and hairy.

She fell down onto all fours; somehow it felt more comfortable like that. Her arms and hands were black and hairy too. She felt a massive strength in them. She ran her hands over her now huge body and felt more hair. Strangest of all she somehow knew that she was now male. Naoko felt the odd, alien sensation of a penis and testicles between her legs, buried deep in fur. They seemed tiny in relationship to the bulky body she now inhabited.

"It must be some sort of lucid dream," she reasoned. Naoko looked around her. She was in a cool, misty upland jungle, surrounded by giant celery and huge nettles, as well as towering tree ferns and hydrangeas. A noise from behind made her turn. There were a group of mountain gorillas not forty feet from her. They seemed to be composed of females and young, who were busy feeding and playing respectively. Naoko realised that *she* was a gorilla, a silverback. It seemed natural, and she sat and began to feed, deftly grabbing handfuls of vegetation and wrapping them up in leaves into tortilla-like parcels before transferring them to her mouth. She found she was enjoying the earthy taste of the plants.

As Naoko reached for another handful of vegetation, something snapped tight about her wrist. Instinctively she pulled, and something began to bite into her flesh. She saw a cable snare about her wrist and screeched in fury. Her alarm call sent the other gorillas running into the deeper jungle. The more she pulled, the tighter the snare gripped. Instead of pulling, she found where the snare was anchored and ripped it from the ground with her free hand. The snare's grip slackened and she pulled herself free.

As she broke free, she saw a group of men enter the clearing armed with rifles. The silverback instinct to protect the troop kicked in. The gorilla body she inhabited let out a thundering bellow, and she pounded at her chest, filling the clearing with the hollow, drum-like beating.

One of the men raised a gun that spat and boomed. A sharp pain ripped through her left shoulder. Fury rose together with the protective instinct, and she charged, fangs bared, letting loose a scream that was strangely high-pitched for such a big creature. Several guns fired in unison. High-calibre bullets pierced her chest and stomach, stopping her in mid-charge. She felt a searing sensation as she tumbled over and over, finally coming to rest at the feet of the poacher. Even now, as she breathed her, last they dare not come near. They moved hastily back and raised their guns again. More bullets tore through her.

* * * * *

Naoko awoke in her bed in a cold sweat. A dream, nothing more - a nightmare brought on by the repressed feeling of guilt at stuffing poached animals. She rose and splashed herself with cold water from the bathroom sink. Just to be sure, she checked the studio. Nothing was amiss.

The next day she continued with the creation of the mannequin frame for the nue mount, and finally finished it. Now it was only a matter of fitting the skins over the mount, sewing them together and fitting the eyes - that could wait until tomorrow.

* * * * *

Again she awoke to the black smoke coiling under her door. It stood out against the night as it was so much blacker than the darkness around it. She felt compelled to open the door and walk down to the studio. No fear of fire this time, just the odd compulsion. Once more, she met a wall of black fog.

She awoke hungry. It was night but she could see clearly. This time a muggy, tropical heat hung in the air. She stretched, finding that she was a quadruped. As she flexed her hands, she saw they were paws. Great white daggers unsheathed themselves, digging into the dirt. Her skin was covered in short golden-orange fur, and she saw the black stripes on her flank and realised she was a tiger. The odd feeling of being male crept over her once more. She squirted urine onto the base of a tree, marking her territory, then clawed at the trunk. Her whole body felt like a coiled spring of predatory power. She needed to hunt, and with an almost indolent grace slipped out into the shadows of the jungle.

There seemed few game animals, no samba deer or chital, and the monkeys slept in the jungle canopy above her. She knew the thin branches would not support her; besides a monkey was but a mouthful. She moved on, pad-pad-padding through the jungle, silent as a ghost. She stopped briefly to drink at a river, but did not enter the deep water. She knew that in that element she was the prey, not the predator; there were crocodiles in the dark water that could make a meal even of her. Returning to the darkness of the jungle, she sniffed the air. There was the scent of prey on it, and she followed.

In a clearing she saw a white tethered goat, fat, dull-witted, and made lazy by man. It was blissfully unaware of the tiger in the shadows so close to it. The goat had the smell of man about it. The tiger usually avoided men and their villages, but sometimes herdsmen took their livestock into the forest to graze - then their slow, stupid beasts were fair game.

Soundlessly she flowed through the night jungle, hardly disturbing a leaf with her passing. The goat was busy feasting on the lush grass. She was almost close enough for her hot breath to have tickled its pale flanks.

A single leap, and her fangs were in its neck before it could bleat in alarm. The canine teeth had dislocated the vertebra as her claws drew lines of scarlet on the white. The goat hardly twitched. She lapped warm blood from her muzzle and was about to sink her teeth into the flesh to feed, when another smell intruded on her senses. Human, it had been downwind, and she had been preoccupied with the kill.

A man holding a rifle stood up from the bushes and fired. She dropped instinctively, and the bullet whizzed past her, burying itself in a tree. She sprang again before he could fire, claws rending his face, destroying eyes, nose and mouth, raking to the bone. His screams mixed with another sound - a second rifle shot. She cursed herself for her lack of caution as the bullet penetrated her skull. She fell back, clawing at nothing in a death spasm.

* * * * *

Naoko jerked awake in her bed once more. Her breath was fast and harsh. Her heart thundered in her chest. Two horrid, lucid dreams in a row. She would be glad when this commission was finished. She drank strong coffee as she tried to get a grip on herself. She was still shaking. She thought of the yen and gradually the shivering subsided.

In the daylight the whole thing seemed stupid. She resumed work on the nue, fitting the animal skins over the frame dummy; such was her skill that they slid on like gloves. The empty skins seemed to eerily inflate, gaining mass and life once more. Then she set about stitching the skins of the three beasts together to make one chimeric creature. Finally, she fitted in the glass eyes. They were not the dark, gentle eyes of a gorilla, but the fire-orange eyes of a lion. Contrasting with the grimacing ape face, they made for a daemonic visage.

She had posed the nue on three legs, with its right front leg raised. The ape head was slightly cocked, as if listening or mocking. The snake tail, with its irridescent scales, swept upwards in an 's'-shaped curve. It did not have the Tanuki's body, racoon dogs being far too small to fit into such a creation; nonetheless, it looked impressive and disturbing.

Looking at the nue, Naoko realised that it affected her in a way none of her other creations did. It made her skin crawl. In its separate parts it did not have this effect, but as a whole the nue appalled her. She could not bear to be in the same room as it. She hoped that Yamaguchi Mikio would be back to collect the horror very soon.

Naoko decided she needed to get out of the studio and the pokey apartment. She spent the day drifting from shop to shop and from café to café in downtown Tokyo. She walked in the park and later ate a fine meal at a nice restaurant. By the time she got back to the studio, it was dark. She went straight to her apartment, avoiding the room where her creation lurked in its listening, mocking stance.

She had tried to stave off sleep as long as she could, drinking coffee and watching late-night movies. She had not even gone to bed, but nodded on the sofa in front of the flickering television.

* * * * *

When she awoke, she felt as if she was in a sleeping bag. She tried to flex her arms and legs, but found she had none. She sensed that this time she was female, but despite that, this was the most alien body she had inhabited. Its rhythms were more alien - slower, cooler but somehow stronger and older. She needed to bask in the rays of the rising sun to energise her elongate body, the body of a python.

Once sufficiently warmed, she flexed muscle groups that she had never possessed before, sending ripples along her underside that moved her long body with sinuous grace.

She moved like a living river of muscle through the scrub. Her eyes, not having lids, were permanently open, another weird sensation she had to adjust to. Her forked, flickering tongue tasted the air, picking up particles and transferring them to her Jacobson's organ. She could literally taste prey on the air, to such a degree that she could tell in which direction the warm-blooded animal had been moving.

She slithered after the mammal that had recently passed, drawing closer, her excitement growing along with the taste in the air. The swamp wallaby had not noticed her, preoccupied as it was with browsing on some shrubs. She stole closer, to within striking range. Pulling the front portion of her body back, she sprang forward like an uncoiling spring. Rows of needle-sharp, backwards- pointing teeth ripped into the wallaby's neck, halting the alarmed squeal in the throat before it could reach the air. Coil after coil whipped around the hapless macropod. The muscular loops gripped tighter and tighter, preventing air being drawn into the lungs and causing a massive rise in pressure in the body cavity of the marsupial. The animal's heart gave out under the pressure, and its struggling ceased.

She loosened her coils and move to the head of the dead wallaby. She began to swallow, the elastic ligaments on her jawbones allowing her to work her mouth around the prey. She found that her lower jaw consisted of two separate bones rather than one. Working these one at a time, she used the backward-pointing teeth to drag the wallaby into her maw and swallow it, whilst her trachea was pushed forwards and out of her mouth like a straw to breathe in air.

Finally, when the wallaby was swallowed, she crawled off to digest the meal in peace. She fell into an odd stupor where time had no meaning, being vaguely aware of her stomach acids breaking down flesh, fur and bone.

She was awakened from the digesting slumber by the sense of movement. She picked up vibrations in the ground as something approached. She was still sluggish; it seemed early morning and she was just coming out of the digestion phase. Two human figures approached. At first they shrunk back, but then seemed to notice her prone state. She made to move off sluggishly, but one man came forward. In his raised hand he held something that had a metallic gleam in the morning sun. The heavy machete blade fell down, decapitating her.

Now she could see her own body writhing and looping in its death throes. She could still feel the body despite her head being separated from it.

* * * * *

The blankets were twisted serpent-like around Naoko when she awoke. She threw them down. A wave of determination swept over her. She needed to cast off this subconscious guilt, or fear, or whatever was causing these nightmares. She also needed to get over the uncomfortable feeling she had when she looked upon the nue; it was her creation after all.

She walked down into the studio and threw on the light. The horrid thing looked more uncanny than ever. The cocked head now made the monster look as if it were waxing sly. The gorilla face seemed to have a mocking grin on it. The iridescence of the scaly tail made it look almost as if it were moving.

* * * * *

The papers had gone wild. Tokyo, after all, was one of the safest cities in the world. Violent crime was very rare. Never had the capital seen a murder like this. The prominent artist Koizumi Naoko had been murdered and preserved in the manner of one of her specimens. Nothing was ever found of the artist aside from her skin. Of the flesh, bones and organs there was no trace, almost as if they had been devoured. Security cameras had revealed nothing. Her skin had been preserved and mounted on what the police at first took to be a taxidermist's frame. Her eyes had been replaced with glass ones and her naked, stuffed body had been positioned in a position of repentance. Police surgeons who had dissected Naoko's remains found not a wood wool and wire mannequin, but money. The woman had been stuffed full of compressed money - thousands and thousands of yen. Exactly one hundred and twenty-five thousand yen had been found inside her flayed hide.

The murder caused such a furore that two other killings on the same day hardly registered on the media. Yakuza saiko komon, or senior advisor, named Chikamatsu Yoshinori, had been found killed in his penthouse apartment along with his Wakagashira, or second in command, one Yamaguchi Mikio. It seemed that they had been attacked and killed by some kind of animal, but for the second time in as many days the police forensics team was baffled. It had seemed like a veritable menagerie had savaged the men. The bite marks were from some animal with powerful jaws but relatively flat teeth, like an ape. The claw marks that had relieved the men of their innards seemed to be the work of a big cat. Last but not least were the marks on the broken necks of the men, as if some huge serpent had throttled them, crushing windpipes and vertebra like cardboard tubes and popcorn. M Once more the security cameras had shown nothing. Both men had repeatedly fired off powerful handguns, but the only blood in the apartment belonged to them.

25. Fruits of the Forest

Sugai Yori had parked his car in a lay-by several miles away and continued to the forest on foot. The thickness of the trees provided an almost absolute silence. The smell was earthy, damp and fresh, there having been recent rain. Yori switched on his torch as he walked along the path. Its yellow beam illuminated the weirdly-gnarled shapes of the trees, festooned with hanging moss and lichen, like organic ghosts.

He wandered a mile along the tourist path before turning off onto one of the less-well-trodden paths. There were several signs along the way pleading with anyone considering the act to think again, to seek help, to turn back.

"Sorry, too late for that. *Far* too late," he whispered to himself.

The ground was madly uneven underfoot. The rock below had been formed of a lava flow from the eruption of Mount Fuji in the year 864 by the Roman calendar. The trees blanketed the nutrient-rich laval rock, their roots burrowing deep in search of sustenance. They were canted at weird angles, the roots emerging like maggots from some vast carcass. How appropriate - this was Aokigahara, famed across the world as 'the suicide forest.'

It was a popular tourist spot. Aokigahara was beautiful, with its caves and the nearby Saiko Lake. Its setting on the northwest base of Mount Fuji meant that many visitors, both from Nippon and overseas, came here; few, however went deep.

Just why Aokigahara was a suicide magnet was unclear, but such things had been happening at least as far back as the 19th century. Aokigahara was the second-most-popular suicide location on earth, after the Golden Gate Bridge. Sometimes over 200 lost souls took their lives here every year. There was even a squad of bodyhunters who went into the forest each day, specifically to search for bodies.

Some, who were undecided as to whether or not to go through with the act, would uncoil rolls of coloured tape behind them, like polychromatic Theseae, in order to find their way back if their nerve failed at the vital moment. Yori had no such worries; this would be his last journey.

He checked his backpack again. The nylon rope was coiled snake-like, ready to form the noose. The jar of painkillers was nestled next to it. Yori had researched suicide on the net. He was unsurprised that there were websites dealing with the best method. Hanging was painful, but could be dulled with enough tablets. This also provided a convenient second line of death if you happened to have tied the noose wrongly.

He was deep enough now. No one would be here at this time of night in such a remote part of the forest. He felt no fear, no apprehension, just an odd kind of relief, as he methodically prepared the noose. Suddenly he was aware of someone standing behind him.

"Good evening," said a pleasant-sounding voice.

Yori turned and almost dropped his torch. The face in front of his was deeply strange, despite its amiable grin. It was a human-looking face, round and seemingly-Oriental in its form yet the skin was red - not like that of an American Indian, but bright red. The long hair that fell well past the shoulders was also bright red, as was the monk-like robe that the odd man was wearing.

"Wh... who are you?", mumbled Yori, nonplussed by the red man's sudden entrance.

"I'm Shōjō," beamed the red man. "And you are?"

"Yori," answered Yori.

"Welcome to my home, Yori."

"Where is your home?" Yori was confused.

Shōjō threw up his arms, indicating to the whole forest.

"Here, the forest of Aokigahara, is my home. Now, as you are a guest, it would be remiss of me to not offer you a drink." Shōjō fumbled in the bag at his side and produced a bottle of sake and two glasses. He poured out two shots and offered one to Yori, who found himself taking it without question.

"Good health," the red man said, and began to drink.

Thinking of the irony of those words, Yori found himself drinking. The sake was the finest he had ever tasted. It seemed warm, too, although he had not seen Shōjō warm it up; he had taken it straight from his bag.

"Are you a monk?", Yori asked, looking at the stranger's apparel.

"Me, a monk? Heavens, no - I'm far too fond of my drink." He poured another and they drank the sweet rice wine. Yori felt warm.

"So what do you do here, Shōjō?"

"Well, I suppose I sort of help out. You could say I'm a kind of guide."

"A guide, for the national park?"

"In a way. I'll show you around if you like."

"At night?"

"Night is the best time to see Aokigahara." Shōjō produced a folding paper lantern and candle from his seemingly-bottomless bag and lit it with a modern-looking match and matchbox.

Yori felt compelled to follow as Shōjō walked deeper into the forest. He had quite forgotten the noose he had just tied. He followed the strange man as he walked between the trees by the reddish lantern light.

"Yes, all the wildlife comes out at night; it's really quite amazing what you can see."

A greenish glow was illuminating a clearing ahead. As Shōjō and Yori drew closer, they saw a group of animals sitting around a flickering flame.

"Foxfire," whispered Shōjō.

Foxes and raccoon dogs were sitting about the clearing. Suddenly one of the raccoon dogs stood up like a man on its hind legs. It began to slap its round belly with its forepaws. Several more did likewise. The drumming sound filled the night air - POM-POKO, POM-POKO. The foxes and dogs stood up like men and began to dance, twirling about as if doing some strange waltz.

Yori was too amazed to speak; he simply gazed silently at the breathtaking spectacle. Then, out of the trees another group of animals came to join the dance. They moved close to the crowd, almost like snakes, until they reached the dance, then they stood up and began a sinuous dance, moving their bodies like reeds in a summer breeze.

"Otters," gasped Yori. "I thought they were extinct in Nippon."

"Here in Aokigahara we call them Kawa-uso. The world believes them to be extinct, and they would rather that it continued to believe that was the case."

Yori could have watched the animals dance all night, but Shōjō tugged at his sleeve and whispered, "Come, there is more to see."

They moved away from the dancers and deeper into the forest. Soon another light was drawing them closer. There was a rustling sound from a stand of bamboo. Every so often a jet of flame licked out from the undergrowth, lighting the area in green. The flames seemed not to harm the bamboo as they coiled and lapped about it.

As Shōjō and Yori crouched to observe, a bird as tall as a man emerged from the bamboo grove. Yori was amazed to see it was a giant rooster. Its feathers were gold and red, save the tail feathers, which were a vibrant green. The comb and wattles that decorated its head were as red as Shōjō himself. The great bird paused and scratched at the ground with its claws, then it threw back its head. Yori thought it was going to crow, but instead it breathed out a jet of shimmering green fire.

"This is a Basan. Originally they come from Shikokou Island in Ehime Prefecture. The male breathes fire to attract a mate."

Another Basan, slightly smaller than the first, with less well-developed wattles and comb, shyly approached from the forest darkness. The male puffed out its chest and spat more of the cold flame; that seemed to impress the female.

"I think they need to be alone," said Shōjō and led Yori away.

Next they stopped at a tree that was heavy with fruit. The growths that hung from its branches resembled large pears in shape.

"Jinmenju" said Shōjō. "Take a look at its fruit." He lifted his red paper lantern to illuminate some of the tree's lower branches. The fruits each had a serene-looking human like face on them.

"These fruit grow on the Jinmenju and live their whole life in but a few weeks. They are born, grow up, grow old and die when they fall from the branch, yet to them it is a full and happy life. Their seeds go on to grow into new Jinmenju trees. They are happy with their lot."

Indeed, all of the fruit bore smiles to rival even Shōjō's beam.

Yori remembered why he had come to Aokigahara.

"You have shown me beauty and magick, Shōjō; thank you for that. Can we go back to where we first met?"

The red man smiled and nodded. They walked back through the forest. Sometimes Yori glimpsed blue lights dancing among the branches.

"Fireflies?", he asked

"After a fashion," his guide replied.

Yori could never have found his way back, but Shōjō seemed to know the wood as if it were his own back yard.

"Well, here we are my friend - back where we started."

"I came here to kill myself, Shōjō."

"So many do."

"I had clinical depression. Nothing helped - tablets, psychiatry, hypnotherapy. 'Chemical imbalance in the brain,' they called it. 'Imbalance of the soul,' I called it. The down periods were growing longer, more severe. I lost my job, couldn't hold on to any kind of relationship. I'm in my mid-forties and I have achieved so very little. This condition has always held me back, like some dark storm cloud hanging over me, but tonight you showed me things that I never thought could exist. You have shown me that there is wonder and mystery and something to live for."

The red man smiled. "I have one last thing to show you," he said. "Turn around."

Yori turned and saw himself. He was hanging from a tree not three feet behind himself. The rope was taught, and cut into the flesh of his neck. His eyes bulged frog-like from their sockets, and his tongue lolled from his open mouth, looking absurdly like a pound of liver. The slight breeze stirred the body, making it sway.

"What... when...?"

"A few moments before you met me. You hanged yourself in the forest. That is why you can see me and the other inhabitants of Aokigahara. So many came here to die that I became their guide. I show them the forest as it is after death. See, now you are one of the fruits of the forest, just like the fruits of the Jinmenju.

"And like them you will now grow into something new here in the forest."

Yori looked down at himself and saw human hands and human legs.

"But I am the same."

"No, you only think you are - force of habit, like a person who loses a limb and swear that they can still feel it. Let go of Yori - Yori was sad. Be something new, something wonderful."

His mind shed the form like a butterfly emerging from a chrysalis. He shed the habit of being Yori, and of being human and all that it carried. The new life that emerged pulsed a beautiful blue, like some gleaming jellyfish, as it rose to meet the swarm of other Hito-dama that swam among the ancient trees.

* * * * *

The first rays of dawn were peeping through the trees of Aokigahara. Shōjō's shift was over. Soon the bodyhunters of the day shift would come to clear up what the thing that had once been Yori had left behind.

Fortean Fiction

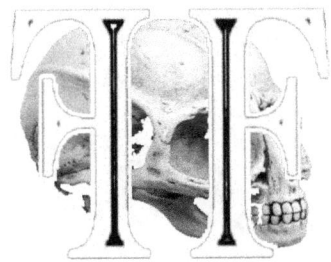

A new imprint from the CFZ Publishing Group dedicated to fictional books with a Fortean or cryptozoological theme.

Green Unpleasant Land by Richard Freeman

Left Behind by Harriet Wadham

Dark Ness by Tabitca Cope

Snap! By Steven Bredice

Hyakumonogatari: Book One by Richard Freeman

Death on Dartmoor by Di Francis

Dark Wear by Tabitca Cope

The Museum of the Future by Andrew May

CFZ PUBLISHING GROUP

www.cfzpublishing.co.uk